☆ ☆ ☆ ☆ ☆ ☆

LEWIS B. PATTEN has written dozens of Western novels over the last twenty years, including several which became films. Also in Signet Brand editions are RED RUNS THE RIVER, MAN OUTGUNNED, AMBUSH AT SODA CREEK, THE TRIAL AT APACHE JUNCTION, THE GALLOWS AT GRANEROS, DEATH OF A GUNFIGHTER, A KILLING IN KIOWA (winner of the coveted Spur Award of the Western Writers of America), and others. A native of Denver, he lived on a ranch before turning to writing full time.

☆ ☆ ☆ ☆ ☆ ☆

More Westerns from SIGNET

GUILT OF A KILLER TOWN

and

MASSACRE RIDGE

by Lewis B. Patten

A SIGNET BOOK

NEW AMERICAN LIBRARY

TIMES MIRROR

Guilt of a Killer Town Copyright © 1971 by Lewis B. Patten
Massacre Ridge Copyright © 1971 by Lewis B. Patten

All rights reserved. Originally appeared in paperback as separate volumes published by The New American Library.

 SIGNET TRADEMARK REG. U.S. PAT. OFF. AND FOREIGN COUNTRIES
REGISTERED TRADEMARK—MARCA REGISTRADA
HECHO EN CHICAGO, U.S.A.

SIGNET, SIGNET CLASSICS, MENTOR, PLUME AND MERIDIAN BOOKS
are published by The New American Library, Inc.,
1301 Avenue of the Americas, New York, New York 10019

FIRST PRINTING (DOUBLE WESTERN EDITION), NOVEMBER, 1977

1 2 3 4 5 6 7 8 9

PRINTED IN THE UNITED STATES OF AMERICA

GUILT
OF A
KILLER
TOWN

Chapter 1

AT SUNDOWN, Frank Kailey halted his horse at the edge of the bluff and stared with somber eyes at Medicine Arrow, New Mexico, sprawling at his feet.

Toward the west, a loop of river caught and reflected the gold of the dying sun. He could see the bluish cast of head-high sagebrush beyond the town. He could see the faint sheen of green lying over everything because now, in April, grass was beginning to poke up through the ground.

It had been April when he went away, he thought. April, two years ago. And suddenly it all came back— the crowded courtroom and the judge sitting behind his bench, frowning, sentencing Frank's father to die by hanging for the crime of murder in the first degree. He thought that now after two years the people of Medicine Arrow should have been able to forget. He hoped they had because this was the only place he knew and the only place where he was known. If he couldn't make it here, he couldn't make it anywhere.

Clouds, high thunderclouds, were piled up in the north. All day they had been spreading slowly south. Now, suddenly, they obscured the setting sun and laid a uniform gray across the land. Frank Kailey touched his horse's sides with his heels and headed him down the precipitous trail through the rimrock. He zigzagged to the bottom along the half dozen sharp switchbacks that had been cut across the steep slope below the rim.

A couple of miles west of town, close against the river bank, he thought he glimpsed the cabin where he and his father had lived, but he could not be sure because of the willows and cottonwoods growing in the river bottom close to it.

Again he wondered uneasily if the people would accept him here. He wondered how he would live if they did not. He shook his head impatiently. No use setting up obstacles

5

in his mind. Enough obstacles would present themselves without any help from him.

His horse slid on his haunches the last twenty feet to the valley floor. A little avalanche of loose rocks and gravel followed him. Frank Kailey lifted him to a jogging trot. He made a loose and relaxed figure in the saddle. He still wore the cheap, ill-fitting suit they had given him when he left the prison in Santa Fe. His hat had been worn out and thrown away by some cowhand in a town fifty miles north of there. His horse and ancient saddle had been purchased with fifty dollars that had suddenly and mysteriously arrived in a plain envelope a couple of days before his release.

He was hungry, and tired, and depressed tonight. He dreaded what lay ahead. He dreaded the memories that would return when he reached the cabin he and his father had shared before he had gone away. The truth of the matter was, he thought ruefully, he felt guilty because he had run away. He felt guilty because he hadn't been able to help the old man in the lonely years that followed his mother's death.

He shook himself as though he could shake off all his unwelcome thoughts. Skirting the town, he followed the river bottom toward the cabin. In the last gray light of day, his unshaven face was grim and almost ugly with its deep-set, bitter eyes. His gaunt body seemed thinner than it really was in the tight, poorly-fitting suit.

While still half a mile from the cabin, he felt the first drop of rain. Lightning slashed suddenly down through the clouds and thunder rolled ponderously across the skies. He felt another drop of rain, and another, and kicked his weary horse into a lope.

Ahead, now, he could see a curtain of rain rolling across the land. It enveloped him several minutes before he reached the shack. He swung to the ground, landing in a rapidly forming puddle immediately in front, tied his horse to one of the posts that supported the sagging porch roof, ducked through the water streaming from the eaves, and plunged inside.

The door hung, sagging, from its hinges. He left it open momentarily even though rain was blowing through it and halfway across the room. He stared around at the gloomy interior with dismay.

He didn't know what he had expected. Maybe he had expected it to be the same as it had been when he went away. But it wasn't. There was cow manure on the floor, left by cattle that had sought shelter here. There were the scurrying sounds of mice in the cupboards. There was the smell of dust dampened by the rain coming through the leaky roof and blown in through the open door.

Frank Kailey shrugged and made a rueful smirk. He crossed to the cupboard beside the stove where the lamps had always, in the past, been kept. He opened it and was surprised to find a dusty but unbroken lamp. He took it down and shook it, discovering that it was still half full. He raised the chimney, fumbled in his pocket for matches, found one and struck it on the stove. He touched it to the lamp wick which caught fire reluctantly. He lowered the chimney, trimmed the wick, and put the lamp on a shelf. He stared around the room.

Rain was beating hard against the roof. In half a dozen places it dripped or trickled through onto the dusty floor. At one end of the cabin were two bunks, one over the other in cow camp style. Both of the mattresses and all the bedding had been piled on the top bunk by someone, but that hadn't saved it from shredding by the mice. Frank Kailey crossed the room to the sagging door. Lifting it clear of the floor, he swung it shut.

The stovepipe was down. He gathered up the scattered pieces, fitted them together, and replaced them. He lifted one of the lids off the stove and found ashes still in the firebox. He shook them down, found a stick of firewood and, drawing a knife from his pocket, began shaving it into the firebox. When he judged he had enough shavings, he piled larger sticks judiciously on top and touched a match to the shavings underneath.

Now, to the sound of rain and the ponderous roll of thunder outside the shack was added the roar of the growing fire in the stove. And to the smell of rain-dampened dust was added the smell of more dust burning on the stove. He backed up to it, grateful for the fire's warmth. This wasn't much but it sure as hell beat a cell in the prison at Santa Fe.

He was hungry, but he knew food was out of the question until tomorrow. He crossed to the bunks and began to pull the bedding down. Most of it would have to be thrown away but maybe he could find something that was usable for tonight. He tossed both mattresses into a corner on the floor. He spread a ragged quilt on the wooden slats, and found a couple of moth-eaten wool blankets to spread over it. He returned to the cupboards beside the stove. Rummaging through them, he found a coffeepot.

7

Cheered by the prospect of coffee, he lifted open the door and went out onto the porch.

Rain still slanted in on a driving wind. He removed his saddle and carried it inside. He took the coffeepot outside, rinsed it and filled it from a stream pouring off the eaves. Returning, he put it on the stove. From his saddlebags he got a small sack of coffee. He put a handful into the pot.

Once more he went outside, this time to lead his horse beneath the porch roof. It was poor shelter at best for the animal, but it was all there was.

Inside again, he took off his soaked coat and hung it on a nail. He hung the ragged, dripping hat on another nail. He began to pace restlessly back and forth.

Faces were now appearing in his memory, and names. He had been born and raised right here in Medicine Arrow, New Mexico. And then, one terrible day when he was fifteen, his mother had been killed in the middle of Juarez Street by a runaway.

Perhaps her death was all the more shocking because of its suddenness and violence. But equally shocking had been what it had done to his father. From an able, hard-working man, Amos Kailey changed almost overnight into a sodden drunk. He seemed to have forgotten that he had a son. A little more each day, he retreated into a fog of drink until he scarcely knew anything or anyone.

The cattle they'd run in the river bottom west of town were sold one by one to pay for the whiskey Amos Kailey now consumed. If he ate, it was because his son Frank prepared the meals. If he slept in a bed instead of in an alley someplace it was because Frank brought him home and put him there.

Six months after his wife's death, Amos Kailey threw a lamp against the wall in a fit of drunken rage. He staggered out, and the house and all it contained burned.

The last of the cattle bought material for this shack. Frank and several good-hearted neighbors built it. But there came a time when Frank couldn't stand remaining anymore. He could see no hope that his father would ever change. After a particularly bitter and disgusting quarrel, he ran away from home.

He doubted if his absence even penetrated the fog his father was almost always in. He doubted if he was even missed.

The coffee was boiling now and its aroma filled the room. Frank found a cup in one of the cupboards, went

8

out, and rinsed it in the rain streaming off the roof. He came back in and poured it full.

After righting a bench, he sat down dispiritedly at the table, sipping the scalding coffee and staring gloomily at the rain blowing through the broken window beyond the door.

Suddenly his horse nickered. From out in the driving rain he was answered by another horse. Frank put down his coffee, went to the door and opened it.

A man in a slicker dismounted stiffly and led his horse to the porch. He tied the reins to one of the posts that supported it. He crossed the porch and came inside.

Frank pushed the door closed after him, and stared warily at the newcomer.

Ray Coates had been sheriff of Juarez County for as long as Frank could remember and before. He opened his slicker but he didn't take it off. He said, "I saw you ride down off the bluff."

He was a short, stocky, powerful man with a wide red moustache and a crop of thinning, reddish hair. His eyes were blue and cold. He could smile and he smiled at Frank right now, but as always the smile only creased his ruddy face. It did not extend to his eyes.

Frank waited. The gleam of the sheriff's silver star beneath the slicker made him nervous and he wondered if the time would ever come when a lawman's star wouldn't have this effect on him. After all, he wasn't an ordinary criminal. He'd been sent to prison for assaulting the judge that had sentenced his father to hang, but at the time he'd been nearly out of his mind from grief and shock.

Coates asked bluntly, "Why the hell did you have to come back here?"

Frank said, "It's the only place I know. This shack still belongs to me."

Coates shook his head. "It was sold for taxes three months ago."

For a moment Frank Kailey was stunned. Then he remembered that property sold for taxes could be redeemed. He said, "I can redeem it. How long do I have?"

"A year. Three months of that is gone. In the meantime, it doesn't belong to you."

"Who bought it?"

"Doesn't matter. You'll have to get out."

"In the rain?" Frank stared at him incredulously.

Coates shrugged. "I guess you can stay tonight." He was silent for several moments. At last he said, "If you're

9

smart, you'll leave in the morning before anybody knows you're here."

Frank Kailey frowned. "Why? I served my time. I paid my debt to society. I'm entitled to do anything I want."

"People around here feel different. Your name's Kailey and in Medicine Arrow that means grief. Your pa was hanged for murder and you were sent to prison for assaulting the judge that sentenced him. Seems to me you'd want to go someplace where you weren't known."

Frank Kailey stared at Coates' face. It was hard to meet those cold blue eyes, but he forced himself and in the end it was Coates who looked away. The small triumph made Frank's heart begin to pound.

It came to him very suddenly. Something was wrong. There had to be a reason why the sheriff hadn't been able to meet his gaze. It wasn't like Coates to look away from any man.

Frank said, "There's something wrong. There's something you're not telling me."

Coates's face turned a dark and angry red. His eyes narrowed and his mouth thinned out. He said, "You didn't learn much down in Santa Fe."

Frank said stubbornly, "I'm going to stay. This is my home and I'm going to stay."

Coates closed his slicker and buttoned it. He stared coldly at Frank a moment, then turned and went out into the rain. Without looking back, he mounted his horse and rode away. He disappeared into the dripping darkness in the direction of town.

Frank Kailey closed the sagging door. He dropped the bar into place. He walked to the table, picked up his cup and finished it.

He blew out the lamp. Wearily he lay down on the bunk and pulled the ragged blankets over him. He was tired but he didn't sleep. Figures from out of the past kept parading through his mind.

Chapter 2

IT RAINED all through the night, not with the furious intensity of the first thunderstorm but steadily, softly, and continuously. In the first gray of dawn Frank Kailey awoke from an uneasy dream of prison to look at his surroundings with relief. He was cold, but he lay still several moments, staring around the room. He remembered the visit from Ray Coates last night and he remembered the way the sheriff had failed to meet his glance. Frowning, he swung his legs over the side of the bunk.

There were many obstacles to staying here, not the least of which was the sheriff's antagonism. But there would be obstacles no matter where he went. He was twenty-one and two of those twenty-one years had been spent behind bars, wasted and thrown away. Another couple of years had been wasted drifting around, picking up a few weeks work in one place, a few in another. Before that he had spent two bitterly frustrating years trying to help his father climb out of the pit into which his grief had toppled him. He wasn't going to waste any more of his life, no matter what the sheriff said.

He thought now, guiltily, that perhaps if he hadn't run away, perhaps if he had stayed, he might have prevented the killing for which his father had been hanged. A little more patience on his part might have made it possible for Amos Kailey to give up drinking.

Impatiently, he shook his head. All that was past. There was nothing he could do to change it now. What mattered was the future. What mattered was a job, and a place to live, and something to wear other than this prison-issue suit that looked like exactly what it was.

He pulled on his shoes. There was a rusty bucket in one corner of the room that looked as if it would hold water. He carried it outside, walked through the mud to the river bank, filled it and returned.

11

There was soap, a comb and a razor in his saddlebags. He washed and shaved and combed his hair. Somehow, he thought, he had to raise the money necessary to redeem this shack and the land that went with it. That was first. Maybe the bank would lend the money to him, he thought.

He brushed off his clothes as best he could, went out and saddled up his horse. He mounted and headed toward town.

Rain had raised the level of the river and what had, last night, been a clear and placid stream was now a muddy, roily one. The road skirted the river all the way to the edge of town where it crossed on a wooden bridge that paralleled the railroad trestle.

The skies were still cloudy, but here and there was a patch of blue and occasionally the sun shone briefly through. Frank rode past the railroad depot and up Juarez Street at a trot, his horse throwing up clods of mud behind them.

The bank wouldn't be open until nine, so he pulled in at Ferguson's Restaurant, dismounted, and tied his horse. He had three dollars and some loose change. Enough to eat for a week, but not enough to also pay for a room at the hotel.

This early, there was no one eating in the restaurant. Ben Ferguson came from the kitchen, wiping his hands on his apron. He stared at Frank a moment without recognizing him.

Frank said, "Hello, Mr. Ferguson."

Ferguson's face lost color. He continued to wipe his hands, even though they now were dry. His hands were shaking visibly.

Ferguson was a skinny man, bald, with prominent teeth in front that made him look like a rabbit or a squirrel. He breathed, "Frank Kailey! I thought—"

"I finished my sentence, Mr. Ferguson. I've come home."

Ferguson swallowed and his Adam's apple bobbed. He asked in a shaking voice, "What do you want with me?"

Frank stared at him, puzzled. He said, "I want some breakfast. Maybe some flapjacks and ham."

Ferguson stared back at him unbelievingly. Then he turned, mumbled something, and disappeared.

Frank sat down at the counter, frowning lightly at his thoughts. People were sure acting peculiarly. Last night the sheriff had been unable to meet his eyes. This morning,

12

Ferguson acted terrified. But why? Did they think he had come back here for revenge?

And even if he had, revenge for what? His father had been legally convicted and legally sentenced to death. Frank had attacked the judge immediately afterward, but his act had been more because of shock at the judge's diatribe than because he had thought the verdict was unfair.

He could hear Ferguson moving around in the kitchen. After what seemed a long time, Ferguson brought his breakfast. The man filled his coffee cup, spilling coffee because his hands were shaking so. He ducked back into the kitchen and Frank heard the back door close.

He wolfed the food. He hadn't eaten for almost twenty-four hours. He gulped the last of the coffee. Ferguson had not returned.

Behind him, the street door opened. He turned his head. Sheriff Coates came in and closed the door. He sat down beside Frank. "You gave Ferguson a start. He figured maybe you were after him."

"What for? Why would I be after him?"

"He was on the jury that convicted your pa."

Frank said, "I'm not after him. I'm not after anyone. All I want is a chance to start where I left off. I want a job and I want to work and I want to be left alone so that maybe, one of these days, I can forget."

The sheriff shook his head. "You ain't going to find any of those things here. Move on, Frank. Get on that horse and ride out of here and don't come back."

"What about pa's place?"

"I told you it was sold for taxes. But maybe I could get you a hundred dollars for a quitclaim deed."

Frank Kailey frowned. The sheriff didn't look at him. He was staring out the window instead.

Frank called, "Mr. Ferguson!"

Ferguson came from the kitchen, drying his hands. Frank asked, "How much?"

"Twenty cents."

Frank laid down a dollar. With shaking hands, Ferguson made change. Frank put it in his pocket and got to his feet.

The sheriff asked, "Want me to see if I can get that hundred dollars for you?"

Frank shook his head.

Coates said warningly, "I can make you leave."

"How?"

13

"You're a vagrant. If you don't leave, I can throw you in jail."

Frank felt anger stirring in him. He said, "I made a mistake and I attacked that judge. But I was only nineteen years old. I'd just heard my father sentenced to be hanged. Now I've served my time. The law says I've paid my debt. Why don't you just let me alone?"

Coates said unyieldingly, "Get on your horse and ride out of town. I'll give you until sundown tomorrow."

Frank Kailey shook his head. The sheriff repeated stubbornly, "Sundown tomorrow."

Frank stared steadily at him and this time the sheriff met his stare. His face reddened and his eyes grew progressively colder and angrier. It was a foolishly stubborn contest of wills and when Frank realized how furious it was making Coates he deliberately looked away, shrugged and went out the door. Coates remained behind, presumably to talk to Ferguson.

Frank was frowning as he untied his horse. He hesitated a moment holding the reins. He had worked at Mendelbaum's Mercantile years ago before he went away. Maybe he could get a job there now. Maybe he could work for Mendelbaum at least long enough to get some clothes.

He mounted and rode up the street toward the store and found Sol Mendelbaum sweeping the walk in front. Frank drew his horse to a halt and said, "Hello, Mr. Mendelbaum."

The old man stopped sweeping and peered up at him through the thick-lensed glasses he always wore. Frank could see he hadn't been recognized so he said, "It's Frank Kailey, Mr. Mendelbaum. I need a job. I thought maybe you'd give me one."

Mendelbaum started sweeping again. He made his broom fairly fly. It was as if Frank Kailey wasn't even there. Frank said, "Mr. Mendelbaum?"

Without looking up or slowing down, Mendelbaum shouted. "You get away from me! I only did what the law said. There were twelve of us and we did what we thought was right. You go away or I'll get Sheriff Coates."

Frank stared down at the old man, frowning with puzzlement. He started to protest, but suddenly changed his mind. It wouldn't do any good. Mendelbaum was as frightened as Ferguson had been. He wasn't going to get a job from Mendelbaum and he might as well leave before Mendelbaum got more excited.

He turned his horse and rode back down the street to-

14

ward the livery barn. The animal hadn't had anything to eat since the night before last. It would take fifty cents from his dwindling supply of money to stable the horse but it had to be done.

Medicine Arrow was not a large town. It contained about three hundred people. It existed to supply the needs of the ranches that surrounded it, and to supply the Navajo Reservation at Chimney Rock.

Juarez Street ran the length of town and contained most of the town's adobe business establishments. Juarez Street began on the open prairie at the upper end of town and terminated at the railroad depot down at the lower end. There was a Plaza about halfway down Juarez. In the middle of the Plaza was a bandstand and a few benches painted green. Otherwise it was just bare ground and trees.

At the corner of the Plaza nearest the depot, Frank Kailey stopped his horse. This was the spot where his mother had been killed. She had stepped into the street before crossing when a runaway horse drawing a buggy came galloping out of the sidestreet and knocked her down. One of the horse's hoofs struck her head, killing her almost instantly.

A man was walking diagonally across the Plaza toward him now. Frank recognized him as Domingo Feliz. Feliz had not seen him, but was walking hurriedly, his head down, apparently oblivious of everything. He was a small, quick, dark-skinned man who, even two years ago, had a wife and a start on a family. He'd had two children then. Frank supposed that by now he had at least two more.

When Feliz was less than a dozen yards away, Frank said, "Hello, Domingo."

Startled, Feliz looked up.

Frank waited for the familiar reaction, the nervousness, the fear, but it didn't come. And suddenly he knew why. Feliz had not served on the jury two years ago. He had not been old enough. Feliz stared up at him a moment, then grinned. "Frank! Frank Kailey! When did you get back?"

Frank swung from the back of his horse. He extended his hand and Feliz gripped it. Frank said, "I got back last night."

The smile faded from Domingo's face. "Was it pretty bad?"

"Prison?" Frank shrugged. He didn't want to talk about it or even to think about it. He said, "It's over now."

15

"What are you going to do? Where—"

"I stayed out at our shack last night. But the sheriff tells me the shack and pa's land have been sold for taxes."

Domingo's expression said he hadn't known. His surprise at Frank's arrival said he hadn't been the one who sent the fifty dollars in the unmarked envelope. He said, "I'm sorry, Frank. Is there anything I can do?"

Frank shook his head. He swung to the back of his horse. He was grateful for Domingo's friendliness but he didn't want Domingo to incur the sheriff's displeasure because of it. He said, "I'll be around a while. I'll see you again."

Feliz nodded, still grinning up at him, and Frank rode away in the direction of the livery barn.

One thing continued to puzzle him. Why had the sheriff been unable to meet his eyes last night? And why had both Ferguson and Mendelbaum acted so damned terrified?

It was true that he had attacked the judge. Terrified and shocked at hearing the death sentence passed on his father, angered by the judge's gratuitous lecture on the wages of sin, he had lost his head and attacked the man. But that didn't mean he had come back here to take revenge on the twelve members of the jury that had found his father guilty. Or on the arresting sheriff who had assembled the evidence. Or on anyone else who had been involved.

Frank stared bleakly at the town, at its muddy street, at the people now beginning to appear on the walks along Juarez. A few of them stared back, recognized him and quickly looked away. Slow, smoldering anger began to grow in him. Maybe in the end they would force him to leave. But he wasn't going to make it easy for them. He'd fight back just as long as he was here.

Chapter 3

THE LIVERY BARN was one of the few frame buildings in town. It loomed above the surrounding one-story adobe buildings and, as if its size did not make it noticeable enough, was painted a garish yellow-orange. Behind it stood a system of corrals, and in a vacant lot on the south side there were a couple of dozen rigs of various sizes and kinds, from buggies to a ponderous Concord stagecoach that had once belonged to the Butterfield Company.

The barn's tall double doors opened on the street and there was a plank ramp leading from the street up to the doors. Frank Kailey rode his horse up the ramp and dismounted just inside. There it was gloomy and dark, but a welcoming voice called from the depths, "Just a minute! I'll be right there."

Frank waited. After several minutes a man came shuffling toward him, a man he recognized immediately in spite of the dim light. It was Dell Aker, middle-aged, stooped, smelling, like always, of horse sweat and whiskey and manure.

Frank stepped out from behind his horse and handed the reins to the stableman. "Give him both hay and oats. Is it still fifty cents a day?"

Aker started visibly. He peered at Frank, the reek of whisky on his breath reminding Frank suddenly and unpleasantly of his father. Frank said, "You're right. It's Frank Kailey. I served my time and I've come home."

Aker licked his lips. He cleared his throat but he didn't say anything. Frank asked with sudden impatience, "What the hell's the matter with everybody? You all act like. . . ." He stopped. Nothing he could say was going to change the fact that Aker was afraid of him. Aker, like Mendelbaum and Ferguson, had served on the jury that con-

17

victed Amos Kailey of murder. All three apparently thought his son had come back for revenge.

Frank turned and tramped disgustedly down the ramp and out into the street. There was an unpleasant chill running along his spine, and its coldness began spreading through his chest. It was the coldness of desperation. How could he combat this irrational fear he seemed to generate in everyone he met? How could he get a job and live a normal life when everyone seemed to expect only vengeance and violence from him?

Maybe Ray Coates was right. Maybe he ought to ride out of this town and never come back to it. That would be simpler all around, for everyone.

He looked up and down the street. All his memories were here, good and bad. Here he had gone to school, riding in bareback from the ranch in the river bottom every morning, riding back out every evening. He had spent his first penny in Mendelbaum's Mercantile at the age of five.

He thought of the sheriff's offer to get him a hundred dollars for a quitclaim deed to the ranch and the shack that stood on it. A hundred dollars would buy him clothes, a gun, and would keep him until he got a long ways from here and found himself a job. By leaving, perhaps he could put a lot of unpleasant memories behind, memories of sitting in the crowded courtroom and hearing the judge say implacably, "You have been found guilty of the crime of murder by a jury of your peers. Have you anything to say?"

And his father's voice, "No sir," shaky and almost inaudible.

And the judge's voice again, "I sentence you to be hanged by the neck until you are dead, said sentence to be carried out at dawn two weeks from today. May God have mercy on your soul."

For a long moment after that, there had been silence in the court. Frank sat stunned in his front row seat. But the judge wasn't through. He suddenly and unexpectedly launched into a tirade about the heinousness of Amos Kailey's crime. He said hanging was too good for him but was, unfortunately, the maximum allowed under the law.

Frank remembered the coldness that had crept through his body as he sat listening. And as the judge went on and on, he remembered the wildness that had replaced it. The next thing he remembered was yelling, "Shut up! Shut up!"

18

and trying to smash the judge's thin, grayish lips with his fists. Then hands were pulling at him, the judge was screeching, and Frank was dragged from the room.

The judge sentenced him to two years in prison a couple of days afterward, his face showing the marks of Frank Kailey's fists. Frank was spared the spectacle of his father hanging in the alley behind the jail, but he saw the scaffold being built. Sheriff Coates escorted him to Santa Fe, returning in time to officiate at the hanging. Frank was not even notified that his father was dead. He read about it in the newspaper a couple of weeks afterward.

Up at the courthouse, the clock began to strike. It struck nine times. Frank turned and headed for the bank.

There was neither hope in him now, nor enthusiasm. Otis McCurdy, the banker, had also been on the jury that had found Amos Kailey guilty of the murder of Juan Trevino. Frank's chances of getting a loan from him would be mighty poor if McCurdy reacted to him the way all the other jury members had.

But he had to try. Before he let the sheriff get that hundred dollars for him, he at least had to give staying here a try.

Walking toward the bank, he wondered who had bought the tax title to the land. And he wondered why the sheriff had refused to tell him the buyer's name. Could the buyer be Sheriff Coates himself?

He reached the bank, a low, adobe building with a long gallery in front and brass bars on the windows. Inside, there was a girl behind the brass-barred teller's window, a girl whose face stirred an elusive memory in Frank. He walked toward her, and suddenly recognized her. She was Kate Guerrero, who had sometimes gone to dances with him down at the Odd Fellows Hall.

She was a dark-eyed, dark-haired girl, descended from an aristocratic Spanish family that had been in New Mexico for at least a hundred years. There was genuine welcome in her eyes as she recognized him. "Frank! Frank Kailey!" She flushed with pleasure. "It's good to see you back!"

He stood at the barred window, grinning foolishly at her. She put both hands through and took one of his. She squeezed it hard and released it again.

He said, "Kate, you look the same."

"Well, *you* don't. You look like you haven't had a decent meal for months. You come for supper tonight. You hear?"

He nodded, for the moment not willing to trust himself to speak. He cleared his throat. "Is Mr. McCurdy here?"

"Of course. I'll tell him you want to see him."

She turned and left the window. She went into McCurdy's office near the rear of the bank. She was gone for what seemed an awfully long time. When she returned, her smile had disappeared and her face was pale. "He'll see you, Frank. Just go on back."

Frank said, "He's scared to see me, isn't he?"

She nodded wordlessly.

He said, "Why? Why are they all afraid of me? Do I look that mean?"

"Maybe their consciences bother them."

"Why should their consciences bother them?"

She looked at him strangely a moment, then repeated, "Go on back to his office, Frank."

Frank opened the gate and walked back to McCurdy's office. The door was ajar so he knocked lightly, pushed it open and went in.

McCurdy was standing at the window looking out. The bars on it suddenly reminded Frank of the bars on the window of his cell. McCurdy turned.

He was a short, bowlegged man in a dark gray suit. His thinning hair was as gray as his suit. His complexion was florid, and red veins were visible in his cheeks. He wore gold-rimmed glasses pinched to his nose. A black silk cord dangled from them and was secured to a button on his vest. Across his bulging middle, from vest pocket to vest pocket, was a heavy gold chain on one end of which, Frank remembered, was a ponderous gold watch. On the other end was a small gold pocket knife.

Frank nodded. "Hello, Mr. McCurdy."

"Kate said you wanted to see me. But if you've come here to threaten me—" Frank could see the veins stand out on McCurdy's forehead now. His face had grown redder and it was obvious that he was under heavy strain.

Frank said, "The sheriff says my place has been sold for taxes and I want to redeem it from whoever has it now. The sheriff says I still have nine months. I'd like to borrow the money from the bank."

McCurdy turned his back. He walked to the window and stared out. Frank waited, shifting his weight from one foot to the other. McCurdy didn't apparently have the courage to look at him. He didn't have the courage to

20

say no straight to his face so he was going to say it while his back was turned.

McCurdy said, "You're not very good security. You've just come back from two years in prison. Nobody will give you a job and you can't make a living on that ranch unless you have cattle to run on it."

"The ranch is good enough security for the loan. If I don't pay you, you can take the ranch."

"We're not in the business of taking ranches to pay off loans. We don't make loans unless we think there's a good chance they'll be paid back."

"Then you're saying no?"

McCurdy turned. His voice was pleading. "Why don't you get out of Medicine Arrow? Go someplace else and make a brand new start. I can work something out so that you'll have a stake. That land of yours is worth more than what the delinquent taxes were. Let me talk to the buyer. I might be able to get you a couple of hundred dollars for a quitclaim deed. Maybe even three hundred. That would give you a new start someplace."

Frank stared at him. The uneasy certainty that something was wrong kept growing in him. The sheriff had offered him a hundred dollars for a quitclaim deed. Now McCurdy was offering three. It looked like somebody wanted to be rid of him mighty bad.

He felt anger stirring inside of him, but when he spoke, his voice was calm. "Who bought that tax title, Mr. McCurdy? Who owns my place?"

McCurdy wouldn't meet his eyes. "How should I know? I'd have to go to the courthouse to find out."

"Then how can you be sure you can get me three hundred dollars for a quitclaim deed? Sheriff Coates thought he couldn't get more than a hundred dollars for it."

McCurdy looked up now. His face was red and his eyes were furious. He licked his lips. His chest was rising and falling rapidly. He shouted, "Get out of here! You get out of here before I have you thrown in jail!"

Frank stared. McCurdy's hands began to shake. Suddenly his face twisted, as though with pain. He grabbed the edge of his roll-top desk and eased himself into his chair.

His face was ghastly now, pale, almost gray, with sweat beads standing out on it. He gasped, "Doc! For God's sake, get Doc!"

Frank turned and ran out the office door. He could

21

see Kate Guerrero standing in the front of the bank looking toward him. He shouted, "Kate! Something's wrong with Mr. McCurdy. He says to get Doc!"

Kate didn't hesitate. She ran out the front door, leaving it open. Frank turned his head and glanced back toward McCurdy's office. There ought to be something he could do to help, but he didn't know what it would be. He didn't even know what was the matter with McCurdy.

He did know that anger at him had brought it on. Going back now could only make it worse, so he walked to the front door and stepped out onto the walk. He didn't want to be alone in the bank. He didn't want anyone saying later that he had helped himself to anything.

All along the street, people were standing and staring at him or staring in the direction Kate Guerrero had gone. One man hurried toward the sheriff's office in the long, adobe courthouse across the Plaza. He disappeared and a moment later reappeared with the sheriff running at his side. The two came toward the bank. Coates dragged his revolver from its holster and came on with it in his hand.

When he was close enough, he shouted breathlessly, "What the hell's going on up here?"

Frank gestured with his head toward the door of the bank. "It's McCurdy. Something's the matter with him. He told me to send Kate for Doc and that's what I did."

Coates ran into the bank, followed by the other man. After several moments Frank saw Kate reappear half a block away with Doc Baker following her, a black bag in one hand. The two hurried toward the bank.

Before they could reach it, Sheriff Coates and the other man came out the door. Coates looked at Frank. "What the hell did you do to him?"

"I didn't do anything. He just suddenly had a pain and sat down in his chair. He said to get Doc so I sent Kate after him."

"Well, it's too late for Doc to do any good. McCurdy's dead."

"Dead?" Frank felt stunned.

"Yes." Doc Baker and Kate arrived. Coates said, "He's dead, Doc, but I want to know what caused his death."

Kate's face was white, her eyes numb with shock. Coates said, "You'd better go home, Kate. I'll lock up when we're through in here."

She stared at Frank. "What happened, Frank?"

"He had a pain. That's all I know."

22

She nodded, accepting his explanation unquestioningly. She said, "I'll be looking for you tonight at six."

He nodded. Coates watched Kate walk away, then turned to Frank. "Don't leave town today. Don't leave until I hear what Doc's got to say."

Frank Kailey shook his head. He wasn't going anywhere until he knew what was going on, and until he knew what was scaring the people in this town.

Chapter 4

FRANK KAILEY walked uptown toward the courthouse feeling as if everybody on the street was watching him, and just about everybody was. Not much happened in Medicine Arrow and when something like a trial or a hanging—or the return of a convict thought to have come back for revenge—did occur, then people paid attention.

When McCurdy had said he didn't know who had bought up the tax title on the ranch, Frank had been sure he was lying. But McCurdy had also mentioned checking the records in the courthouse to find out. And that was what Frank intended to do now, to find out who held the tax title on the ranch and the amount that he'd have to raise to redeem it.

The courthouse resembled the famous old Palace of Governors in Santa Fe, although smaller. It was a low, adobe building with log beams extending out from the adobe walls in front to form a gallery. The gallery was paved with adobe bricks that had been worn smooth by thousands of feet over the years.

The sheriff's office and the county jail were at one end of the building, the courtroom at the other. In the center were the offices of the county treasurer, the county clerk and the county assessor. Frank glanced over his shoulder as he went through the open door and saw Sheriff Coates standing in the doorway of the sheriff's office, scowling angrily at him.

Frank ignored him and went into the county treasurer's office. John Littlehorse, the treasurer, looked up, saw him and, with a wary neutrality, said, "Hello, Frank. I'll bet you're glad to get back home."

John Littlehorse was half Comanche Indian, half Spanish. Only in a community where Indians and Spanish and Anglos mingled so well could he ever have been elected county treasurer. Frank remembered that Littlehorse had not been on the jury that convicted his father. He nodded and grinned sparingly. "I thought I would be but now I'm not so sure. People have been treating me like they'd rather I'd just disappear."

Littlehorse ignored the remark. He asked, "What can I do for you?"

"I want you to look up the name of the man that bought the tax title to our ranch."

"I can tell you that without looking it up. The sheriff did. Sheriff Coates."

Frank wondered fleetingly why he wasn't more surprised. If the sheriff owned tax title to the ranch, it explained his offer of a hundred dollars for a quitclaim deed. It also explained why he was so anxious for Frank to get out of town.

Frank asked, "Can you tell me how much it's going to take to redeem it from him?"

"I'll have to check on that." Littlehorse got down a huge ledger and laid it on the desk. He was a muscular man of medium height, with a dark complexion inherited from both his Spanish and Comanche ancestors. His hair was black and straight, his hands strong and stubby-fingered. He found the place in the ledger he was looking for, ran a finger down a column and said, "The delinquent taxes were $143.88." He figured rapidly on a piece of paper and said, "It'll cost you close to $175.00 to redeem the land. The house got burned a long time ago, didn't it?"

Frank nodded. "There's a shack out there that I built before I went away. It's pretty run down but I could fix it up."

"Know where you're going to get the $175.00?"

Frank shook his head. A hundred and seventy-five dollars wasn't much for two sections of river bottom land but right now it seemed like several thousand to Frank. It was going to be that hard to raise.

With McCurdy dead, his best chance of borrowing the money had disappeared. Now, he didn't know who to ask.

He went out and stood for a moment on the gallery. He hadn't come back for revenge, but suddenly, standing there in his soiled and rumpled prison clothes, he felt resentment stirring him.

It was true that he had attacked the judge. It was true that his father had been executed for robbing and killing Juan Trevino, who had run a cantina for the town's Mexican laborers. But the debt had been paid. He had served his time. Now that he was back, he thought he deserved something better than all this suspicion and hostility. Furthermore, it seemed to him highly unethical for the sheriff to buy tax title to his ranch just a few weeks before his release.

He heard a door close and turned his head. Sheriff Coates had come out onto the gallery in front of the jail. He looked at Frank and said, "I want to talk to you."

"Yeah. And I want to talk to you." Frank walked toward him.

The sheriff gestured toward the office door. Frank went in. He said, "Now I know why you've been so damn anxious to get rid of me."

Coates' face flushed but his eyes were hard and his mouth was an angry line. "You don't know any such goddam thing. Why shouldn't I buy the tax title to that land? It's a good piece of land and I had no idea you'd ever come back here."

"Well, I did come back and now I want the land."

"You can have it if you can raise the money to redeem it from me."

"I thought I was supposed to get out of town by sundown tomorrow."

Coates uttered an angry obscenity. He glared at Frank. "What in the hell do you want from me anyway? You came back here looking for revenge and because you did, McCurdy's layin' down there dead. You seem to think this town owes something to you. Well, it don't."

"I didn't say it did. All I said was that I wanted to stay. I said I wanted to get a job and work and be let alone."

"Well, you're not going to be let alone. You've got the people in this town half scared to death."

"Why should they be scared? I haven't done anything to scare them. I haven't threatened anyone. I haven't said I came back for revenge."

"You don't have to say some things."

Frank Kailey stared at Coates, realizing that for some reason he had the upper hand. He asked, "Well, what do you want me to do? Make up your mind. Do I have to get out of town at sundown tomorrow or are you going to let me stay and redeem my ranch?"

Coates opened his mouth to say something, then closed it like a trap. He said, "Just get the hell out of this office! And by God, if you bother any more of the jurymen that convicted your old man, I won't wait until

26

sundown tomorrow. I'll run you out of town tonight!"

Frank shrugged. He turned and went out onto the gallery. From here he could see the corner where his mother had died in the dust of the street. He could suddenly remember her lying there with blood matting and drying on her hair. . . .

He shook his head impatiently and walked away. He didn't know where he was going, but suddenly he found himself walking toward Kate Guerrero's house. Maybe Kate could tell him what was the matter with the people here. Maybe Kate could tell him what was going on.

Medicine Arrow, like most unplanned Spanish communities, had its share of narrow, twisting alleyways that, from necessity, served as streets. The route Frank took to Kate Guerrero's house led through the Spanish section of town, between rows of squat, adobe houses along bare, dusty alleyways sometimes no more than eight or ten feet wide.

A block from the courthouse, he came out of a narrow alleyway into one that was somewhat wider, and he was suddenly face to face with four men.

He recognized them immediately. One was Floyd Hapgood, big and fat and mean, who ran the Red Ram Saloon. Another was Sam Ford, the town blacksmith. Ford's hands were enormous, their backs thickly covered with fine black hair. Ford wore a beard, as black as the hair on his hands. He was a short, squat man whose legs seemed too short for the ponderous torso and oversized head they were forced to support.

The third was Jules Trevino, the son of the man Amos Kailey had been hanged for murdering. The fourth was Jess Cozzins, who owned a horse ranch about twenty miles from town. All four were red-faced and out of breath as though they had been forced to run to head him off.

Two blocked his way on the right, two blocked it on the left. Frank stopped suddenly. He took a backward step. He had spent two years in prison in Santa Fe. He had seen this before. He knew what they intended to do to him. Nobody had to explain.

He took another wary, backward step. Immediately Cozzins jumped into the alleyway behind him to cut him off.

Frank sidled sideways until he felt an adobe wall at his back. He said, "All right. You can beat hell out of me but what's that going to prove? I didn't come here looking for

27

revenge. Nobody seems to believe it but it's the truth."

Only one man blocked the alleyway on his right. Cozzins was behind him blocking the direction from which he had come. The other two blocked the alleyway on his left.

A dog came from between two houses on Frank's right. Startled by the men he began to bark shrilly. Sam Ford began to curse the dog.

Frank said, "I know all four of you. I can give your names to Coates."

Ford chuckled humorlessly. Hapgood said, "Coates wants you out of town as bad as we do."

Cozzins said, "Let's get it over with. Jules, go down to the stable and tell Aker to give you Frank's horse. We'll put him on it after we're through with him and head him out of town."

Frank glanced around, looking for some weapon with which he might even up the odds. He saw nothing. He began to edge along the adobe wall toward the opening from which the dog had appeared. He knew it would do no good to talk. Nor would it help to plead. They intended to beat him and tie him, unconscious, on his horse.

He said, "What the hell is the matter with all of you? I told you I didn't come back for revenge. All I want is to be left alone."

Again Ford laughed. "Tell that to McCurdy."

"I didn't touch McCurdy."

"No. Sure not. But he's dead just the same. And by God you're not going to stay here and pick us off one by one."

Jules Trevino had disappeared. As the three began to close in on him, Frank made a sudden dive for the passageway where the dog had appeared earlier. He didn't make it. Sam Ford's body struck him and slammed him hard against the adobe wall. Ford's enormous hands seized him and flung him violently across the alleyway. He struck the opposite adobe wall with his head and slid, stunned, to the dusty ground.

He could see their three pairs of feet advancing toward him through the dust and suddenly a wild kind of fury sprang in him. He wasn't going to take a damn bit more from the people of this town. Maybe these three would beat him senseless but they were going to have to work at it.

He shook his head furiously, trying to clear it. He

28

flung himself at a pair of legs half a dozen feet away and felt the man sprawl on top of him as he fell. It was Ford and now Frank twisted around, seized Ford's beard in both his hands and began to beat Ford's head rhythmically on the hard-packed ground.

A kick landed in his ribs and drove the breath out of him. He rolled aside, wickedly jubilant because Ford lay stunned. Another kick caught him in the back and for a moment the pain was nearly unbearable.

But the pain was having a strange effect on him. Instead of weakening his will, it only made him more furious. Crawling, he made it to the adobe wall and fought to come erect. A fist slammed into his mouth. He tasted blood and felt his lips smashed against his teeth. But he was up now, and he swung a haymaker at Cozzins that happened to connect. Cozzins went to his knees and remained there a moment, shaking his hanging head.

Now Ford was up again, his eyes red and savage. Floyd Hapgood had a stick of firewood in both his hands, easing in cautiously, looking for a chance to strike.

Frank suddenly whirled and ran. He made it to the passageway where the dog had appeared and ducked into it. He either stumbled or was caught from behind. He sprawled face down in the narrow, trash-littered passageway. Hapgood sprawled on top of him, hitting with the stick of firewood. The first blow struck Frank between the shoulders. The second hit the back of his head, driving his face into the dirt. His mouth tasted brassy and he could feel his senses slipping away. Vaguely he thought that if Hapgood hit him again with that damned stick of wood it was going to kill him for sure. He exerted all the will he could muster to hold onto his fading senses. He rolled, and saw the stick of firewood descending, and put up his hands to ward it off.

It struck, but now he had his hands on it. He twisted it away from Hapgood, and fought furiously to free his body from Hapgood's heavy one. When he had, he slammed the stick down repeatedly on the top of Hapgood's head. The man slumped.

Frank tried to crawl away, but Ford came plunging into the narrow passageway and aimed a booted foot at his face. The boot toe connected with his jaw.

Ford stooped and yanked the stick from Frank's grasp. Savagely now and with plain intent to kill, he began to beat on Frank's unprotected head.

Frank faintly heard a voice, "Sam! For Christ's sake,

that's enough! We don't want to kill the son-of-a-bitch!"

He lay there several moments more. Then somebody grabbed his ankles and dragged him out of the passageway. Grit and dirt got into his mouth. He was conscious but he couldn't move.

Cozzins and Ford were now apparently trying to get Hapgood's great bulk out of the passageway. He heard Cozzins say, "That's a hell of a lump on Hapgood's head." Not long afterward, Cozzins said, "Here comes Jules with the horse."

Hands raised Frank and slung him over the back of his horse. His hands and feet were tied beneath the horse's belly. Someone lashed the horse's rump and the animal galloped down the narrow alleyway.

Terror touched Frank Kailey's thoughts. What if the horse galloped out on the prairie and never stopped? What if he couldn't get his hands and feet untied? He could starve, and die, and rot on this horse's back unless the horse managed to dislodge him or unless he managed to free himself.

He tried to open his mouth and cry out for help but no sound came. The horse continued on past the limits of the town and onto the empty prairie beyond. The inert burden on his back and the lack of a controlling hand on the reins terrified and puzzled him. He ran as though some nameless terror were pursuing close behind.

Chapter 5

THE DRUM of the horse's hoofs died away. Sam Ford stood staring in the direction the animal had gone, hands on hips, legs spread. He growled, "That ought to take care of the son-of-a-bitch! By the time he gets his hands and feet loose, he'll be a long ways from here and in no mood to come crawlin' back."

Jules Trevino was kneeling at Hapgood's side. He looked up, his face pale. "Senor Ford! Senor Ford, come here!"

Ford turned. He knew what Trevino was going to say even before he said it.

"Senor Hapgood is dead."

"Dead? He can't be dead!"

Cozzins, lanky, long-haired, and red-faced, knelt and picked up Hapgood's fat wrist. He tried to find a pulse, couldn't and dropped the hand with a disgusted curse. "He's so damned fat I couldn't find a pulse even if there was one."

Ford said, "He ain't breathin'. I ain't seen his chest move once."

Cozzins growled, "That's a big knot on his head. You reckon that could have killed him?"

"I don't know. What I do know is that we'd better fix up some kind of story before Coates gets here."

"Story? What kind of story can we fix up—that Kailey attacked the four of us? Even Coates wouldn't swallow that."

"We could say we stopped him to talk to him, to try and persuade him to leave. We could say he grabbed the stick of wood and attacked us with it. Hell, he attacked the judge in his own courtroom two years ago with nothing but his bare hands, didn't he?"

Cozzins nodded. "Maybe you're right. Anyhow, it's about the only story we *can* tell." He turned his head

31

and looked at Jules. "Go get the sheriff. And while you're downtown, get the doc. And tell Burt Vigil to bring the hearse to pick Hapgood's body up."

Jules Trevino ran obediently down the narrow alleyway toward the center of town. Before he reached the courthouse, he slowed, so that he would not be too out of breath to talk. He went into the sheriff's office. It was cool and dark and smelled of cigar smoke. The sheriff looked up from his desk.

Trevino said, "Senor Sheriff, they have sent me to bring you. Senor Hapgood is dead."

Coates got up, scowling. "How the hell did that happen? Who—?"

"It was Frank Kailey. He hit Senor Hapgood with a stick of firewood."

"What?"

"Yes, Senor." Trevino was a slight, dark-skinned young man of sixteen. Since his father's death, he had helped his mother run the cantina his father had operated.

"Where is Hapgood?"

Trevino told him. "Senor Ford told me to get the doctor and to tell Senor Vigil to bring the hearse."

"All right. You do that and I'll go see what's going on down there. You say Ford's there? Who else?"

"Senor Cozzins is also there."

Coates nodded, his expression saying he was beginning to understand. "And where is Frank Kailey? Is he dead too?"

Trevino shook his head. "They tied him on his horse. They whipped the horse and he ran away."

"Then I take it Kailey was unconscious when they tied him on his horse?"

"Si, Senor."

"Did you see what happened before that?"

"Si." Trevino shifted from one foot to the other and eyed the door.

Coates stared steadily at the floor. He was afraid of Sam Ford. He was afraid of Cozzins, too. He said in a voice that was barely audible, "They stopped Senor Kailey to tell him to leave town. He attacked Senor Hapgood with a stick of firewood."

"And what were the rest of you doing all this time?" The sheriff's voice was dry.

"Fighting him, Senor. He was like a wildcat."

"And you three finally subdued him after he had killed Hapgood with the stick of firewood. He was unconscious so you tied him on his horse and whipped the horse out of town."

"Si."

Coates said, "You're a liar, Jules. The four of you attacked Kailey. I don't know what you were doing with those other three, but they were trying to get Kailey to leave town, weren't they?"

Trevino nodded reluctantly.

"Why were you with them?"

"They said if I was with them, Senor Kailey would listen. He would be ashamed because I was the son of the man his father killed."

Coates snorted disgustedly. "Go find the doc. And get Burt Vigil to hitch up his hearse."

Trevino escaped and ran down the street. Coates went out onto the gallery and turned toward the Mexican section of town where Jules had said Hapgood's body was. Puzzled, as he walked, he growled to himself, "What I can't understand is how come Kailey doesn't know. Seems like somebody would have told him by now."

It didn't really matter to Coates who had started the ruckus that had resulted in Hapgood's death. What did matter was that because Frank Kailey had returned to Medicine Arrow last night, two men were dead. McCurdy's heart had stopped. Hapgood had died from a blow on the head. Even if the blow had been struck in self-defense, the fact remained that if Kailey had not come back, both McCurdy and Hapgood would be alive.

An uneasy premonition ran a chill along the sheriff's spine. He shook it off impatiently. He was behaving like an old woman or a superstitious Indian, he told himself. But the uneasiness remained, as did the thought that had prompted it. What if McCurdy and Hapgood were only the first to die. What if more of the jurymen died off?

He told himself it was silly to think this way. Kailey didn't even know the truth. And if he didn't know the truth, why should he be thinking of revenge?

The trouble was that the jurymen weren't aware that Kailey didn't know. Their own guilty consciences were making them afraid. Fear had certainly caused McCurdy's death. It had caused Hapgood's death as well.

He reached the place where Ford and Cozzins waited for him. A small crowd of Mexicans had collected. A dog was sniffing at Hapgood's body, the hackles raised on the back of his neck. Coates said, "All right, let's have it. And don't bother trying that stupid story you cooked up on me. I want the truth."

Ford looked at him sheepishly. "What did Trevino say?"

"What you all agreed you'd say. But I know different. You were going to beat Frank Kailey up, weren't you? You jumped him and it was three against one even if Jules didn't take any part in it. Frank fought back and Hapgood got hit in the head with a stick of wood. Isn't that how it was?"

"Damn it, who's side are you on? You tried to get rid of him yourself, didn't you?"

Coates said, "You dumb bastards, Frank Kailey doesn't even know the truth. *He doesn't know his father was innocent.*"

Ford and Cozzins stared unbelievingly. Coates nodded. "He thinks his father was guilty. He thinks the trial was fair. He believes you brought in an honest verdict based on the evidence."

"Well, we did! We made a mistake, that's all. We're only human. Anybody can make a mistake."

"Sure. *If* it was a mistake. Except that you and I know different. This whole damned town wanted to get rid of Amos Kailey only they didn't know how to manage it. When Juan Trevino was murdered it was made to order. There didn't have to be any evidence."

"But there *was* evidence. You arrested him yourself."

"Sure, I arrested him. Because he was the only suspect I could find. He'd had a fight with Trevino and threatened him because Trevino wouldn't give him any more whisky on the cuff. But that isn't evidence."

"You arrested him and charged him and testified against him at the trial. The jury relied on your word. So don't lay the blame on us." Cozzins' face was red with anger. "He was a burr under your saddle too."

Coates shrugged. There was no use arguing about something that was over and done with and could not be changed. What mattered now was that Frank Kailey didn't yet know the truth. And if he could be persuaded to leave before he learned the truth, then life would be better all around, both for him and for the people of the town. Coates asked, "Which way did his horse go?"

"You're not going after him, are you? You're not going to bring him back here to stand trial? That would bring the whole stinking mess out into the open, Coates. That's the worst possible thing you could do."

34

Coates said bitterly, "If I brought him back maybe we could convict him of killing Hapgood and get him sentenced to be hung. That would get rid of him for good, wouldn't it?"

Ford glared at the sheriff. He said savagely, "Don't be so high and mighty, Coates. You couldn't wait to buy the tax title to Kailey's land. You're the one that stands to lose most if Frank Kailey stays."

Coates repeated, "Which way did his horse go?" He didn't want to argue the question of Kailey's land. He hadn't done anything wrong in buying it at the tax sale three months ago. But the fact that he held it was going to make every action he took with respect to Frank Kailey suspect in the eyes of the people here.

Ford pointed. Coates said, "You two wait for Doc and for the hearse. I'm going to see if I can't find Frank."

He walked back toward the center of town, scowling to himself. Why the hell did Kailey have to come back anyway? Why couldn't he have gone someplace else? Coates wanted to keep that land. He wanted it for when he retired as sheriff or for when he was defeated by a younger candidate. He could use what he had saved to build a house on it. He could buy cattle a few at a time out of his salary. He could even buy calves now, put them out on that river bottom grass and wait for them to grow.

He reached Juarez Street and turned toward the stable that loomed so prominently above the rest of the town. He was sweating when he reached it and went inside, and the coolness in the stable felt good to him. It was only April but the sun today was hot. He thought of Kailey, tied belly down over the back of his horse, unconscious, beaten, unable to free himself.

He had a brief and cold blooded thought—and was instantly ashamed. If he failed to find him—Kailey would die. And the problem he had dumped in the lap of this town would be solved.

Aker came shuffling to the front of the stable, peering to see who it was. Coates said, "It's me, Dell. Get my horse and saddle him."

"What you goin' to do about Frank Kailey, Ray?"

"Never mind that now. Just get my horse."

Aker hesitated a moment, turned and shuffled away. Coates fished a cigar from the breast pocket of his coat, bit off the end and rolled it back and forth for a moment in his mouth. He lighted it and puffed furiously, the frown remaining on his face.

He knew how the jurymen that had convicted Amos Kailey felt because he felt the same way himself. They felt guilty because they had condemned an innocent man to death. They felt doubly guilty because they had brought in their verdict on insufficient evidence simply because Amos Kailey was a quarrelsome, abusive, unpleasant drunk who, when refused a drink, had been known to go so far as to spit on the men refusing him. He had been thoroughly disliked by everyone in town. He had even driven his own son away. But that didn't justify hanging him for a murder somebody else had committed. And every one of the jurymen knew it.

Aker brought the horse and Coates took the reins from him. He swung to the horse's back and rode him out into the street. He rode out of town, knowing he ought to hurry, but keeping the horse at a steady walk. He would try to find Frank Kailey. He told himself he would. But deep inside he admitted that he didn't want to find Kailey at all. At least he didn't want to find him alive.

Chapter 6

FRANK KAILEY'S HORSE ran for a couple of miles without stopping or slowing down. At the end of that distance he plunged sliding into a deep ravine, starting a small avalanche. Frank's body sagged forward. The rough back and forth motion of the horse going down the precipitous grade made his body flop helplessly back and forth, further terrifying the horse. When he reached the bottom of the slope, he began to buck, frantically trying to rid himself of his burden.

Frank slammed viciously back and forth between pommel and cantle. At the top of each jump there was daylight between him and the saddle but each time the horse hit bottom, Frank slammed down painfully.

Motion and pain brought a return of his senses and a return of his muscular control. He struggled to free himself. The rope had cut cruelly into both his wrists and ankles and now was slippery with blood. Frank pulled against it, gritting his teeth against the pain. The horse had stopped bucking and stood with its head hanging wearily.

Frank's hands could almost, but not quite, slip free. He exerted more pressure. There was raw terror in him now. He knew if he didn't get loose soon both his hands and his feet would swell. When that happened, any chance he might have had before would be gone for good.

Struggling, he worked his body off balance without realizing it. Suddenly and with terrifying finality, his body slid out of the saddle, made a half circle and ended up hanging beneath the horse's belly where his hands and feet had been a few moments before.

The shift of weight again terrified the horse. He galloped away along the rocky floor of the ravine. Frank's body banged against his legs, front and rear. The horse began to buck again, and this further frightened him because when he bucked, Frank slammed repeatedly against his belly and his flanks.

The horse stopped bucking at last. He lay down and rolled, and when he caught Frank's arm between the saddle and a rock, Frank screamed with pain. Sobbing, he cursed the horse and he cursed the men who had tied him here. He cursed the sheriff and he cursed the town.

Once more the horse got to his feet. He stood in one place now, raising his hind feet one by one, trying to kick Frank free, and although he couldn't kick Frank solidly, his hoofs grazed Frank's body painfully several times. Once more Frank's senses began to fade.

He knew he had to get loose, for his time was running out. Again he yanked against the ropes that tied his hands and feet.

This time, perhaps because the ropes were more slippery, one hand came loose. The other followed and Frank fell limply to the ground beneath the horse. The horse, free, kicked at him as he plunged away. A hoof struck Frank's shoulder, numbing it. But he was loose. He was free again.

For several minutes he lay completely still, breathing heavily, sweating copiously. He felt weak with relief. He didn't even care right then if the horse did get away.

At last he stirred and raised himself to his hands and knees. There was a small trickle of water in the middle of the ravine. He crawled to it and scooped out a hole in the gravel and watched the hole fill with muddy water almost immediately.

He plunged his hands in and splashed water on his face. He lowered his face and drank. He splashed water onto his head and the back of his neck. He began to tremble, suddenly, as though he had a chill. It was a reaction, he supposed, but his inability to control it infuriated him. He got to his feet, staggered and fell and got up again. He peered up at the sun, trying to decide which way Medicine Arrow was from here. In his confused and befuddled state, he had no idea. He looked around for the horse, but now the horse was gone. The animal would probably return to town, he thought, to the stable where he had fed last.

He blinked his eyes and stared at the wet gravel in the bottom of the ravine. His horse's tracks stood out plainly, the deeper ones already filling with water. He stumbled along in the direction the horse had gone. He had to catch the animal if he could. In the condition he was in, he could lose himself and die out here.

38

He must have walked half a mile before he saw the horse grazing quietly in a clearing a little higher than the bottom of the ravine. Frank forced himself to straighten up. He forced himself to ignore the pain in his ankles and wrists. He shook his head, forcing it to clear.

He must approach the horse from downwind, he told himself, or else the animal would spook when he smelled the blood. He circled around and then began to speak soothingly. He got to within a dozen feet before the horse whirled and plunged away. Frank halted, holding his breath. The horse ran fifty feet and stopped. He stared at Frank, then lowered his head to crop a mouthful of grass.

Frank approached again, more deliberately, speaking softly. He covered twenty feet of the distance separating him from the horse. He covered another twenty. The horse raised his head and Frank halted, once more holding his breath. The horse continued to stare at him, trembling. Frank began to talk soothingly again. Inch by inch, he eased closer. Finally he was able to put a hand on the horse's neck. With the other he seized the bridle and held on.

The horse smelled blood and whirled. He plunged away, down toward the trickle of water and across the gravel floor of the ravine. Grimly Frank held on. His weight pulled the horse's head sharply to the side. The horse stopped and stood, trembling.

Frank soothed him with a soft monotone, but the words he spoke were savage and profane. "Hold it, you miserable, stupid, hammer-headed son-of-a-bitch. Hold it or I'll beat some goddam brains into you. You give me a time like that again and I'll see that you're made into glue."

He got hold of the reins. He got a foot into a stirrup and swung astride.

His head whirled and he thought he was going to faint from pain. But he held on and when his head had cleared, he guided the horse up the steep side of the ravine in the direction from which he had come earlier.

He had lost his hat. He had lost what little money he possessed. His prison-issue suit hung from his body in filthy rags.

Anger that had begun back there in town earlier now began to grow anew in him. He had come back to Medicine Arrow wanting only peace, wanting only a chance to forget and start where he had left off. The people there had denied him that. McCurdy had refused him a loan. Coates had ordered him out of his own shack in the river bottom. Ford and Cozzins and Hapgood had attacked and beaten him and in the end had tied him on his horse and whipped the animal away.

There had to be a reason why they were treating him so savagely. Now he meant to find out what that reason was. But not yet. Not today. First he had to get cleaned up. He had to have a change of clothes. He needed bandaging and he needed rest. Who, of all the people in Medicine Arrow could he count on now? Domingo Feliz? John Littlehorse? Kate Guerrero?

Suddenly he thirsted just to look at Kate. He knew he could count on her if he could count on no one else.

When he slacked the reins and kicked the horse's sides with his heels, the animal broke into a trot that was a painful gait. Every bruise Frank had sustained hurt. His skinned and bleeding wrists and ankles were on fire. His head throbbed and at times his vision blurred. But he held on.

The landmarks looked right to him. He could see the bluff he had ridden off last night. He could see the cottonwoods that marked the course of the river on his left. The moisture that had rained down during the previous night was already drying fast. The mud was gone. By this time tomorrow, there would be dust again.

Medicine Arrow became visible ahead. Then between him and town, Frank suddenly saw a horseman proceeding toward him at a walk. Quickly he guided his horse into a nearby arroyo, dismounted and, holding onto the reins, climbed to the lip. The horseman was closer now, close enough to recognize. . . . Sheriff Coates.

Coates had his eyes and his attention on the ground. Trailing, thought Frank. Probably trailing him. The sheriff had heard about the beating Ford and Cozzins and Hapgood had given him. He probably knew how they had tied him on his horse and whipped the horse out of town.

Frank's mouth twisted bitterly. Coates sure as hell didn't seem too worried or concerned. But then he probably didn't want to catch up with the runaway horse. It would suit Coates if he died on the horse's back, of thirst, of starvation, of head injuries. It would save everybody a lot of trouble if he was dead when his horse was found. Coates probably figured that if he could stall around until dark, then he'd have to give up for the night.

When Coates had disappeared behind a long ridge, Frank mounted and climbed his horse out of the arroyo. He continued on toward town, circling so that he could approach it from the east, at the edge where the Guerrero

40

house could be found. When he arrived in the dusty street in front, Frank dismounted at the gate. He yanked on the bell rope and winced when the bell rang almost above his head. He waited and several moments later, the gate creaked open.

Kate cried, "Frank! What in the world happened to you? There's blood all over you! And your clothes!"

Frank tried hard to grin. "It's a long story, Kate, but I need help. You're the only one I could think of—"

"You come on in." She took his horse's reins from him and led the animal through while Frank closed the gate behind them.

They entered an adobe walled courtyard, in the center of which was a well. Kate called, "Miguel!" and an elderly man who looked like a Pueblo Indian appeared and took the horse's reins from her. He led the animal away, while Kate and Frank walked on to the house.

There was a long gallery in front with a roof supported by thick pine pillars and a floor paved with adobe bricks. Inside the house was cool. Kate's father sat in a chair, a serape over his shoulders and another across his knees. His face was like a dried apple and his eyes were like black shoe buttons. He looked at Frank with neither recognition nor concern. He must be past ninety, thought Frank.

Kate put a hand affectionately on her father's head as she passed his chair. She turned her head and smiled at Frank. "He lives in a world of his own these days. He doesn't know anyone."

She took him to the kitchen and had him sit down in a chair. She got a pan of water, a cloth and a towel. He winced as she washed the bloody lumps on his head.

She worked silently for a while but at last she asked, "What in the world happened to you, Frank?"

"Ford and Hapgood and Cozzins. They jumped me and beat me up. They tied me on my horse and whipped him out of town."

"Why? In heaven's name, why would they do a thing like that?"

"They wanted me out of town—for good."

She nodded. "I can understand why they wouldn't want you around. You remind them of the terrible mistake they made."

"What do you mean—the *mistake* they made?" he asked slowly.

She took a backward step and stared at him. "Do you mean to tell me that you don't know?"

"Don't know what?"

"That your father was innocent. He was wrongly convicted. He died for a crime committed by another man."

For a moment, Frank was stunned. Shocked, he stared unbelievingly at her. She said, "About a year ago, a man committed a robbery and murder in Santa Fe. He was convicted and executed, but before he died, he confessed killing Juan Trevino and robbing him. So your father was innocent. He didn't do anything."

Suddenly the pieces of the puzzle began to drop into place in Frank Kailey's mind. He understood why McCurdy had been so desperately afraid of him. He understood the fear he had seen in Ferguson, in Aker, in the other jury members he had encountered in town today. He understood why Ford and Hapgood and Cozzins had wanted to be rid of him, why they had been willing to beat him to force him to leave town.

The whole town had despised Amos Kailey. They had wanted to be rid of him for years but they hadn't known how to manage it. When Juan Trevino had been killed after being threatened by Amos Kailey, it had been like handing the townspeople what they had all wanted on a silver platter. They suddenly had their chance to be rid of Amos Kailey once and for all.

Conviction had been a certainty. They would have convicted him on any kind of evidence.

Now, for a year, the jury had lived with the knowledge that they had wrongfully convicted and wrongfully executed a man innocent of any crime. Guilt had gnawed at them until it had become nearly intolerable. The return from prison of that man's son had terrified them because they thought he knew, because they naturally assumed he had come back for revenge.

He'd had no thought of revenge when he first came back. But this changed things. This changed many things.

Chapter 7

WHEN KATE FINISHED washing the abrasions on Frank's head, she raised his hands and looked at each of his cut wrists. "I want to bandage those but maybe you'd like to take a hot bath first."

He nodded. She went out to the kitchen and he followed her. There was a metal bathtub in an adjoining shed. He carried hot water from the stove and cold water from the pump to fill it with. In the meantime, Kate had found some clothes that belonged to her father. Pants, a shirt, underwear, socks and boots. She said "I'm pretty sure the clothes will fit but I'm not sure of the boots. You'll just have to try them on."

Frank felt a surge of gratitude at her matter-of-fact assistance. He said, "Helping me isn't going to make you popular in this town."

"Then I'll have to be unpopular." She went out and pulled the shed door closed. Frank got out of his filthy clothes and climbed into the tub. Water and soap made the abrasions on wrists, ankles, and the rest of his body burn savagely. He sat there soaking for a long time, letting the hot water take some of the soreness out of him. But his thoughts seethed. Damn their lousy souls to hell! It was bad enough for them to have wrongfully convicted and executed his father, to have sent him to prison for an involuntary and tormented attack on the judge who had sentenced him. But now for them to try and rid themselves of him as cold-bloodedly as they had rid themselves of his father simply because his presence reminded them of their own wrongdoing! That was too much.

He was determined now to stay. Kate had given him clean clothes (he was sure she had sent the fifty dollars with which he had bought his horse), but he couldn't accept any more from her. That left only one way to obtain the money necessary to remain in Medicine Arrow. He would have to sell the horse.

He got out of the tub, dried himself, and dressed. Every movement hurt. His head ached savagely and his vision sometimes blurred. Carrying the boots and socks, he went into the kitchen again.

Kate had bandages and salve. She bandaged his ankles and wrists and Frank put on the socks and boots, which fit surprisingly well. He returned for the bathtub and for his discarded clothes. He burned his clothes in the stove and emptied the tub onto the ground behind the house. Every movement hurt but he knew if he let himself remain still his muscles would stiffen and hurt even more.

Kate had some soup waiting when he had finished and she sat across from him while he ate. She asked, "Frank, what are you going to do?"

"I'm going to stay. I'm not going to let them drive me away. And somehow or other I'm going to raise enough money to redeem the ranch."

Her expression remained worried but her eyes told him she was glad. He asked, "You sent me that fifty dollars, didn't you?"

She flushed faintly, hesitated, and finally nodded. He said, "Thank you, Kate. I'll pay you back."

For several moments there was an awkward silence between them. Frank continued to study her and her flush deepened. She avoided looking at him for a time but at last raised her eyes and steadily met his glance. This time, it was Frank who looked away.

It came as a shock to him, the realization that Kate had counted the months until his return, just as he himself had counted them. Kate had waited for him. The realization made a pleasant warmth flood through him. He had been alone but he was alone no more.

He got up. "I'm going back into town."

"Why, Frank? Why don't you rest? You're only human and you've been beaten terribly."

"Does the supper invitation stand?"

"Of course it does."

"Then I'll see you at suppertime."

He limped into the courtyard. Miguel brought his horse, which he had rubbed down and saddled again. Frank mounted, grinned at Kate, and rode away toward the center of town.

He needed money to live until he managed to find a job

or until he could borrow enough to redeem the ranch. But he also needed enough to buy a gun. He had been waylaid and beaten by Hapgood, Ford, and Cozzins and he was damned if anything like that was going to happen to him again.

As he rode down Juarez Street, he felt everyone staring at him. But each time he met someone's glance, that person would look away. He rode past the courthouse. The sheriff's door was closed. He wondered if Coates knew about the attack.

He reached the livery stable and rode up the wooden ramp. He dismounted just inside the doors.

For a long time there was utter silence inside the place. In spite of that, Frank knew Aker was here. Aker was always here, even at night. He had a bed in the tack room. The only time Aker wasn't here was at mealtime and right now it was midafternoon. Frank called, "Mr. Aker! I want to sell my horse."

He waited another long interval. At last he heard a shuffling sound and saw Aker approaching from the rear of the stable. Aker carried a pitchfork in his hands, the tines pointed menacingly at Frank. He carried it like a weapon that he fully intended to use.

Warily, Frank stepped behind his horse. This morning he would have ruled out the possibility that Aker might attack him with the pitchfork but since the attack in the alley by Hapgood, Cozzins and Ford, he knew it was possible. He said, "You don't need that. All I want is to sell my horse."

"I'm not buying horses. And you get out of here. You're not going to do me like you did Hapgood."

"What are you talking about? Take a look at what Hapgood did to me." He pointed to some of the bloody bumps on the side of his head.

"You're alive. That's the difference."

"And Hapgood isn't?" There was a sudden emptiness in Frank's chest.

"That's what I said. You killed him. Just like you killed McCurdy earlier. But don't try anything with me or I'll run this fork right through your gut."

Frank said patiently, "I want to sell my horse. That's all. This is a livery stable. You buy horses all the time and he's a good one. You know he is."

Aker peered at him suspiciously. He eyed the horse, a calculating expression coming into his face. He was scared but not so scared he wouldn't try to buy the horse cheap if he thought there was a chance.

He put the pitchfork down and looked into the horse's mouth. Frank stepped back so as not to further frighten him. Aker wiped his hands on his pants and said, "I'll give you ten for the horse just like he stands. Saddle and bridle too. Take it or leave it. It's the last offer I'm goin' to make."

Frank felt a sudden unreasoning fury, fury like that which had consumed him the day of his father's sentencing. It wasn't enough that they had wrongfully convicted and executed his father, or that they had sent him to prison for two long years. It wasn't enough that they had stolen his ranch and beaten him, and ordered him to leave town by sundown tomorrow. Now Aker was trying to steal what little he had left. Horse and saddle were worth thirty-five or forty dollars at the very least. But Aker knew he was desperate.

Frank lunged at Aker and seized him by the shirtfront with both his hands. He held him there, while Aker struggled frantically to be free. Aker was drooling with terror and his face was gray. Frank raged, "You son-of-a-bitch, you don't want me in town, but you don't mind robbing me while you're waiting for me to leave! You're as bad as Coates!"

Aker tried frantically to speak, but only an incoherent mumbling came out. Frank said disgustedly, "Well, you're not going to rob me. I want forty dollars for that horse. I paid fifty in Santa Fe less than a week ago."

"All right! All right! I'll give you forty! Only please, let go of me! Don't do anything!"

Frank flung him away. Aker stumbled and fell on the manure-littered floor. He got up and lunged for the pitchfork but Frank reached it first. Aker changed his mind and headed for the tack room at a shambling run. Frank blocked his way. "Oh no. You don't keep your money in there. You keep it in that greasy pocketbook in your pants."

Aker stopped. He fumbled in his pocket and came up with the leather pocketbook. He opened it and dumped part of its contents into his hand. He selected two twenty-dollar gold pieces and handed them to Frank. "I want a bill of sale."

"All right. Make one out. But I'll just go along with you so you won't get any ideas about shooting me."

46

He followed Aker into the tack room. Aker got a bill of sale form and filled it out. Frank signed it. He said, "Now go back out into the stable. I wouldn't put it past you to shoot me in the back and claim I robbed you."

Aker glanced once, swiftly, at a rifle standing in the corner. Meekly, then, he preceded Frank out of the tack room. Frank said sourly, "Thank you, Mr. Aker. Now I can stay in Medicine Arrow long enough to find out what's going on."

He went out into the street, elated for the first time since his return. He had these clothes that Kate had given him. He had forty dollars in gold. Things looked much less bleak.

He headed for the hotel. Glancing around cautiously in case Aker tried something, he saw the stableman come running out of the stable door. Aker crossed the street and ran uptown toward the courthouse. Frank supposed he was going to tell Coates his tale of woe. He was probably going to claim he had been robbed, or that he had been forced, under threat of violence, to pay forty dollars for a ten-dollar horse.

Frank went into the hotel. It was a two-story adobe structure. The lobby had a white-tile floor and was filled with horsehair sofas and chairs. Beside each was a brass spittoon. On his right a door opened into the hotel bar. The desk was on the far side of the lobby. Frank crossed to the desk and rang the bell.

A man came out of an office behind the desk. He glanced at Frank and Frank recognized him as Leon Sellers, another member of the jury that had found his father guilty two years ago.

Sellers knew him instantly. He stopped momentarily, then came on determinedly. "I warn you, Kailey, don't you try anything on me! I was on that jury, but eleven other men were on it too. If you're going to blame me you've got to blame the other eleven equally."

Frank said, "I want a room."

"For how long?"

Irritably Frank asked, "How do I know how long? The way things are going, I may not live until tomorrow. Besides, the sheriff told me to be out of town by sundown tomorrow."

Sellers was a portly, white-haired man. Frank had never known him well since he'd never had much occasion to enter the hotel. He'd been in the hotel bar often enough though before he went away. He'd been in there to drag

47

his father out and take him home. Most times he'd only gotten cursed for his pains.

He stared at Sellers as the man pushed a room key across the desk. He said, "You all had a reason, didn't you? Each one of you had a reason for wanting to be rid of him. He was a hell of a pest. He was always cluttering up the hotel bar, begging people to buy him drinks, passing out, vomiting. But he didn't kill Juan Trevino and you knew it down deep all the time, didn't you? The evidence was flimsy and you all knew it but you convicted him because it was a way of getting rid of him."

Sellers looked as though he'd rather be anywhere in the world right now than here. He said, "The sheriff arrested him and charged him and the county attorney brought him to trial. All I did was sit on the jury."

"How many times did you vote? How many ballots did you take? Or were you all agreed when you walked into the jury room?"

Sellers didn't answer that. His failure to answer told Frank that they had been agreed when they walked into the jury room. Only one vote had been taken and it had been unanimous. Amos Kailey had been found guilty of murder in the first degree.

Frank asked, "And what about the money he was supposed to have killed Trevino for? Didn't it seem peculiar to any of you that the money wasn't found? It was missing from Trevino's saloon, but it wasn't found in my father's possession."

Sellers stared pleadingly at him. "Please, Frank. We're all sorry for what we did. We've been living with it for more than a year. We made a mistake but we're human, Frank. Men make mistakes."

"That mistake cost a man his life. How do you think he felt walking up those steps to the scaffold with all of you looking on? Can you even imagine how he felt? He hadn't had a drink for days and he was sick. He was scared. He knew he was innocent, but he also knew nobody in this whole damned town would believe it because they were sick of seeing him around. They were sick of seeing him lying filthy and drunk in the gutter and they were sick of hearing him curse them because they wouldn't buy him a drink. Only I don't care how unpleasant he was, he was a man and he was hanged for something he didn't do!"

His voice had risen. He became aware that people in the lobby were staring at him. There were only three, but they

48

all looked scared. Frank picked up the key and headed for the stairs.

He knew the town was afraid of him. He knew they were wondering what he was going to do. The hell of it was, he didn't know himself.

Chapter 8

THE SHERIFF'S OFFICE had whitewashed adobe walls. The floor was paved with adobe bricks, worn smooth and uneven by years of use. At the rear of the office iron bars from floor to beam ceiling separated the office from the jail. A barred, iron door opened into this area, and in the rear of the building was another door, this one of two-inch oak planks. It was used to escort prisoners to the outhouse behind the jail.

Ray Coates was sitting at his roll-top desk, his booted feet resting on its top, when Aker burst through the door. "Ray! Sheriff! Kailey attacked me! Kailey threatened me! He forced me to buy that damned horse of his for three times what it was worth. I want him arrested and thrown in jail!"

Coates put his feet down on the floor. The cigar in his mouth, he puffed and exhaled deliberately in Aker's direction. He asked, "How much did you pay for his horse?"

"Forty dollars. I offered him ten and he attacked me and forced me to pay forty."

Coates said, "And you expect me to believe that the horse wasn't worth more than ten? I suppose you got the saddle and bridle too."

Aker nodded. He studied the sheriff speculatively, suddenly a lot less excited than when he had come in. He said, "So maybe the horse is worth forty dollars. That ain't the point. The point is that Kailey put his hands on me. He threatened me. That's assault. You can arrest him and bring him to trial and send him to prison again."

"And when he comes out, you'll be the one he's looking for."

"You're supposed to be the law. You're supposed to be able to protect people from the likes of him."

Coates studied the stableman thoughtfully. The man's smell offended his nostrils, composed as it was of stale

50

sweat, horses, manure, and whisky. He doubted if Aker ever changed his clothes.

Two of the jurymen who had found Amos Kailey guilty already lay dead down at Vigil's Undertaking Parlor, he thought. Now, Aker claimed Frank Kailey had threatened him and forced him to pay more for his horse than the animal was worth. He supposed the accusation was at least partly true. Sourly he reflected that no matter how afraid Aker was he had not been sufficiently afraid to quiet his everlasting greed.

Coates had assumed that Kailey had made it back to town and had given up searching for him because he'd found the place where Frank had freed himself from his horse. He had read the tracks and had figured that Frank would probably arrive back in town before he did. He had not, however, been able to locate Frank when he returned.

He asked, "Where did he go when he left your place?"

"He was headed for the hotel."

"What did he look like? Was he beat up pretty bad?"

"There were bruises on his head and scratches on his face. His mouth was smashed and he had bandages on his wrists."

"Bandages?"

"Uh huh. He had clean clothes on, too."

Coates said, "All right. I'll talk to him." He hadn't expected his reply to satisfy Aker and it didn't. The stable-man scowled at him several moments resentfully, then went out into the street and shuffled away in the direction of the livery barn.

Coates knew who had given clothes to Frank. He knew who had bandaged him. Kate Guerrero. She had even sent money to him at the prison less than a month ago. Hank Thibault, the postmaster, had reported it. The man had turned brick-red when asked how he'd known money was in the letter, confirming what Coates had suspected for a long time—that Thibault wasn't above steaming open an envelope to see what was inside. He'd been glad to have the information, though. Knowing that Frank was coming back had given him time to think about what he ought to do. The trouble was, he hadn't reached any conclusions and he still didn't know what to do about Frank Kailey's presence here in town.

He couldn't arrest Kailey for killing McCurdy. Nor could he, in good conscience, arrest him for killing Hap-

51

good. There was ample evidence that he had only been defending himself.

Furthermore, Aker had invited Frank Kailey's anger when he offered him only ten dollars for his horse. Besides, in that incident, it was Aker's word against Frank's.

He waited until Aker had disappeared into the stable. Then he walked slowly toward the hotel. He still had no idea what Frank Kailey would do when he found out his father had been innocent of the crime for which he had been hanged. Kailey hadn't come back for revenge, but he would probably change his mind when he knew the truth.

Leon Sellers crossed the lobby to meet him when he walked in the door. Sellers was sweating. He said, *"He knows,* Ray."

Coates nodded fatalistically. He should have realized he wasn't going to get away with hustling Frank Kailey out of town before the young man found out that his father had been innocent.

"What did he say? Did he threaten you?"

Sellers frowned, as though trying to remember Frank's words. "I guess he didn't exactly threaten me. He was pretty worked up, though."

"What room's he in?"

"Eight."

"All right. I'll go talk to him." Coates wished he'd handled Kailey differently last night. He wished he'd made a substantial offer for the ranch—maybe five hundred dollars for a quitclaim deed. That might have given Frank the incentive he needed to go away and he could have raised five hundred dollars easily enough. Or a thousand, for that matter. McCurdy would have loaned it to him with the ranch as security. McCurdy would have stretched a point, being as anxious as anyone to see Frank settle someplace else.

They were afraid of young Kailey, he thought as he clumped up the stairs. But there was more to it than fear of his taking vengeance against them individually. His continued presence in town would forever be a reminder to each of them of what they all had done.

He reached the door of room eight. From here he could see the whole lobby over the rough-hewn balcony rail. Frank came to the door and opened it. Coates said gruffly, "I want to talk to you."

"Sure. Come on in." The young man looked older than his twenty-one years, the sheriff thought. He looked almost thirty now. His eyes had a flat, expressionless quality that

52

Coates found upsetting because he had seen it in other men before. He knew it masked violent thoughts and emotions that were only temporarily suppressed.

He said, "So you know," stepped into the room and pulled the door closed at his back.

"I know."

"What are you going to do about it? Are you going to try revenging yourself against them, one by one?"

Frank Kailey stared expressionlessly at him. "What would you do if you were in my place?"

"Maybe what you're thinking about. I don't know. But I do know it isn't smart. You'll only wind up dead. You didn't miss it far this afternoon. It was just plain lucky that you got loose from that horse before he killed you."

"Maybe I was lucky Ford and Hapgood and Cozzins didn't kill me before they put me on the horse. By the way, Sheriff, have you arrested Cozzins and Ford?"

"For attacking you? They say you attacked them first."

Kailey grinned humorlessly. "Are you going to arrest me?"

"Maybe I should."

"That would be consistent, anyway."

The sheriff scowled. "You still haven't told me what you're going to do."

"Maybe I don't know. Maybe I'll just stay around town and see what *they're* going to do."

Coates shook his head. "Don't, Frank. What good will it do? Will it bring your father back? The truth of the matter is, you feel just as guilty about him as those jurymen do. You keep telling yourself that you ran away when he needed you. It isn't true, but that's what you keep telling yourself. You think that if you can make the jurymen pay, it's going to ease your guilt. But it won't."

Kailey continued to stare at him with that disturbing, expressionless look upon his face. He said, "I told you last night, Sheriff, I just want to stay. This is my home. I want to redeem the ranch. I want to get married and settle down and raise a family."

"Like hell you do!" The sheriff burst out angrily. "All you want is to tear the guts out of the people in this town! Well, let me tell you something, boy. You can only push so far. Sooner or later these people will start pushing back. You've already seen some of that and it pretty near cost you your life."

Frank waited, unspeaking, showing the sheriff no emotion of any kind. Disgustedly Coates turned and opened

53

the door. He went out, slamming it violently. He stamped down the stairs, scowling savagely at Sellers as he crossed the lobby to the door.

Upstairs in his room, Frank Kailey stared at the door which the sheriff had slammed so violently. He really hadn't come back here for revenge, he told himself. He hadn't even known there was anything he might have to avenge. He had believed his father guilty of the murder of Juan Trevino, and in that respect, he admitted reluctantly, he was as guilty as the jurymen. He had accepted the flimsy evidence because he had been so soured he would not give his father the benefit of the doubt.

It had shocked him when Kate told him the truth. For a while he had been angry enough to want to go out and harm the jurymen as they had harmed his father and himself. And he was still angry, but he no longer wanted to hurt anyone. He only wanted justice for himself. He wanted to be given an opportunity to redeem his ranch. He wanted to be safe from attacks like the one made on him this afternoon.

He turned and walked to the window. He stared down into the street. He looked at the bank, thinking that McCurdy was dead because of him. He looked at the Red Ram saloon down beyond the livery stable, thinking that Hapgood was also dead. Because of him? He shook his head wearily. Neither man was dead because of him. They were dead because each had done something wrong. They were dead because they had helped kill Amos Kailey as surely as if they had fired a bullet into him.

The sun slid below the rim of the bluff and the shadow of the bluff marched across town and out onto the rolling prairie beyond.

Frank remembered that he had intended to buy a gun. He turned from the window and went out the door, closing it but not locking it. He went down the stairs to the lobby. He could feel Sellers staring at him from behind the desk.

It was probably about five-thirty, he thought. The gunsmith's shop would close at six.

He remembered who the gunsmith was. Hans Keegle had also been a member of the jury. He also would be afraid. But Frank had no choice. Only two places in town handled guns. One was Sol Mendelbaum's Mercantile. The other was Keegle's Gun Shop.

54

For several moments as he walked toward it, Frank considered the wisdom of buying a gun. Word that he had it was certain to get around, only frightening the remaining jurymen more.

And he admitted that it was time for complete honesty with himself. Did he really want to torment the jurymen into actions that might result in their deaths? Was he being honest when he said he only wanted to live here in peace?

He scowled. The hell of it was, he couldn't answer either question with complete honesty because he didn't know. What he did know was that it was going to be dangerous to remain. Ford and Cozzins and Hapgood had proved that to him this afternoon. He really did need the gun.

Hapgood and Ford and Cozzins had failed to kill him this afternoon. But they certainly had tried. Ford had been determinedly beating him to death with the stick of firewood when Cozzins intervened. Neither Ford nor Cozzins had cared if he died with his hands and feet tied beneath his horse's belly out on the prairie miles away from town.

Keegle's Gun Shop faced the Plaza diagonally across it from the courthouse. Like most of the buildings in town, it was built of adobe with poles extending out in front to support the roof of the gallery. Frank went inside.

A bell tinkled as he opened the door. He stood in the semidarkness waiting.

He heard footsteps behind a partition and a moment later Keegle appeared. He was a slight man of medium height. He was, perhaps, thirty-five, with thinning yellow hair that he wore rather long in back. He had slim, tapering hands and with a revolver he could hit a tin can five times in five seconds at about a hundred feet.

Frank said, "Hello, Mr. Keegle. I want to buy a gun."

At the sound of his voice, Keegle tensed. Frank knew in that instant that he was in more deadly peril than he had been since his return last night. There were half a dozen loaded guns within the reach of Keegle's hand.

Slowly, slowly Keegle relaxed. He said, "All right, Frank. What kind do you want?"

Chapter 9

IT WAS DUSK when Frank left Keegle's Gun Shop. Around his waist was strapped a Colt's single action .36 caliber Navy Revolver which had been converted by Keegle to accept .38 caliber cartridges. He had paid ten dollars for it, the belt, and a box of cartridges. He hurried toward Kate Guerrero's house, knowing he was late.

Keegle left immediately afterward. He locked the door behind him and pocketed the key. He headed straight across the Plaza toward the sheriff's office, in which a dim light burned. He walked with quick, wary steps, from long habit. It wasn't known by anyone in town except Coates, but Keegle hadn't always been a gunsmith. Nor had his name always been Hans Keegle. He didn't wear his gun in an exposed holster with a belt anymore. He wore it in an unobtrusive holster strapped beneath his left armpit.

The sheriff was about to blow out the lamp and leave when he entered. Coates turned his head, saw him and straightened up. Keegle said, "Frank Kailey was just in my place."

"Bought himself a gun?"

Keegle nodded. "You've got something you can use now, Coates. A convicted felon isn't allowed to carry a gun. You can arrest him. You can hold him a while because Judge Lavasseur isn't due for several days. Then you can give him a choice of leaving town or standing trial."

Coates studied Keegle. He said, "Neat. He walked right into it, didn't he?"

"What's wrong with it? Everybody wants to be rid of him—almost as badly as they wanted to be rid of his old man."

Coates said, "It's against the law to sell a gun knowingly to a convicted felon. Did you think of that?"

"I did. But who are you trying to get rid of, him or me?"

Coates shook his head disgustedly. "A gun in Frank

Kailey's hands doesn't scare you, does it? You know you can outdraw and outshoot him and you're pretty sure he won't shoot you from ambush or in the back. But what about the others? Did you stop to think about them when you sold that gun to Frank? Seeing him wearing it will scare those jurors worse than they're already scared. They think he came back for revenge anyway and when they see him with a gun, they'll be sure of it. And I'm supposed to keep the lid on things."

"Why don't you just run him out of town?"

"I tried."

Keegle said, "Come on now, Coates. You don't expect me to believe you can't run him out of town."

Coates said wearily, "I made the mistake of buying the tax title to his ranch when they had that tax sale several months ago. I didn't think Frank would be coming back and anyway if I hadn't bought it someone else would have. Only now you can see how I'll look if I run him out of town. He'll have something he can take to the governor, if he happens to think of it."

Keegle stared at Coates suspiciously. He nodded. "I'm beginning to understand more than you think I do. If you let him stay, you figure somebody might kill him and that would solve your problems for you once and for all."

Coates reddened. His eyes narrowed and his mouth became a thin line. "Watch the way you talk to me. Your hands aren't so clean you can twist my tail. I know who you really are. All I'd have to do would be to spill it and in two weeks there'd be ten men here trying to outdraw the famous Jim Scull. Besides, you're wrong."

He was irritated, doubly so because Keegle had touched a nerve. He wasn't completely sure in his own mind that he didn't want Frank Kailey killed.

He walked to the lamp and blew it out. Keegle went to the door and Coates followed him. He locked the door but before he walked away toward Mrs. Murphy's boarding-house where he lived, he said, "You let Frank Kailey alone."

"Sure, Ray. Sure." Keegle stood in the shadow of the gallery and watched the sheriff disappear into the darkness. Then he walked indolently down Juarez Street toward Ferguson's Restaurant.

Sometimes, facing the prospect of eating at Ferguson's, he wondered why he didn't marry a Mexican girl, one that could cook. But he never considered it seriously. He would have felt like a caged hawk. Not even good cooking and the comfort of having someone look after him could change that. And when he got tired of her, as he surely would, he'd have to leave Medicine Arrow to be rid of her.

Ferguson was busy in the kitchen. A Mexican girl named Dolores was waiting on customers. Several men were lined up at the counter, and a man and woman were at one of the tables. Keegle nodded to the men at the counter and sat down.

Dolores took his order. A few moments later she came back. "Mr. Ferguson wants to talk to you."

He got up and went back into the kitchen. It was hot, with the big cast-iron range going full blast. Ferguson was sweating heavily. He had to talk loudly to be heard above the noise of the fire, the noise of frying meat, the noise of Dolores handling dishes. "There's going to be a meeting at Sol Mendelbaum's at seven o'clock."

"A meeting of who?"

"The men who were on Amos Kailey's jury. What's left of them. Cronin died over a year ago and Iverson was killed when a horse fell on him last fall. McCurdy and Hapgood died today. But the eight that are left are going to get together at Mendelbaum's tonight."

Keegle nodded.

"You'll be there?"

Keegle nodded again.

"You don't look worried."

"Worried about what?"

"About Frank Kailey."

"Maybe I figure I can take care of myself."

Ferguson stopped a moment and stared closely at him. "What if he shoots you in the back?"

"I don't think he will. I don't think that's Frank Kailey's style."

"How do you know what his style is? He's been in prison for two years. Before that he was gone two years and before that he was just a kid."

"I don't think there's anything to be afraid of. Just because he bought a gun—" He stopped suddenly but it was too late. Ferguson asked, "He's got a gun?"

Keegle nodded. "He bought it half an hour ago."

"From you?"

Keegle nodded.

"Are you out of your goddamn mind? Why did you sell it to him?"

58

"I'm in the business of selling guns. If I'd told him no, he'd have gotten it someplace else."

Ferguson stared at him unbelievingly. Deliberately, then, he turned away and put his attention on the meat he was frying on the stove. Keegle lingered a moment. When he saw that Ferguson didn't intend to talk to him anymore, he returned to the front part of the restaurant irritably and sat down.

Sam Ford came in, saw him and sat down next to him. "Did you hear about the meeting up at Mendelbaum's?" he asked.

Keegle nodded.

"You'll be there, won't you?"

Keegle said, "Sure. I wouldn't miss it for the world."

Ford scowled. "You sound like it was some damn kind of joke. Like maybe you weren't part of it. You were on Amos Kailey's jury too. You voted against him just like the rest of us. That makes you guilty too."

Ford was bearded, short, powerful and without any sense of humor at all. Keegle asked, "Guilty of what? We just happened to be on the jury that found Amos Kailey guilty. The sheriff arrested him and charged him and testified against him at the trial."

"But Kailey swore he was innocent. He swore to it with tears in his eyes. The trouble was, what we saw wasn't a man but a slobberin', puking drunk that slept in gutters and alleys and stunk to high heaven and cussed us and tried to panhandle from us in the same damn breath."

Keegle said, "All of a sudden you sound like only eleven men voted him guilty. You were there too and the vote was unanimous. Besides, weren't you one of the bunch that tried beating Frank up this afternoon?"

Ford scowled again. "We thought maybe we could scare him off."

"And all you did was make him more determined to stay."

"It might've worked. It still might if the sheriff had the guts to charge Frank with killing Floyd."

"What do you think you're going to decide at the meeting? How to get rid of him?"

"Maybe. Before he gets rid of us. He knows now that his father was innocent. If he didn't want revenge before, he sure as hell wants it now."

Keegle couldn't resist needling him. "And now he's got a gun. I sold it to him less than an hour ago."

"Oh for Christ's sake! What did you do that for?"

Keegle shrugged. "He'd have got it someplace else if he hadn't gotten it from me."

Ford stared at him as unbelievingly as had Ferguson. Keegle said, "Frank Kailey is barely twenty-one. I don't know what all of you are so damn stirred up about."

Ferguson said, "You should have seen him when we jumped him this afternoon. You should have seen his face. Two years in that prison down in Santa Fe toughens up a man. And Frank was a mean son-of-a-bitch even before he went away. You saw the way he attacked Judge Lavasseur."

Keegle did not reply. The waitress brought his food and he began to eat. A fleeting frown crossed his forehead. He was thinking about how dull his life had been since he buried the name Jim Scull and came to live here. It was right after the hotel fire in Wichita in which he had been burned around the face and throat. When the bandages came off, he didn't even look like Jim Scull anymore. It had come to him that he could disappear. He could start fresh someplace else. So he did disappear. He came to Medicine Arrow to live.

What vanity had made him keep his gun he'd never know because it was the gun that Ray Coates had recognized. And suddenly there was someone who knew his old identity.

Coates promised to keep the knowledge to himself so long as Keegle behaved. And then, too late, Keegle got rid of Jim Scull's gun. He threw it in the river and watched it sink from sight. He opened a gunsmith's shop. Eventually the blotched, parchment-like quality of his burned skin changed, but he never resembled Jim Scull again.

Sometimes though, he missed the excitement of Jim Scull's life. He missed the adulation he had once been given in each new town. He missed the excitement of knowing he might be challenged at any moment of any day. He even missed the challenges themselves, when he laid his life on the line like a poker bet shoved into the middle of the table and called by another man. And maybe there was something else he missed. Maybe he even missed that fleeting, unbelievable exhilaration that came to him when he saw a man go down before his gun. In that brief instant he soared, above the earth, above all men as though for a split second in time he was a god.

He finished eating. Dolores had brought Sam Ford's plate and Ford began to eat noisily, his head only four inches above his plate. Keegle put a quarter on the counter, got a toothpick from the whiskey glass and left. Picking his teeth thoughtfully, he headed uptown toward Mendelbaum's Mercantile.

A possibility kept occurring to him, but each time it did he pushed it irritably away. No matter how often he pushed it away, it kept coming back. If he wanted to he could feel that old heady adulation and he could feel the old exhilaration again. All he had to do was challenge Frank.

The trouble was, if he killed Frank Kailey he would risk his new identity. Even if Coates remained silent, there was a chance someone else would put two and two together when they saw the way he used his gun. It was known that Jim Scull had been burned in the fire in Wichita. The story had later been circulated that he had died as a result of his burns. But now if a man whose face showed evidence of having been burned were to show unusual speed with a gun. . . .

He reached Mendelbaum's and went inside. Mendelbaum was waiting on a woman customer. He nodded at Keegle and said, "Go on back to the office, Hans. The rest of them ought to be showing up pretty soon."

Keegle went down the long aisle and into Mendelbaum's office in the rear. He sat down on the long, leather-covered sofa. He fished a cigar from his pocket, bit the end off thoughtfully and put it into his mouth. He lighted it, suddenly feeling the gun in its holster at his armpit as a pressure, as something almost having a warmth and life of its own.

He began to try justifying what he would like to do. Maybe the rest of them were right. Maybe Frank Kailey did want revenge. And maybe he was being stupid saying Frank wouldn't shoot from ambush or behind. How did he know what Frank Kailey might do? Kailey had been in prison down in Santa Fe for two long years. In two years a man can change. He can learn a lot of things. He can turn into an animal.

He was still frowning with indecision as the others began filing in.

Chapter 10

DELL AKER was the first to arrive and Keegle wished irritably that the stableman had cleaned himself up before he came so that he wouldn't smell up the room. He glanced up and said, "I could tell it was you the minute you came in the front door."

Aker scowled, getting the reference immediately. He said sourly, "If you had to work around horse manure the whole damn day, you'd smell, too."

Keegle didn't carry it further. Sam Ford came in, followed by Jess Cozzins. The three sat down.

Leon Sellers came next, followed by the postmaster, Hank Thibault. Ferguson and Sol Mendelbaum were the last to come into the room. Sol looked around. "I guess we're all here."

Sellers said, "The sheriff isn't here."

Mendelbaum said, "I thought we could talk this out without Coates."

Keegle said mockingly, "In case we decide to do something that isn't legal. Is that what you mean?"

Mendelbaum frowned at him then decided to ignore the question. He said, "I don't know about the rest of you, but I'm scared." His forehead was sweating and he wiped it with his hand. "You can say it's just chance, but McCurdy and Hapgood are dead and Coates says he can't do a thing. He says McCurdy's heart stopped and that Kailey killed Hapgood in self-defense."

Cozzins growled, "What I don't see is how the son-of-a-bitch got loose from his horse. We tied him on there belly down and he was unconscious to boot."

Aker said, "His wrists were bandaged when I saw him so I suppose the rope cut into them. Maybe the blood made his hands slippery enough for him to get them loose."

Hank Thibault said, "If nobody gives him a job and if

nobody helps him, it seems to me that sooner or later he's *got* to leave."

Mendelbaum said, "And in the meantime, he's going to be picking us off, one by one."

Thibault said, "You don't know that."

Ford said, "You didn't see his face this afternoon before we tied him on that horse."

Sellers said, "And you didn't talk to him. He came in and got a room and talked to me for a while. If you ask me, he's dangerous."

Aker broke in, "He came into the stable to sell his horse. He threatened me with a pitchfork. He made me pay him four times what the damn horse was worth."

"What did Coates have to say about that?"

"Coates excused him. Said I tried to rob him and deserved to get manhandled."

Keegle grinned sardonically. "What did you offer him for his horse? Ten bucks?"

Aker flushed and refused to meet Keegle's eyes. Keegle taunted, "So if you ended up paying him four times what you say the horse was worth, you paid him forty dollars. Right?"

Again Aker refused to answer him. Sellers said, "It's not going to do any good to argue among ourselves. If we're going to do something about Frank, we'd better quit bickering and try working together for a change."

Keegle asked, "What would you suggest?"

"He's got forty dollars and it won't last long. All we've got to do is see that he doesn't get any more."

Keegle said, "He's got thirty dollars and a gun. I sold one to him a while ago."

Sellers breathed, "Christ!"

Mendelbaum stared unbelievingly at Keegle. "You sold him a gun?"

Keegle shrugged. "Why not? I'm in the gun business. He had the money, so I sold him a gun."

"Ever think he might turn the damn thing on you?"

"I wish he would. That would put an end to this whole stupid business."

Ford said sarcastically, "Big talk!"

Keegle opened his mouth then closed it suddenly. He'd been about to tell Ford who he was. But nobody would believe him even if he did. Maybe, he thought, he *could* kill Frank Kailey without giving his identity away.

Ferguson said, "So he's got thirty dollars and a gun.

Thirty dollars won't last long. A month at the most. If nobody helps him or gives him any more."

"Who'd help him? Who'd give him any more?"

"Kate. She gave him some of her father's clothes."

Thibault broke in, "And she sent him fifty dollars a few days before he was released. That's how he got his horse."

Keegle stared at the postmaster. "How the hell did you know that?"

Thibault flushed guiltily. Keegle said, "Why you son-of-a-bitch! You opened her letter, didn't you?"

Mendelbaum broke in, "Wait a minute. Why do we have to fight among ourselves? Frank Kailey's here to kill us off one by one."

Ferguson said, "And a month is too long to wait. Too much can happen. But what if somebody was to relieve him of both the thirty dollars and the gun tonight?" He looked at Keegle. "Where is he now? Where'd he go when he left your place?"

"He was headed toward Kate's house."

"Then he's probably going to have supper there. Some of us could wait outside and get him when he leaves. We could take that thirty dollars away from him."

Aker shook his head. "That wouldn't do any good. Unless a couple of us was to have a talk with Kate. She'd only give him more."

Several of the men looked at Mendelbaum. "What do you think, Sol?"

Mendelbaum plainly didn't want anything to do with robbing Frank. He said, "I'd be willing to talk to Kate. Sellers, why don't you and me do that?"

Ford said, "By God, I wouldn't mind taking that thirty dollars away from him. Keegle, you and Cozzins can help."

Mendelbaum said, "Somebody ought to keep an eye on Coates."

Aker said, "I'll do that."

Mendelbaum looked at Cozzins. "Would you want to help Sam?"

Cozzins nodded. "I sure as hell would. I got a couple of things I'd like to settle with Kailey."

Mendelbaum looked at Keegle. "How about you?"

Keegle shrugged. "I'll go along."

"All right, let's get started then." Mendelbaum stood up. Thibault and Ferguson were the only ones without something to do. Thibault said, "How about me? What am I supposed to do?"

Keegle taunted, "You just keep an eye on the mail. If anything comes for Frank, let us know what's inside."

The men filed out of the office, along the darkened aisle of the store and out into the street. Except for the stars, the sky was now completely black. There were a few lamps burning along Juarez Street and there were a few people on the street.

Mendelbaum shivered even though the air was warm. He said, "I suppose the five of us had just as well go over to the Guerrero house together. We'll have to keep an eye on it until Frank leaves."

He had an uneasy feeling that tonight someone else was going to die here in this peaceful town. But he also knew the eight of them had no real choice. They had to get rid of Frank Kailey any way they could. If they didn't get rid of him, he was going to get rid of them, one by one. Besides, Keegle and Cozzins and Ford didn't intend to kill Kailey. All they wanted was his gun and the money he was carrying.

In virtual silence the five walked toward the Guerrero house. Their route led through the narrow alleys of the Mexican section, and dogs began to bark, marking their progress with progressive noise. Two or three of the dogs came out, but were cursed into silence by one or another of the men.

It must be about quarter of eight, thought Mendelbaum. He wondered how long they would have to stand in the darkness waiting for Frank Kailey to come out.

They reached the Guerrero house. The gate in front was closed. Keegle lighted a cigar, cupping his hands to hide the flare of the match. Cozzins sat down and put his back against an adobe wall. He said, "We're going to be here a while. We'd just as well be comfortable."

"How are you going to manage it?" asked Mendelbaum. "How are you going to keep him from shooting you?"

Cozzins said, "He ain't going to try anything with three of us holding guns on him. He ain't that stupid. But if he does, he'll be dead and we won't have to worry about him anymore."

"Coates—"

"Damn Coates! How's he going to know who did it if all of us are in the back of your store still talking about how to get rid of Frank? Just remember this, both of you. If you hear shots, get to the store as quick as you can. If the five of us swear we never left it, what's Coates going to do?"

The talk subsided. Keegle puffed comfortably and imperturbably on his cigar. The five waited, watching the front gate of the Guerrero house.

Inside the house, Frank Kailey sat across from Kate at the heavy oak table in the dining room. Her father sat at the head of the table because he was the head of the house but he didn't seem to be aware of anything. Kate got up once and cut his meat for him. She spoke to him several times but he did not respond. It was as if he were off in some strange world of his own, a world into which the sounds and sights and smells of this world could not penetrate. He ate slowly and patiently as if the plate of food in front of him was the center of his universe.

Frank remembered him as a sharp-eyed if elderly man who had never quite approved of Anglo ways and once he asked in a low voice, "How long has he been this way?"

"Almost two years now. He lost his land and cattle three years ago and he never got over it. All we have left now is this house. A lot of the things that had value have been sold. A little over a year ago I finally had to ask Mr. McCurdy for a job." She smiled. "At least I had to if we intended to continue eating, and once you get the habit it's hard to break."

"That fifty dollars. I'll find a way to pay it back."

She flushed with embarrassment. "You're not to mention it again. I wouldn't have sent it to you if we had needed it."

Frank hadn't had a meal like this one for years and he told her so. Their conversation lagged and to start it again she asked, "Have you decided what you're going to do?"

He shrugged. "I want to stay. I want to redeem my land. But I'm not sure they're going to let me stay. After what happened this afternoon—"

"Is that why you bought the gun?"

There was a strange tension in her as she asked the question. It was the first time she had mentioned the gun, which he had laid aside when he came into the house.

He grinned. "You too? Do you think I came back for revenge?"

"I guess I couldn't blame you if you had. Your father *was* innocent. He *was* convicted on evidence that was pretty shaky to say the least."

Frank finished his supper and laid down his knife and fork. He shook his head when she offered to refill his plate. For a moment he studied her. Her skin had a warm olive color, a legacy from her Spanish ancestors. Her hair was black, gleaming and tonight piled high upon her head. Her eyes were brown and warm, her mouth humorous and full. She wore a simple cotton gown that she had probably made herself.

He said, "I was mad when they beat me up and tied me on that horse. I was madder when I found out Pa was innocent. I have to admit that I've had some ideas about revenge today. But I didn't act on them. If it turns out I can't redeem that land and can't get a job, I suppose I'll have to go whether I want to or not. But I think I can get Coates to give me three hundred dollars for a quit-claim deed. That would get me started someplace else." The thought of giving up and going away suddenly seemed intolerable to him. The thought of never seeing Kate again—

They waited, reminiscing about things that had happened before Frank went away, until Kate's father had finished eating. After that Kate led him from the room. She returned fifteen minutes later. "He's in bed."

"I've got to be going. It's been a long day. I hope I don't have to take a beating like this one every day."

She went with him to the door. He hesitated nervously for a long time but at last he lowered his head and kissed her lightly on the mouth. "Thank you, Kate. Without you, I don't think this town would be worth staying in."

She flushed slightly, but met his glance steadily. "Good night Frank. Will I see you tomorrow?"

He nodded, buckling on his holstered gun. "What will you do about the bank?"

"I suppose I'll go down as usual tomorrow. I can keep it open until Mr. McCurdy's wife makes other arrangements for running it."

Frank went across the small courtyard to the gate. Going through it he turned and waved. Kate made a straight, lovely figure against the lamplight of the room.

Chapter 11

FRANK smelled cigar smoke the instant he stepped through the gate. He stiffened and the short hairs on the back of his neck seemed to rise like hackles. He knew that Mexicans and Spanish people rarely smoked cigars, not this kind of cigar at least. He knew the Anglos did. They were waiting for him somewhere in the darkness here; but how many—he could not tell.

His hand touched the gun in its holster at his side. He was suddenly glad he had bought the gun, glad he wasn't as defenseless as this afternoon. A light breeze was blowing out of the west. They must be waiting, then, directly across the narrow street. He tried to penetrate the darkness with his glance but the shadows were too deep and the stars gave off too little light.

He crossed the street diagonally toward the center of town. As a boy he had known every twisting alleyway. He hoped he hadn't forgotten them. He was going to need his knowledge now. He heard the low rumble of a voice and the scuff of feet. Walking as quietly as possible, he hurried on, hearing them coming swiftly after him. He ducked into an alley that was so black he couldn't see a yard ahead. He kicked a tin can and it rattled along the ground. Someone called softly, "There he is! Come on!"

They were running now, their footfalls gaining rapidly. One of them kicked another tin can, perhaps the same one he had just kicked, and it rolled noisily only to trip another of the men and send him crashing to the ground cursing angrily.

No longer was there need for silence. They knew Frank had heard them and they knew he was running ahead of them.

What did they mean to do this time? Would they murder him and leave him lying here? Would they beat him again, hoping that a second beating would convince him

68

it was wiser to leave town? He knew they meant business. He also knew that if he stumbled, or made a single mistake, they would overtake him. Then he would have a choice—either kill or be killed. He promised himself he would not take another beating like the one he'd taken this afternoon.

A couple of dogs ran out and barked excitedly at his heels, eliminating the chance that he might hide and let the pursuit go past. He turned his head and cursed them futilely.

Too dark to see landmarks, too dark to recognize houses and sheds and adobe walls. He swung left into an intersecting alleyway and sped along it toward the opening at its end. He slammed headlong into an adobe wall. Stunned, he realized that he had made the one mistake he didn't dare to make. He was cornered here in a blind alley. The only escape route was over an eight foot adobe wall. Reaching up, he seized the top of the wall. He tried to pull himself up but the wall was rounded at the top and his hands kept slipping off.

Behind him they were nearing, no longer running headlong for they sensed they had him cornered now. Perhaps they were more familiar with this section of town than he. Perhaps they knew this alley had no exit by which he could escape.

A voice said softly, "Spread out. Don't let him break back."

The two dogs, at bay, continued to bark excitedly. Frank put his back against the wall and drew his gun.

The dogs suddenly realized they were between their quarry and the other men who were pursuing him. Cornered and terrified, they whirled and sped back in the direction from which they had come, tripping one of the men who cursed as he went to his knees. Then the dogs were gone and Frank was alone, facing those who had been pursuing him.

One said, in a voice disguised either with a hand or a handkerchief, "This is a holdup. Turn around and put your hands against the wall."

Frank didn't move. He knew they couldn't see him any more than he could see them.

The same disguised voice said, "All right then. Have it your way. You got ten seconds to throw your gun down and put up your hands."

Frank took a careful, silent step to his right. He took

another step. He took a third, but this time he scuffed his foot against the ground.

Blindingly and with shocking suddenness, a gun flared not ten feet in front of him. The report and the concussion of it nearly deafened him. Dust showered from the adobe wall where the bullet struck.

In that instant Frank knew: this was no holdup—it would be no beating to persuade him to leave town. This was to be murder and unless he fought back he would soon be dead. He fired at the flash of the gun. Before he knew whether or not his bullet had found its mark, he pushed himself away from the wall and charged headlong at those spread out across the alley in front of him.

His body struck one of them but the impact scarcely slowed Frank down. Running hard, he bowled the man aside and went on. Behind him, two more guns flared. One of the bullets struck an adobe wall beside him and whined away into the black, star-studded sky. The other burned like a hot iron along his right shoulder. Immediately thereafter blood flooded down his arm, soaking his shirtsleeve below the wound.

He didn't slow and he didn't turn to fire at them again. A second volley pursued him down the alley but both bullets went wild. Frank whirled around a corner. He slammed his gun into its holster. Ignoring the increasing, burning pain of his wound, he ran as he hadn't run for years. He burst out of an alley into the Plaza, slowed immediately and crossed it diagonally at a fast walk, heading toward the hotel.

A few people sitting on benches glanced at him incuriously. He knew it was too dark for them to see the blood that had soaked his upper right shirtsleeve. He reached the hotel and went inside. There was no one at the desk and, luckily, no one in the lobby. As he headed for the stairs, he glimpsed a man standing at the hotel bar but the man did not turn his head.

Frank reached the top of the stairs. He paused on the balcony in front of his room to examine the lobby carefully, making certain he had not been seen. Then he opened the door and went inside. He locked the door behind him before he struck a match to light the lamp.

He shrugged out of his shirt immediately. The wound was fairly shallow but the flesh was shredded and the wound was bleeding heavily. He got a towel and soaked it in the washbasin with water that he poured from the white china pitcher on the dresser top. He made a compress of the towel and laid it against his shoulder wound. The water burned but he did not take it away.

He crossed to the bed and lay down wearily. Maybe *he* didn't want revenge but the town did. They seemed determined to kill him unless he left town at once.

As soon as Keegle, Ford, and Cozzins had disappeared, Mendelbaum and Sellers crossed the street to the Guerrero gate. It creaked as they opened it. They crossed the courtyard to the door and let the huge cast-iron knocker fall thunderously.

The door opened almost immediately and Kate Guerrero stood there looking at them. "Mr. Mendelbaum! Mr. Sellers! What are you doing here?"

"We want to talk to you."

Kate looked puzzled but she stood aside courteously. "Come in."

The two went in. Mendelbaum was feeling sheepish now. He stood tall and gaunt with his back to the door, nervously turning his black derby hat around and around in his hands. "It's about Frank Kailey, Kate. You've got to stop helping him. He's a convict and he's back here for revenge and we don't want him to stay. Mr. McCurdy is already dead and so is Floyd Hapgood. The sheriff gave Frank until sundown tomorrow to leave town and we intend to see to it that he leaves."

"And if I go on helping him?"

Sellers broke in. "We don't like threats, Kate, but we mean business. We're not going to stand idly by while Frank picks us off one by one. He's only been here a day and look what's already happened here."

"You say you don't like threats. What, exactly, do you have in mind?" Kate's voice was cool, even and controlled. But her eyes sparkled and her face was pale.

"We're not making any threats. At least not now we're not. We're just warning you. Don't help Frank Kailey any more."

Kate stepped past them and opened the door. "I think that's all, gentlemen."

Both men were highly uncomfortable, but Mendelbaum's voice was firm. "Don't underestimate us, Kate. We're fighting for our lives."

Kate didn't bother to answer him. She slammed the door angrily.

Mendelbaum and Sellers crossed the courtyard without

71

speaking. They reached the gate, opened it and went through. As it creaked shut behind them the first shot rang out a block away.

It was followed by another, by two more and by two more after that. Mendelbaum and Sellers were already hurrying toward the center of town. Both were out of breath now, too much so to say anything. But they were wondering what had happened. Six shots had been fired in all. How many men lay dead? How many wounded?

They reached Mendelbaum's store and Mendelbaum quickly unlocked it and went inside. He led the way in darkness down the long aisle to the office at the rear. Here, screened partially from the big windows on the street, he lighted a lamp and trimmed the wick with a hand that trembled violently.

Sellers paced nervously back and forth. "What do you think has happened, Sol? Do you suppose they got Frank? I didn't think there'd be that much shooting. Cozzins said Frank wouldn't be stupid enough to fight back with three men holding guns on him. Looks like he was wrong."

"We'll soon find out." Sellers continued to pace back and forth. Mendelbaum went to the office door and stared toward the street. Once he turned his head and said, "Stop that damn pacing, will you?"

Sellers stopped. "See anybody yet?"

"Uh uh. But I'll bet Coates is down there by now. He's had time enough."

Suddenly a man came through the front door. A second followed him. The first man called softly, "Sol? Is that you?"

Mendelbaum stepped back. "It's me. What happened?"

"Wait until we get inside the office."

Mendelbaum backed into the office. The first man in was Cozzins. The second was Keegle. Keegle closed the office door behind him.

Both men were out of breath. Cozzins had dirt and dust on his clothes. He began to brush it off. Sellers asked, "Where's Sam?"

Keegle said bluntly, "He's dead. He's layin' back there in that alley, dead."

"What happened?" Mendelbaum looked at Cozzins accusingly. "I thought you said—"

"I said Frank wouldn't be stupid enough to fight with three guns on him. Well, I was wrong. We got him cornered and he fought. He got Ford with his first shot after Ford had shot at him."

"Oh Lord! Oh good Lord, I knew something was going to go wrong tonight."

Cozzins said irritably, "Well this is no time for wringing your goddamn hands. Sit down and get hold of yourself. Coates is going to be back here looking for us pretty soon."

"Why don't we just tell Coates that Frank shot Sam?"

"Because then we'd have to tell him where we were at the time."

Mendelbaum sat down. His forehead was shiny with sweat. He kept licking his lips nervously. "I wish we hadn't started this."

"It was as much your idea as anyone's. But now it's started and we'd better finish it. Did you and Sellers talk to Kate?"

Mendelbaum nodded. "We talked to her but I don't think it did any good."

"What makes you think it didn't?"

"She practically told us to go to hell."

"Maybe you didn't convince her you meant what you said. Maybe somebody that can convince her ought to go see her."

Keegle looked at Cozzins. He narrowed his eyes. "Like you, I suppose. What would you do, beat her up?"

Cozzins scowled.

The front door opened and closed again. Footsteps came along the aisle.

Mendelbaum had turned a ghastly shade of gray. Keegle said, "For Christ's sake, get hold of yourself!"

But it wasn't Frank Kailey. It was Sheriff Coates. He stood in the doorway and glared at them. He said, "Sam Ford is dead."

Cozzins asked, "Frank Kailey again?"

Coates looked at him disgustedly. "Don't play dumb with me."

Keegle said, "What the hell are you talking about? We've been here for more than an hour trying to decide what we're going to do about Frank."

Coates continued to stare at them disgustedly. At last he said, "Like hell you have!" He turned and went back through the store to the street slamming the door.

73

Chapter 12

COATES stood in the street a moment, scowling savagely. He was furious because he knew damned well who had shot Sam Ford. He was willing to bet that Ford had been shot while he and several others had been trying either to beat or kill Frank Kailey. Kailey had gone to Kate Guerrero's house for supper. They had probably waited for him outside and waylaid him on the way back to the hotel.

And the hell of it was, he had *believed* Frank when he said he hadn't come back for revenge. He believed Frank only wanted to live here in peace. Apparently he was the only one who did believe. The men who had been on Amos Kailey's jury were sufficiently scared to try and get rid of his son any way they could. Their own fear had killed three of the remaining ten. Only seven now were left.

Gerda Mendelbaum approached him from uptown. "Good evening, Sheriff Coates. Do you know if Mr. Mendelbaum is here?"

He removed his hat. "Yes, Ma'am. He's here."

She started to go past him and enter the store but the sheriff said, "Wait a minute, Mrs. Mendelbaum. I want to talk to you."

"Yes?"

She was an impressive figure of a woman, tall, with bosoms like the prows of ships sailing through heavy seas. Her gown was of black silk and she wore a bustle that made her look very fashionable. Coates said, "You probably know that Frank Kailey is back in town."

"I know."

"You probably also know that your husband and the rest of the jurymen who convicted Frank's father are scared to death. They think he came back for revenge."

"Didn't he, Mr. Coates?"

"I don't think so."

"Mr. McCurdy is dead. So is Mr. Hapgood."

"And so is Sam Ford. He was shot less than fifteen minutes ago."

"And you can say Frank Kailey did not come back for revenge?"

Coates said, "McCurdy scared himself to death. His heart just stopped. Frank never laid a hand on him."

"What about Mr. Hapgood and Mr. Ford?"

"Hapgood and some others tried to beat Frank up. He killed Hapgood in self defense. I figure it was the same thing a little while ago when Sam Ford was killed. I think several of them were trying to murder Frank."

"And my husband was one of those?"

"I think so, Mrs. Mendelbaum, and I thought maybe you could talk some sense into him. Get him to let Frank alone. Have him persuade the others to do the same."

She stood there a moment in the darkness. He couldn't see what her expression was. At last she said in her richly Jewish voice. "Thank you, Sheriff Coates. I will talk to him."

She went into the store. Coates headed for the hotel. He doubted if he could prove Frank Kailey had shot Sam Ford. He wasn't even sure he wanted to prove it. In his own mind he was reasonably sure that if Frank had done it it had been in self-defense. He had heard at least six shots.

Furthermore, he wanted no part of arresting Frank. He wanted no more trumped-up cases against men innocent of any crime.

He went into the lobby of the hotel. In the adjoining hotel bar, he could see several men, but there was no one in the lobby and no one at the desk. He climbed the stairs and knocked on the door of room eight. Frank's voice called, "Who is it?"

"It's the sheriff—Coates."

He heard the bed creak and heard footsteps approach the door. It opened. Frank stood there, without a shirt, holding a bloody, wet towel against a shoulder wound. Coates closed the door. "Let's look at that. Is it bad?"

Frank took the towel away. Coates saw immediately that the wound wasn't serious. But he could tell from Frank's sweating, grayish face that it hurt like hell. He said, "As soon as I leave, I'll get the doc to come up here to look at that."

Frank sat down on the side of the bed. Coates said, "Sam Ford is dead. Did you shoot him, Frank?"

Frank shrugged, then grimaced with the pain the movement caused. "Hell, I don't know. Some men chased me from Kate's house and cornered me in a blind alley. One of them shot at me and I shot back. I may have hit Sam Ford. I don't know. It was too dark to see anything."

"Then you don't know who the men that chased you were?"

"Uh uh."

Coates walked to the window. He stared gloomily down into the street. Vigil's black hearse was just turning off Juarez Street, heading toward the alley where Sam Ford's body lay.

There were going to be some repercussions from the three deaths today. Floyd Hapgood hadn't had any family but McCurdy and Sam Ford both had wives and children. Tomorrow a lot of pressure was going to develop and all the pressure would be on him—to arrest Frank Kailey and charge him with the murder of Hapgood and Ford.

And maybe that *was* the best solution to the problem in the long run. Frank would be in jail and off the streets. At least no one else would have to die.

He said, "I ought to arrest you, Frank."

Frank looked bitterly at him. "That would solve everything for everyone, wouldn't it? Get me out of the way. Convict me and send me back to the prison in Santa Fe. Well, let me tell you something, Sheriff Coates. You do that to me and I *will* be looking for revenge. Against you, and against the men that tried my father and against the jury that sends me back. You know I haven't done anything but try to defend myself. What am I supposed to do, let them kill me without even trying to fight back?"

Coates shook his head wearily.

Frank said, "If I were you, I'd get those men together and talk to them. Tell them I'll let them alone if they'll do the same with me."

Coates said, "I'll play hell making them believe that now. You've only been here a day and three of those jurymen are dead."

Frank didn't reply. He sat with his head hanging, obviously in pain. Coates went to the door, opened it and stepped onto the balcony. "I'll send Doc over to bandage you. I won't arrest you unless I have to, but there's going to be a lot of pressure on me tomorrow."

Frank Kailey did not reply.

Coates went out and closed the door. He went down the stairs heavily. He had an uneasy feeling that things were rapidly getting out of hand. Frank had been badly beaten today and now he had a bullet wound. He was going to hurt tomorrow and he was going to be irritable and edgy as a result. He wasn't going to be in any mood to be reasonable.

Nor would the remaining jurymen, nor the town at large for that matter, be willing to accept his assurance that Frank didn't want revenge. Frank's father had been unjustly hanged and his own two years in prison had been a direct result. His ranch had been sold for taxes and he had been refused a loan to redeem it with. To make things worse, he had been beaten and shot, all in less than a twenty-four hour period. Nobody was going to believe that Frank didn't want to strike back now.

His job was to keep the peace. Somehow he had to see to it that no more of Amos Kailey's jurymen died. More important, he had to try and keep the remaining jurymen from killing Frank.

He met Sellers coming into the lobby as he went out. He stopped the hotel man. "Get off Frank Kailey's back. You and the others are pushing him. Let him alone and he'll let you alone."

Sellers stared at him. There was resentment in his eyes. "You know he killed Hapgood and you know he caused McCurdy's death even if he didn't actually murder him. Now Sam Ford is dead and you know damned well it was Frank Kailey that shot him. When are you going to do what you're supposed to do? When are you going to arrest him?"

"I'm not going to arrest Kailey for defending himself. There was only one bullet in Sam Ford. I heard six shots, and Sam's gun had only been fired once. Add that up for yourself. Somebody fired those other four shots and they sure as hell weren't Kailey's friends. I figure that Frank was attacked down there in that alley and he only defended himself.

Sellers stared at him unbelievingly. "Do you mean to stand there and tell me you're not going to do *anything*? Three men are dead and they all were respected members of the community. And what's Frank Kailey? A convict. A jailbird. He's got nothing and he'll never contribute anything."

77

He brushed past Coates angrily and went into the lobby of the hotel. Coates stood on the walk in front and lighted a cigar. Then he turned and headed for Doc Baker's office two blocks up the street. He had to admit that Frank Kailey didn't look like a harmless kid. He'd changed in prison during the last two years. They'd toughened him and they'd changed him from a boy into a man. He was hard and lean and there was a spare competence about him that did its share toward convincing people he was dangerous.

He reached the stairway leading up to Doc's office and climbed it wearily. He was tired. The day had been difficult.

A lamp was burning in Doc's office. There was a small sign behind the doorglass that said "Walk In." He went inside.

Doc was sitting at his desk. Coates said, "Frank Kailey is down at the hotel with a bullet wound in his shoulder. Maybe you'd better go down and take a look at it."

"Bullet still in the wound?"

Coates shook his head. "Nope. But the flesh is shredded and Frank's mighty sick."

Doc got up, shrugged into his shabby coat and picked up his bag. "What about Sam Ford?"

"Oh. You heard about that?"

"Everybody in town has heard."

Coates followed him out the door. He said, "They keep wanting me to throw Frank in jail, but I'm not going to do it, Doc. I arrested his father and I presented what evidence I had against him at the trial, but I never was convinced he was guilty."

Doc turned his head. "Is that hindsight, Ray?"

"I don't think so. I remember being uncertain at Amos Kailey's trial."

Doc asked disconcertingly, "Then why didn't you tell the judge?"

Coates scowled. He said, "Damn it!" And stopped. Then he said more reasonably, "All right, I was wrong. I should have told the judge and I should have told the prosecutor. The fact is, I thought that Kailey probably was the one who killed Trevino even if the evidence was flimsy. I figured that if so many of the others were sure they probably were right."

They reached the hotel. Coates said, "He's in room eight."

78

He sat down in one of the rockers on the gallery. His cigar was almost finished but he hated to throw it away.

He puffed comfortably, relaxed for the first time today. Kailey would probably go to bed when Doc got through with him. He'd sleep through the night.

The chances were, then, that nothing more would happen tonight. The townspeople would go home and go to bed. He could get some sleep himself. But he wasn't going to the boardinghouse. He was going to sleep on the cot in the sheriff's office. He wanted to be instantly available if anything else came up.

He waited patiently on the hotel veranda until Doc Baker came out again. He glanced up. "It wasn't too serious, was it?"

Doc shook his head.

"You reckon he'll sleep all night?"

"Uh huh. I gave him some morphine for the pain and that will help him sleep."

"Then maybe I can relax. Until sunup at least."

Baker took time to pack and light his pipe. He looked up at the sky. "Nice evening after that rain we had last night."

The rain now seemed like it had happened a week ago. Riding out to Frank's shack also seemed like it had happened that long ago. Coates did not reply.

Doc said, "Kailey would be a hell of a lot safer if he was in jail."

Coates nodded. "He would. But I'm not going to put him there until he does something I can charge him with. I arrested his pa without sufficient evidence and I'm not going to make the same mistake again."

Doc puffed on his pipe until he had it going. Then he headed up the street.

Coates continued to sit in the chair on the hotel veranda for a long, long time. He watched the lights along Juarez Street go out one by one. He saw Mr. and Mrs. Mendelbaum come out of the store, lock the door and turn toward home. He frowned slightly, then got up out of the squeaking rocker and headed toward the jail. He paused in front of it, looking across the Plaza, his attention drawn by a lamp still burning in Keegle's Gun Shop.

He was thinking that a sheriff ought to be detached in order to do his job the way it should be done. He was realizing that in this case he was not detached. He had a personal interest in the way things came out. He shared the town's guilt for what had happened to Amos Kailey two years ago.

But he was trying. He was trying not to compound that wrong with another, more callous wrong. He guessed that only God knew how it was going to work out.

Chapter 13

THE WALLS of Kate's house were thick but the sounds of shots less than a block away easily penetrated the windows and doors and she had heard each one. She froze at the first shot, listening. Thereafter she counted them, her heart seeming momentarily to stop.

There were six in all in groups of two. Had Frank been attacked by Sellers and Mendelbaum? It didn't seem likely since Frank had left several minutes before they did. Besides, she couldn't imagine either Sellers or Mendelbaum attacking anyone.

Someone else must have been waiting outside for Frank to emerge. They must have followed him while Sellers and Mendelbaum came inside to threaten her. They must have attacked him somewhere in the twisting alleyways between here and the center of town.

Worried and agitated, she wondered what she should do. Common sense told her there was little she *could* do. Six shots indicated that there must have been several men waylaying and attacking Frank. Furthermore, had Frank been killed immediately, she doubted if six shots would have been necessary. One or two would probably have been enough. Frank must be alive, then, although he might be wounded. She had to know for sure. Frank might be lying in an alley someplace, hurt, helpless, desperately needing her.

Quickly she went into her father's room. He was sleeping, snoring softly and regularly. She hurried to the rear of the house and called Miguel. She told him she was going out and to listen for her father in case he needed anything.

Seizing a shawl, she went outside. The gate squeaked as she opened it. Outside, she stood still for several moments, listening. She had been warned not to help Frank anymore. It was possible they had left someone to watch her house.

But nothing moved in the shadows. No small sound came to her listening ears.

Quickly and quietly, she hurried along the street. Inside the house, it had been hard to place the exact direction of the shots. Knowing these streets well, she relied on her intuition and headed directly toward the Plaza by the shortest route.

Suddenly, ahead, she heard the faint, confused babel of many voices. Coldness seemed to seep into her chest. Something clutched her heart, like a constricting hand. She began to run.

Turning a corner, she saw a crowd ahead of her. A couple of figures had lanterns and by this flickering, yellow light, she saw the body of a man lying on the ground.

Was it Frank? Had she been wrong? Could Frank be dead? She pushed through the crowd and knelt beside the man. Instantly she knew it was not Frank. This man had a heavy beard. He was short and powerful, and older than Frank.

One of the men with lanterns approached so that now she recognized the man on the ground. It was the blacksmith, Sam Ford. She seized his heavy wrist and felt for pulse. There was none. Sam Ford was dead.

Kate got to her feet. She looked at the one with the lantern, an elderly man named Luis Lucero. "What happened here, Luis? Who shot this man?"

He shrugged eloquently. "I do not know, Senorita. We came when we heard the shots. There was the sound of running feet so we remained hidden until the sounds had gone. Then we brought lanterns and found Senor Ford lying there."

"You didn't see anybody else?"

"It was too dark. All we heard was running feet. All we saw was shapes."

"May I have the lantern a moment, Luis?"

"Si." He handed the lantern to her. Holding it high, she moved back along the alley in the direction of town. She studied the ground carefully, looking for spots of blood among the scuffed footprints.

Suddenly she stopped, knelt and stared closely. Here there was a cluster of red drops of blood, and a little farther along there were more. Frank was hurt, she thought, and anger touched her unexpectedly. They had no right to treat him this way. He had served his time in prison for attacking the judge and that was the only wrong thing he had ever done. He deserved a chance to start a new life without being harrassed at every turn.

She straightened and returned the lantern to Luis. Nervously she paced back and forth, listening to the excited confusion of Spanish voices.

Suddenly the voices stilled. Turning her head, she saw Sheriff Coates.

He glanced at her as he passed. "Good-evening, Kate."

"Good-evening." She watched while he went to the body, while he knelt and felt for pulse. He straightened, turned and faced the crowd. "Anybody see what happened here?"

They all seemed to speak at once. "No, Senor. We heard the shots and the sound of running feet but we saw no one."

Sheriff Coates came to Kate. "Do you know what happened?"

She shook her head.

"Wasn't Frank Kailey at your place tonight?"

She nodded reluctantly.

"When did he leave?"

"I didn't notice the time."

"How long before you heard the shots?"

Kate frowned, but she did not reply. Coates said, "Never mind. It doesn't matter anyway. I know Frank was in on this."

"How can you possibly know that?"

"Because he's been in on everything that's happened since he arrived."

"I don't see how you can be so sure. It seems to me you're doing the same thing to Frank that this town did to his father two years ago." She wanted to ask the sheriff why he didn't protect Frank from being attacked, but she didn't want him to know she believed Frank had been involved in the shooting here.

She admitted that she didn't trust Sheriff Coates. She didn't trust him to be fair.

She had made a mistake in sending that money to Frank just before he was released. If she had not sent it, he would not have been able to come home. He would have stayed in Santa Fe. He'd have gotten a job and all this wouldn't have happened at all.

She turned and walked slowly back toward home. Every instinct demanded that she find Frank and help him, that she bandage his wounds if they weren't serious, that she get the doctor for him if they were. But she knew if she went looking for him now, she would only be incriminating him. The sheriff would know she believed Frank had shot Sam Ford. He would know Frank had left her house only a few moments before she heard the shots.

The gate creaked again as she opened it and she told herself absently that she ought to have Miguel oil the hinges tomorrow. But she forgot before she had even stepped into the house.

Miguel retired and she paced nervously back and forth, frowning and occasionally biting her lower lip. Frank must have reached safety, she told herself, or else the sheriff would have found him. And if he had outdistanced the pursuit and escaped, he could not have been wounded too seriously.

She found herself remembering the way Frank had been before he went away and she remembered the way he had been when he came home two years ago to stand by his father who had been arrested and charged with the murder and robbery of Juan Trevino. Frank had been filled with remorse because he had left his father in the first place. He had tried desperately to find evidence that would clear Amos Kailey of the crime.

The trouble had been that Amos Kailey wasn't sure himself whether he was guilty of the killing or not. He had been drunk the night Juan Trevino was killed, and when he was drunk he moved in another world, remembering nothing afterwards.

Kate could see Frank Kailey's face, marked by the two years he had spent in the prison in Santa Fe, aged beyond his years by hardship and remorse, thin because of inadequate prison food. She felt tears spring into her eyes.

Did she love Frank or did she only pity him? That was a question she would have to answer soon.

Suddenly she knew she could not stay here. She had to know whether Frank was badly hurt or not. He might need her help desperately. He might die unless he was found at once. She would have to take the chance that she would incriminate him by going to him. Sheriff Coates had his mind made up anyway that Frank had been involved. Nothing she did was likely to change the sheriff's mind.

She hurried out the door, crossed the small courtyard and opened the gate. She went out and hurried along the dark alleyways toward the center of the town. She emerged on Juarez Street a block and a half below the courthouse, turned the corner and went into the hotel.

It was late and Sellers had gone home. The desk was tended by a young man named Chavez. She crossed the deserted lobby and asked, "Is Frank Kailey registered?"

"Si, Senorita. He is in room eight."

"Is he in his room?"

"Si. Doctor Baker has just left."

"Thank you." She hurried across the lobby and climbed the stairs. For a moment she hesitated in front of the door of room eight, then she knocked firmly.

A groggy voice answered and a moment later the door opened. Frank stood there, naked above the waist, a heavy bandage on his shoulder through which blood had already seeped to make a spot of red. She said, "Frank! Is it very bad?"

He stood aside for her to enter, leaving the door ajar. He sat down weakly on the bed. "Doc gave me some morphine for the pain. I'm pretty groggy."

"But the wound. Is it very bad?"

He shook his head. "Doc says no. It's a flesh wound and it will heal."

Relief flooded Kate. He was battered and hurt. He had taken more from the town of Medicine Arrow in a single day than anybody should have to take in a whole lifetime. But he was alive and that was all that mattered now. She said worriedly, "Frank, you've got to leave. They're not going to give up. They'll insist that Sheriff Coates arrest you for killing Mr. Ford. They can put enough pressure on him to make him do it, too. He's an elected official. He can't fight those who put him in office for very long."

Frank said, "It was self-defense. He shot me first."

"Do you think that will matter to the people in this town? They hanged your father for a crime he didn't commit, and they want to get rid of you even more than they wanted to get rid of him. You're their conscience, Frank. Every time they see you they're reminded of the wrong they did."

Frank shook his head. "I'm going to stay. This is my home. I want to redeem that land." He met her glance steadily with his own. "Kate, if I leave, I'm lost. Anyplace but here I'm only an ex-convict and sooner or later, no matter where I go, that will catch up with me."

"Is that worse than staying here and being killed?

They've tried to kill you twice today. They'll try again tomorrow. They won't stop until they're rid of you."

"Why? I can forgive them eventually for the mistake they made even if their reasons for making it weren't very good. Why can't they forgive me for reminding them?"

Kate shook her head. "I don't know, Frank. I guess it's just the way people are. There is nothing more awful to live with than guilt and those jurymen have been living with it now for almost a year. Maybe they were beginning to forget when you came back. Maybe they think if you stay they will never be able to forget."

There was a long silence. He stared at her steadily until she flushed and looked away.

She pleaded, "Please, Frank, leave! I'm afraid for you. I'm afraid of what they're going to do tomorrow."

He shook his head stubbornly. "Two of the ones who tried to kill me are dead. I don't think they'll try to kill me again. Cozzins can't do it alone and I don't think Keegle is even afraid of me. I don't know why, but he doesn't act like the others do."

"Then they'll find another way. They'll try to send you back to prison if they can't get rid of you any other way."

"How can they do that if I don't do anything?"

She reminded him, "Your father didn't do anything and they got rid of him."

There was an implacable stubbornness in Frank's battered face. He shook his head. "No Kate. I've got to stay. No matter what happens, I've got to stay. Maybe it has something to do with Pa. Maybe it's for myself. It's mixed up and I don't really know. But I do know I can't run now."

Tears were streaming down Kate's face. She stared at him angrily through her tears. "Frank Kailey, you're as stubborn as a mule!"

She stood there, furious, for several moments more. Then she crossed the room, went out the door slamming it angrily.

And suddenly she knew. She pitied him for what had happened to him but there was more to it than that. A part of her would die if anything happened to Frank.

Chapter 14

COATES awoke as dawn began to gray the sky. He realized instantly where he was, and that reminded him of why he was here instead of at the boardinghouse. Frank Kailey was back in town. He had been shot last night and had killed Sam Ford. Today there was going to be trouble over it. A lot of pressure was going to be put on him to jail Frank or run him out of town.

He got up, pulled on his pants and boots, then went through the cell block to the door at the rear. He pumped a bucket of water and carried it inside. He built a fire in the pot bellied stove and put the coffeepot on top. When that was done, he washed in cold water and shaved. Only then did he put on his shirt, the same soiled one he had worn yesterday. If he happened to go by the boardinghouse today, he thought, he'd change.

By the time he was shaved, the water on the stove was beginning to get hot. He put a handful of ground coffee into the pot, then went to the front door, unlocked it and stepped outside.

The sky was blue and the air was cool. The sun was just now staining the clouds pink above the bandstand in the middle of the Plaza. Birds were chirping and there was an elusive fragrance in the air from something blossoming.

Coates stared sourly at the beauty of this dawning day. He wished he wasn't sheriff suddenly. He wished he was out at the Kailey ranch instead.

Thinking of the ranch made him feel guilty again. He was irritated at the town. He was irritated at Cozzins and Keegle and the others over the way they were treating Frank, but was he any better? He knew Frank couldn't raise the money to redeem the ranch. The right thing for him to do would be to lend Frank the necessary money himself.

But he knew that he would not. He wanted to keep that land. Right or wrong, he wanted it for himself. He wasn't young anymore. He was past fifty and the time was coming when he wouldn't have this job. They sure as hell didn't pension sheriffs off. They defeated them. And who would hire an ex-sheriff? Particularly one that was well past middle age?

He went back inside. He picked up the broom and began to sweep, but his thoughts didn't stop. They raced on in spite of his attempt to halt them in physical activity.

He was as responsible as the jurymen for the conviction and execution of Amos Kailey two years ago. And he felt as guilty as they did over that affair. He wanted Frank to leave as much as any of them did because as long as Frank was here he'd be reminded of Amos Kailey, swinging from the scaffold behind the jail. Besides, if Frank left it would mean he could keep the Kailey Ranch. The year given Frank under the law to redeem it would pass and it would then belong to him.

Yet he was not without principles, not without conscience. He knew Frank deserved better treatment than he was getting here. He deserved a chance to redeem his ranch. He deserved fair treatment at the hands of the town. He had a right to the protection of the law.

Coates tried desperately to justify himself. Ford and Cozzins had wanted him to arrest Frank yesterday. They had wanted Frank charged with Hapgood's death, and he had refused. He'd done right by Frank in that instance, hadn't he?

Deep down inside he knew that he had not. Frank had been the one attacked. He should have arrested Cozzins and Ford. They were the ones who should have gone to jail.

The truth was, he admitted finally, he was no better than any of those who had been persecuting Frank. He had not joined them in their persecution, but neither had he tried to protect Frank from them.

He poured himself a cup of coffee and gulped the scalding stuff. He walked to the door again, cup in hand, and stared outside. The sun was up now and blazing straight into his eyes.

A group of men were coming down the walk. They nodded at him and he understood that they wanted to talk to him. He also knew what they wanted to talk about. He stepped aside and they entered the office. A few of them had been on Amos Kailey's jury. Mendelbaum was one. Thibault, the postmaster, was another. Sellers, the portly, white-haired hotelman, was a third. But the others had not been on the jury two years ago. One of these was the town mayor, Jefferson Chavez. Another was John Littlehorse, the county treasurer. A third was Burt Vigil, the undertaker.

Coates tugged at the end of his moustache and asked almost defiantly, "Well gentlemen, what's on your mind?"

Chavez, a dark-skinned man of Spanish descent, said, "I think you know, Ray. I think you know what's on our mind. The same thing that's been on everybody's mind since yesterday. Frank Kailey."

Coates waited, refusing to help Chavez, who plainly did not like what he was going to have to say.

Chavez cleared his throat. "Our town was peaceful until Frank came home from Santa Fe but look at what happened yesterday. Otis McCurdy had a heart seizure, which Frank Kailey brought about. Floyd Hapgood was killed by a blow on the head. And last night Sam Ford was shot."

Coates asked wearily, "What do you think I ought to do about it? Kailey never touched McCurdy. All he did was ask him for a loan. He'd never have touched Hapgood if Floyd and a couple of others hadn't attacked and beaten him. And last night, Frank was also shot in that alley down there where Ford was killed. It looks to me like the trouble would stop if people would start letting Frank alone."

Jefferson Chavez was an aristocrat accustomed to being obeyed. He said stiffly, "You are the sheriff in this county, Mr. Coates. Your job is to keep the peace, and the peace is threatened. As citizens, and I might say as voters, we demand that you arrest Frank Kailey and charge him with the death of Sam Ford last night. There are lesser charges than first degree murder, you know. There is voluntary manslaughter. There is also involuntary manslaughter. Judge Lavasseur will be here in a few days. Frank will be convicted and sentenced to prison in Santa Fe. Next time he's released he'll know better than to come back here."

Coates felt a stir of angry defiance. "And if I refuse?"

"Then we may be forced to have you removed. We can appoint an interim law officer who will do what you refuse to do."

Coates could see what anger, defiance, and stubbornness might cost him if he persisted in refusing their demands. He also knew he couldn't give in immediately. He thought of his own self-respect, as well as his need to maintain the respect of the community. He said grudgingly, hating himself as he did, "I'll have to think about it."

Chavez was immediately more jovial. "That's all we ask. We have confidence that what you decide will be right."

Coates stared at him. He was thinking that what they had confidence in was that he'd do what they wanted him to even if it was wrong.

The delegation filed out the door. Coates scowled at their backs bitterly. Anger began to grow in him, but strangely enough, it was directed neither at the delegation of townspeople nor at himself. It was directed at Frank Kailey, whose return had precipitated all the trouble now besetting him. He cursed savagely and kicked the empty spittoon halfway across the room. Ashamed of himself, he picked it up and replaced it beside his desk where it belonged. But his scowl remained.

A block and a half down the street in the direction of the depot, Frank Kailey stepped stiffly from the hotel. His left shoulder and left sleeve were brown and stiff with dried blood. The shirt fit tightly over the bandage Doc Baker had put upon the wound.

Frank was sore in every muscle and the ache in his shoulder came close to being intolerable. His mouth was swelled, one eye was black, and his ribs hurt every time he breathed. Wrists and ankles burned savagely beneath the bandages.

He was scowling; today he was dangerous. Irritability lay close to the surface in him, and violence was scarcely deeper. He wore his gun low against his right thigh; it gave him a feeling of confidence he had not had yesterday.

He crossed the street to Mendelbaum's, entered and walked to the counter where the shirts were displayed. Mendelbaum approached him timidly, having just returned from the sheriff's office. Frank saw Mendelbaum's fear and it prodded his irritability. He said, "For Christ's sake, I'm not going to bite! All I want is a shirt."

With shaking hands, Mendelbaum pulled some shirts out of a drawer. Frank selected a white one his size and paid for it. He took off the bloody one and put the clean one on. He wadded the dirty one up and handed it to Mendelbaum. "You can throw this away."

Mendelbaum took it silently. Frank went out and paused for a moment on the walk. A group of men stood across the street in front of the bank talking quietly among themselves. He recognized the mayor, Jefferson Chavez, Thibault, the postmaster, and Sellers, the hotelman. All looked at him furtively, then looked quickly away when they saw that he had noticed them.

Frank's irritability increased. He was beginning to wish he *had* come back for revenge. He was beginning to hate the people of this town thoroughly. Damn them, they were practically forcing him to do the very things they claimed to fear.

Disgustedly, he turned and walked down the street toward Ferguson's Restaurant. He felt a little sick at his stomach, partly, he supposed, from disgust, partly from his injuries; but he knew he ought to eat.

How was all this going to come out, he wondered suddenly. Would they succeed in killing him? Would they beat him again and ride him out of town? Or would they jail him on some trumped-up charge and railroad him to prison again?

He knew he was foolish for staying. All he had to do was go to Coates and ask to be paid for a quitclaim deed. He could buy back his horse and saddle and ride out of Medicine Arrow a free man, with money in his pocket and all the world ahead of him. And it was something he could not do. Not now at least. Not the way he would have to go right now, like a whipped pup with his tail between his legs.

He reached Ferguson's and went inside. Domingo Feliz was sitting at one end of the counter. He had just finished breakfast and had a toothpick in his mouth. He glanced at Frank, then lowered his glance without speaking. He got up, passed Frank with his head down and ducked out the door.

There was an emptiness in Frank's chest as he sat down. Domingo hadn't been on the jury that convicted his father two years ago. Domingo had no reason to fear.

Even Dolores came to him timidly and asked in a frightened voice, "Yes, Senor."

He scowled at her and saw that his scowl had further frightened her. He said, "Eggs and ham. Coffee too."

"Si, Senor." She scurried away and a moment later he heard her voice talking to Ferguson in the kitchen.

91

Ferguson stuck his head through the door, looked at him, then ducked back again.

He felt like standing up and shouting, "What the hell's the matter with everybody in this lousy town? All I did was defend myself! Is that some kind of crime? What was I supposed to do, let them beat me to death? Was I supposed to let that bunch fill me full of lead last night? Look at this shoulder! Four inches farther to the right and I'd have been the one Vigil's hearse picked up!"

But he didn't move. There wasn't any use. Guilt had instilled fear in the hearts of the jurymen. They believed he had come back for revenge because each knew he was justified in seeking it. Nothing would convince them otherwise.

Filled with fear, they weren't going to let him live here in peace. They'd never be satisfied until he left for good. And if he refused to leave, they'd get rid of him any way they could. They'd kill him or they'd railroad him back to prison on some trumped-up charge.

He made his decision suddenly. He *would* leave. He didn't want to live in a town like this, a town that had committed a deadly sin but which hadn't the courage to admit it and try to atone for it. He could never be happy here. The hanging of his father and the things they had done to him trying to get him to leave would always stand in the way. He'd leave all right, but first he was going to let them sweat a while. He was entitled to that much, in payment for his land, in payment for his right to live here where he had been raised.

Dolores brought his food and he began to eat, with neither appetite nor pleasure, but automatically, scowling at his plate.

Chapter 15

SOL MENDELBAUM, tall and gaunt, watched Frank Kailey as he walked out the door and disappeared. He realized he still held Kailey's bloody shirt in his hands and he threw it on the floor disgustedly. He went to the door of the store.

Jefferson Chavez, Sellers and Thibault were standing with several others across the street in front of the bank watching Kailey as he walked toward Ferguson's. Mendelbaum caught Sellers eye and beckoned him. Sellers touched Thibault's arm and the two left the group and crossed the street.

When they reached the store, Mendelbaum asked, "What do you think? Will Coates arrest him for killing Sam?"

Both men shook their heads. Sellers said, "It's a matter of pride. Coates can't let Chavez tell him what to do. Chavez is a town official and Coates is county sheriff."

Mendelbaum nodded agreement. "That's how I figured it."

Sellers asked, "So what are we going to do? Maybe Cozzins and Keegle could—"

Mendelbaum shook his head. "No. I want no more violence. There is another way."

"What way?"

"We know Kailey needs money. He needs it to redeem his ranch. He tried to borrow yesterday from McCurdy but McCurdy refused. What would be more reasonable than that he would try to steal it since he can't get it any other way?"

"How much does he need?"

"A hundred and seventy-five dollars. Now suppose I was to force a back window open with a crowbar and suppose Sellers was to put a hundred and seventy-five dollars out of my cash drawer in Frank Kailey's room.

Then suppose Aker was to swear he saw Kailey coming out of that back window at dawn—?"

"Coates wouldn't swallow it. He'd want to know why it wasn't reported this morning when we all went down to the jail to talk to him."

"Aker wasn't there. We could say we didn't know about it then. I could go down to the jail right now and report my window forced and the money stolen. Thibault, you go talk to Aker at the livery barn. Sellers, you plant the money in Frank's room while he's down at Ferguson's eating breakfast."

The two hesitated briefly. Mendelbaum said, "Make up your minds. There isn't too much time."

Both men nodded suddenly. Mendelbaum went to his cash drawer and got a hundred and seventy-five dollars in currency. He gave it to Sellers, who left immediately. Thibault followed him out and hurried toward the livery barn. Mendelbaum watched them a moment, then hurried to the back room. He got a crowbar and went into the alley. He glanced cautiously up and down. Seeing no one, he climbed on a box and forced the window open with the crowbar.

He looked up and down the alley again. Still seeing no one, he threw the crowbar into the weeds of the vacant lot next door. Quickly, then, he went back into his store.

Now that it was done, he felt a nagging sense of shame. It was the first really dishonest thing he had done in his life. Unless voting Amos Kailey guilty had been dishonest—and he didn't think it had. He'd had no feeling of committing a dishonest act then the way he did right now.

But it was necessary, he told himself. Coates wasn't going to arrest Frank Kailey for killing Ford. And Frank had to be stopped. If he wasn't a lot of others were going to die.

Nervousness continued to grow in him. He began to pace back and forth in front of the windows opening on the street. At last, satisfied that both Thibault and Sellers had had time to do what they were supposed to do, he left the store and hurried up Juarez street toward the courthouse. He wouldn't have to pretend agitation. He was upset enough to convince anyone.

He burst into the sheriff's office and Coates, startled, glanced up at him. Mendelbaum said excitedly, "Sheriff, I've been robbed! My store's been robbed. A back window was forced and there is money missing from the drawer."

Coates's eyes were instantly suspicious. "Why didn't you tell me a while ago?"

"I didn't know. I just now found the window and when I did I counted the money and most of it was gone."

"Most of it? Wouldn't a thief take all of it?"

"How do I know what a thief would do? I'm telling you, sheriff, that I've been robbed. Are you going to sit here arguing or you going to go out and catch the thief?"

Coates got slowly to his feet. He studied Mendelbaum suspiciously. He said, "We haven't had a theft in Medicine Arrow since Juan Trevino was robbed and killed. Quite a coincidence, wouldn't you say, that the first one happens the day after Frank Kailey comes home from prison?"

"You think Kailey did it?"

Coates's voice was dry. "What do you think, Mr. Mendelbaum?"

Mendelbaum couldn't meet the sheriff's eyes. Coates said, "Let's go down there and take a look at the window you say was forced."

He went out and Mendelbaum followed him. Down the street, he saw Thibault coming out of the livery stable. He hoped Aker wouldn't come rushing up here just yet to tell the sheriff he had seen Frank climbing out of the store window earlier.

They reached the store and went inside. Mendelbaum led the sheriff to the back room and pointed to the window that had been forced. Coates went out into the alley to look around.

Nervously, Mendelbaum followed him. The sheriff studied the ground carefully and Mendelbaum wished he'd thought about tracks. He hadn't, though, and now it was too late. Still, it wasn't likely the sheriff was going to find any tracks he could identify. The ground was hard. All the dust had been turned to mud night before last when it rained and the mud had hardened yesterday.

Mendelbaum withdrew into the store. He went to the cash drawer and counted the money. He never knew exactly how much money was in the drawer. When too much had accumulated there he took it to the bank. He wondered how close he ought to be when he estimated the loss. Maybe he should just tell Coates that more than a hundred dollars was gone.

He saw Dell Aker go past in the street, heading for the courthouse. He nodded to himself with satisfaction. Dell didn't know Coates was here and it would look a lot better if he had to hunt for him.

Now that it was done beyond recall, he began to feel very guilty about it. Frank didn't deserve to be sent back to prison for something he hadn't done. McCurdy's heart had failed, even though Frank had caused it by frightening the man. And Hapgood had been one of those who had beaten Frank. He had therefore deserved what happened to him. Last night, Sam Ford had been trying to kill Frank. He had just happened to be killed himself.

Not one of the three deaths would have occurred if the jurymen hadn't felt so guilty about sending Frank's father to the gallows two years ago. Still, Frank's return *had* been directly responsible. While he might not be to blame, he was responsible.

Coates came back into the store, carrying the crowbar. "Isn't this your bar?"

Mendelbaum nodded. "I must have left it in the alley yesterday. I was opening some crates."

Coates stared at him long enough to make Mendelbaum feel acutely uncomfortable. "How much money is gone?"

Mendelbaum spread his hands. "You know I don't count it every day. But over a hundred dollars, I think. It is at least that much."

Coates continued to stare at him and Mendelbaum couldn't continue to meet his gaze. Coates turned and headed up the aisle toward the door. Speaking over his shoulder, he asked, "Where would you suggest I start? Do you have any idea who it might have been?"

"Me? How should I know who it might have been?"

"I just thought maybe you'd have an idea or two. How about Frank Kailey? He was trying to borrow money yesterday from the bank and got turned down."

Mendelbaum hoped his voice sounded natural. "I'm not accusing anybody. I'm certainly not accusing Frank."

"No. Of course you're not." The sheriff went out into the street. He stopped in front a moment, looking up and down. He saw Dell Aker hurrying toward him from the direction of the courthouse and waited.

Aker drew to a halt in front of him, out of breath. Coates could smell the man—horses and manure and stale man sweat. Aker said, "There's something I ought to tell you, Ray."

"Huh uh. Why don't you let me guess? You were robbed last night."

Aker shook his head. "That ain't it. But I saw Frank Kailey coming out of the back window of Mendelbaum's. It was just about dawn."

96

"What were you doing in the alley behind Mendelbaum's?"

For an instant Aker looked confused. Then he asked defiantly, "Any reason I shouldn't be in that alley? I got a right to go any place I want."

Coates said, "Well. Now all that's left is for me to go down and search Frank's room. I wonder if I'd find the money there. I wonder if it would be exactly a hundred and seventy-five dollars."

Aker looked at Mendelbaum. "What's he talking about?"

Mendelbaum said, "That's the amount Frank needs to redeem his ranch."

Aker asked resentfully, "Are you accusing me of lying, Ray?"

Coates shook his head. "Now what makes you think I'd do a thing like that? I'd just like to know what you were doing in the alley behind this store at dawn."

"One of my horses got away."

"I didn't see any tracks."

"Of course not. He didn't go down the alley behind Mendelbaum's. He cut across through those vacant lots. You don't have to be in the alley to see that window."

"Did Frank see you?"

"I don't think so. He was backing out of the window and he acted like it hurt him considerable when he dropped to the ground."

"All right Dell, I'll want a written statement from you if I should happen to find the money in Frank Kailey's room."

"I'm not going to leave." Aker hesitated a moment, then asked, "You need me any more?"

"Huh uh. I'd say you'd done enough."

Aker scowled, but he turned and trudged away toward the livery barn. Frank Kailey had not yet emerged from Ferguson's.

Coates asked, "Have you got any more witnesses?"

Mendelbaum flushed angrily. "Damn you, Coates, you've no right to talk to me that way!"

"Maybe not. But you know I can't search Frank's room without a warrant. And I can't get a warrant until Judge Lavasseur arrives."

Mendelbaum opened his mouth to protest, then shut it without saying anything. He waited an instant, then said, "You're the one who suggested searching Frank Kailey's room. I didn't."

"No. Of course you didn't. But it would be logical, wouldn't it, in view of the fact that Aker saw Frank coming out of your window at dawn?"

Mendelbaum glared at him. "Maybe you could get Frank to agree to let you search."

Coates said, "I'll bet I could. If a man didn't figure he had anything to hide, he wouldn't mind being searched. Of course, now, something else just occurred to me. Sellers has a key to every room in the hotel, doesn't he?"

Mendelbaum said sulkily, "I'm not going to stand here and let you make your damn insinuating remarks. You go to hell. You're the sheriff and I've been robbed. If you recover the money, let me know. If you catch the thief, throw him in jail. I've got work to do."

"Of course. Go ahead and do your work."

Mendelbaum withdrew into the store. Coates scowled after him. He knew this was a put-up job. He knew it was their way of getting rid of Frank. The hell of it was, it was going to work. In Medicine Arrow, after all that had happened yesterday, Frank wouldn't have a chance. He knew he'd find the money in Frank's room at the hotel where Sellers had planted it. The amount would be exactly a hundred and seventy-five dollars. It would be cut and dried. A jury would find Frank guilty and Judge Lavasseur would sentence him to the prison in Santa Fe again.

Coates cursed savagely, knowing he was as much to blame for this as anyone. *If* he'd done what he should yesterday, *if* he'd arrested Cozzins and Ford after Hapgood was killed—

But he hadn't. And now it was too late.

Angrily he turned and headed for the hotel.

Chapter 16

LEON SELLERS was behind the desk in the hotel lobby when Coates entered. He glanced at the sheriff, then quickly glanced away again. His normally florid complexion seemed even more ruddy this morning.

Coates crossed to the desk. He was damned if he was going to make this easy for any of them. Furthermore, if the case ever came to trial he was going to stand up in court and tell Judge Lavasseur and the jury exactly what he suspected even if it cost him the election in November. He had felt guilty the past year over the conviction and execution of Amos Kailey ever since he had learned of the confession made by the actual killer in Santa Fe. He was damned if he was going to spend the rest of his life feeling guilty about railroading the son back to prison for something *he* hadn't done. Maybe he couldn't refuse to arrest Frank when someone like Mendelbaum wanted to sign a complaint. But he didn't have to keep still about what he thought when it came to trial.

He put his elbows on the desk and stared steadily at the white-haired manager. "I don't suppose you know anything about this, do you?"

Sellers looked up at him guiltily, his sheepish expression betraying he most certainly did. He asked, "Know anything about what, Ray?"

"Ah come on! You know what I'm talking about."

Sellers' color deepened. He couldn't meet the sheriff's eyes no matter how he tried. "I *don't* know what you're talking about."

Coates uttered a single obscene word. He said, "I hope you and Mendelbaum and Aker know what you're doing. If you felt guilty when you found out Amos Kailey was innocent, you're going to feel a hell of a lot more guilty when you see Frank get on the train and head for five or ten more years in Santa Fe, knowing it was your perjured evidence that sent him there."

Sellers finally managed to meet his eyes. "I wish you'd tell me what the hell you're talking about."

"I'm talking about a hundred and seventy-five dollars that I'm about to find hidden in Frank Kailey's room."

"You mean he stole that much from Mendelbaum?" Sellers managed to make his voice sound surprised.

Coates repeated that single, obscene word and turned away from the desk. He crossed to one of the leather-covered chairs and sat down heavily. He took a cigar from his pocket, bit off the end and lighted it.

He had been waiting no more than five minutes when Frank Kailey came in. Frank had a clean shirt on that was tight over the shoulder bandages. He was limping slightly and walking as though every movement hurt. He saw Coates and crossed the lobby to him.

Coates said, "An accusation has been made against you."

Kailey nodded. "I wouldn't be surprised. What kind of accusation?"

"You were seen coming out of the back window of Mendelbaum's store early this morning."

"Who saw me?"

"You admit it, then?" For an instant, Coates felt relief. If Frank had really robbed Mendelbaum's store it was sure as hell going to simplify everything.

Frank grinned crookedly. "You wish I would admit it, don't you? That would be the solution for everybody. Send me back to prison for the robbery. Get me out of your town and off your consciences. But I'm afraid I'm not going to make it that easy for you. Whoever says he saw me coming out of Mendelbaum's is a liar."

"Well, if it wasn't you, then you shouldn't mind if I searched your room."

"Without a search warrant you mean?"

Coates nodded. "That's what I mean. Judge Lavasseur isn't due for several days. I can't get a warrant until he arrives. But if you haven't got anything to hide——" Coates suddenly despised himself. He had condemned what Mendelbaum and Aker and Sellers were about to do to Frank, but he was now making himself a part of it. By getting Frank to let him search, he was making himself a part of it.

Frank said, "I haven't got anything to hide, but this is beginning to have a bad smell as far as I'm concerned."

100

Coates said, "Mendelbaum says he's been robbed. Aker says he saw you coming out of the window at Mendelbaum's. You can see that doesn't leave me much choice. Whether you let me search your room or not, I've got to arrest you and throw you in jail."

"And if I let you search?"

"I'll either find something or I won't. If I do, you go to jail anyway."

"And if you don't find anything?"

"Then I'll have to assume that Aker either lied or made a mistake." Coates didn't like himself much right now. He knew Frank deserved a warning from him. He also knew he couldn't give it. Unless he was prepared to charge Mendelbaum and Sellers and Aker with conspiracy.

And he wasn't prepared to charge the three with conspiracy because he knew he could never make it stick. The three were too respectable.

Frank said wearily, "I've got a feeling I'm going to be sorry, but you haven't given me much choice. Come on. You can search my room."

Coates got heavily to his feet. He followed Frank across the lobby and up the stairs. In front of Frank's room, he glanced down at the desk. Sellers was looking up, watching the two of them expectantly.

Kailey unlocked the door. Coates preceded him into the room. There were few places in the room where anything could be hidden. The bed was one. The dresser was another. The chair was the third. Coates checked the dresser first, pulling out the empty drawers one after another. Frank's saddlebags were in the corner and he looked into them without finding anything.

He glanced at Frank who was watching him with an unreadable expression on his face. He asked, "What's that expression mean?"

"Just trying to figure you out. I know you'd like to get rid of me because you'd like to keep that land. But your conscience won't let you completely disregard the law, will it? Otherwise you would have arrested me for killing Hapgood yesterday. Or you'd have arrested me for shooting Ford last night."

Coates said drily, "When you get me all figured out, let me know."

Kailey ignored the remark. He asked, "What are you going to do if you do find that money here? That's really going to put you in a fix, isn't it? You know I didn't rob

101

anybody. You'll know, if you find the money that some-body put it here. And who's the only one that's got a key to my room besides myself?"

Coates lifted the corner of the mattress up. It didn't surprise him in the slightest to see the thick sheaf of currency lying there. He thought fleetingly that he didn't have to count it to know how much there was.

Frank saw it too and he didn't seem any more sur-prised than Coates. He said, "Well, pick it up, Sheriff. It isn't going to bite."

Coates swung his head. "I'm sorry, Frank."

"For what? Because now I'm out of the way for good? Or because you know somebody planted that?" Frank's tone was light and mocking, but his face was pale and his eyes, for the first time since his return, were scared.

Coates picked up the money gingerly and counted it. It came to a hundred and seventy-five dollars just as he had known it would. He asked, "Can you give me an explanation of how it got here, Frank?"

"You know I can't."

"Then I guess you'll have to go to jail."

For an instant, panic flared in Frank Kailey's eyes. Then it subsided and he nodded resignedly. "All right."

"Give me your gun." Coates realized that his right arm was tense, his right hand poised over the grips of his own gun like a claw.

Frank hesitated for an instant. Coates said warningly, "I'm good, Frank. You wouldn't have a chance."

Frank Kailey shrugged. With thumb and forefinger he lifted his gun from its holster and handed it to Coates. The sheriff stuffed it into his belt.

Coates opened the door and stood aside. Frank stared at it. He would walk out of this room a prisoner, headed for jail, probably headed for prison once again. Only this time it was a put-up job. He wasn't going back to jail for anything he had done but only because he reminded the men in this town of their guilt.

He walked out onto the balcony. The sheriff followed, closing the door behind him. Frank went down the stairs. He felt Sellers looking at him and glanced at the hotelman. Sellers looked quickly away. Sellers had to be the one who had planted the money in his room, thought Frank. Not that it mattered now.

He would go to trial, he thought, when Judge Lavasseur arrived and the judge, mindful of the attack two years ago, would probably give him the maximum sentence allowed under the law. He'd go back to prison in Santa Fe.

A feeling of desperation came over him, a feeling that was as close to blind panic as any he had ever experienced. He wanted to break and run; he wanted to force Coates to shoot him down, to kill him and have it over with. He clenched his fists at his sides. It wasn't over yet. He hadn't been brought to trial, or convicted. There was still a chance, a chance Coates would find the strength to get off the fence and do what he knew was right, even a chance that Mendelbaum or Aker or Sellers would feel so much shame over what they had done that they wouldn't be able to go through with it.

Passing Mendelbaum's Mercantile, Frank glanced that way and glimpsed Sol Mendelbaum's gaunt old face peering at him through the front window. The face instantly disappeared as Mendelbaum drew back. Frank said bitterly, "Now I'm sorry I didn't come back for revenge. I've got the name. I'd just as well have had the game."

Coates did not reply. He paced along steadily a little behind Frank. He had holstered his gun, which made the spectacle a little more tolerable, but Frank was glad Kate wasn't downtown. He was glad she didn't have to be watching this.

They passed the bank. The shades were still drawn over the front windows. The "Closed" sign was still in the glass-paneled door. At the corner Frank stared at the place his mother had been killed six years before. It had all started here, he thought, with an unavoidable accident, but the consequences of the accident had spread, and spread, like ripples spreading from a stone dropped into a pond. His father's life had been destroyed. McCurdy, Hapgood and Ford were dead. His own life had been ruined for the past six years and now promised to be ruined for a much longer time than that.

How much further were the consequences of her death going to spread? At this moment it looked as though the end had come, but he didn't believe it had. He had a feeling this was just another episode in an inevitable chain of events that was far from complete.

He saw Domingo Feliz turn away guiltily, and across the Plaza he saw Hans Keegle standing in front of his gun shop, watching. Then they reached the jail and Frank stepped inside.

The sheriff followed, closing the door behind him. He said, "Pick any cell you want."

He was trying to be agreeable, but Frank could feel nothing but bitterness. Staring at those barred cells a sudden wild rebellion came over him. He turned and scowled at Coates, close to making a break. Coates grabbed his gun. The hammer clicking back was a noise that, in this deadly silence, seemed almost thunderous. Frank said softly, "You won't shoot me. You won't do it because you know it's wrong."

Coates shook his head. "Don't bet on it. Turn around and get into one of those cells."

Frank shrugged. He turned and went into a cell. Coates closed the door behind him, turned the key, removed it and put it into his pocket. He returned to the office, got an envelope out of his desk and put the money into it. He wrote something on the envelope, sealed it and put it into the small black iron safe in the corner of the office.

He rummaged in his desk and finally found what he was looking for, two complaint forms. He asked, "Anything you want?"

Frank shook his head without looking up.

Coates said, "I'm going to Mendelbaum's and get him to sign a complaint. Then I'm going to the stable and get Aker to sign a statement that he saw you coming out of Mendelbaum's window this morning."

Frank still did not look up. Coates hesitated several moments before he said, "Maybe when it comes to signing their names to a lie, they'll back out, Frank."

"Then you admit that it's a lie."

"Let's say I admit the possibility."

Frank said sourly, "I hope I never have to bet my life on you."

Coates didn't answer him. He went out, closed the door and turned a key in the lock. Frank was alone and the silence suddenly seemed almost unbearable.

Chapter 17

FROWNING WORRIEDLY, Dell Aker watched as Coates walked up Juarez Street toward the jail. He had agreed to say he had seen Frank Kailey climbing out of Mendelbaum's back window this morning when Hank Thibault asked him, but he hadn't realized he was going to have to sign a statement and appear in court to swear to it.

But when Coates presented him with a statement to sign, he hadn't had any choice. It was either sign or admit that he had lied.

He saw Coates go into Mendelbaum's store and continued watching until the sheriff reappeared ten minutes later. Coates walked on uptown toward the courthouse. He disappeared into his office.

It was now almost nine o'clock. Aker supposed there would be funerals this afternoon, for McCurdy, for Hapgood, perhaps for Sam Ford too. He saw Kate Guerrero appear at the corner of the Plaza and turn toward the bank. Using her key, she disappeared inside. She didn't act as though she was aware that Frank Kailey had been arrested and charged with robbing Mendelbaum's store.

Still frowning, Aker left the stable, walked uptown toward Mendelbaum's. He had to talk to someone. He was worried about the statement Coates had forced him to sign. Kailey had already killed two men and caused a third to die since his return. If he ever escaped from jail. . . . Even if he didn't escape, they couldn't keep him in prison for the rest of his life. Sooner or later he'd get out and then he'd come back looking for those who had lied and sent him there.

A cold chill ran along Aker's spine as he thought of it. He realized suddenly that he had never fully accepted the idea that Frank had returned this time for revenge. He had admitted the possibility, of course, but the real reason he had wanted to be rid of Frank was because Frank reminded him of the way he and the others had found Frank's father guilty on flimsy and insufficient evidence simply because they wanted to be rid of him.

He reached Mendelbaum's but before he went in, he glanced guiltily toward the bank. Kate was standing at the window, watching him. He averted his glance and ducked inside the store.

Mendelbaum stuck his head out of his office in the rear to see who it was. Aker hurried back. He said, "Coates was just down at the livery barn. He made me sign a statement that I saw Frank coming out of your window this morning."

Mendelbaum wore a small, worried frown. "I know. He made me sign a complaint."

"Did Sellers get the money planted in Frank's room all right?"

Mendelbaum nodded. "The sheriff's got Frank in jail."

Aker looked down at his shaking hands. "What if he escapes? Have you thought of that?"

Mendelbaum nodded. "I haven't been thinking of anything else."

"Or even if he doesn't, what about when he gets out of prison? He'll kill every one of us."

Mendelbaum stared at him irritably. "You didn't have to agree to lie. You could have refused."

Aker started to snap at him, then stopped. He said, "What we'd better do right now is try and figure some way out of this. I'm not absolutely convinced that Frank even came back for revenge this time. Maybe the sheriff was right. Maybe nobody would have been killed if they'd just let him alone. But there won't be no doubt next time. Frank will come back looking for the three of us. He'll kill us for sure unless we manage to kill him first."

"Are you suggesting that we kill him in his cell?" Mendelbaum's voice was horrified.

Aker considered it briefly. The trouble with that solution was that not one of the three of them could do it. Not one of them had the guts. Aker knew *he* didn't. He couldn't stand at Frank's cell window and deliberately murder him.

A sudden idea came to him. He said excitedly, "I've got it, by God!"

"What do you mean?"

"Why don't we fix it for Frank to escape? He'd have to leave the country and he'd have to stay gone because the

106

minute he came back he'd have to go on trial for robbing your store."

"How could we do that? The jail is practically escape-proof."

"We could slip him a gun."

"And how the hell would you manage that? The bars on the windows are too close together for a gun to pass through."

"Then how about a knife?"

"That would go through all right. But he'd have to get Coates right up next to the bars before he could threaten him with it." Mendelbaum frowned. "Kailey could get killed in the scuffle. I wouldn't think a knife would be much good against Ray Coates."

Aker said, "Would that be so bad? Does it matter how we get rid of Kailey, just so we get rid of him?"

Mendelbaum continued to frown, slowly shaking his head. "It isn't right."

"Right?" Aker scoffed. "Is this put-up robbery charge right? Besides, the chances are that Kailey will get away with it. He's not going to threaten Coates with the knife unless he's sure it's going to work. Nobody's going to get hurt. Kailey will get away and Coates won't try very hard to catch up with him."

Mendelbaum hesitated. Aker could see that his conscience was bothering him. He also knew that when you have compromised your conscience once, the second time is easier. And the third time is easier still.

Aker said, "McCurdy and Hapgood and Ford are dead. It seems to me that getting rid of Frank this way ain't so goddamn bad. If we let him go to trial we're going to have to get up in court and swear to a lie. He'll get five years in the pen. But what about when that five years is up? What's the first thing he'll do when he gets out?"

Mendelbaum's face was pale. His hands were shaking. He said, "All right. But who's going to slip him the knife?"

"I don't mind doing that. You go down to the jail and tell Coates you've found something in the store that may have belonged to Frank. Get him to come here and look around. Find out which cell Frank is in. I'll meet you at the corner of the Plaza and if you get the chance you can tell me which cell it is."

Mendelbaum asked, "What—?"

"Oh hell, I don't know. Haven't you got an old pocket-knife? Drop it under that window out in the back. Tell

107

the sheriff you didn't want to touch it for fear he'd say you put it there."

"That's pretty thin."

"You got a better idea for getting Coates away from the jail?"

Mendelbaum shrugged. He put on his coat, which was shiny at the elbows, and headed for the front door. Aker got a butcher knife out of a drawer full of them and followed him. Mendelbaum hurried up the street in the direction of the jail.

Aker followed more slowly, so that he could meet Mendelbaum and the sheriff coming back. At the corner of the Plaza he stopped. He got out his pipe and packed it deliberately. As he lighted it, he saw Coates and Mendelbaum come out of the sheriff's office and walk toward him.

Mendelbaum spoke to him but Coates only stared at him suspiciously. Mendelbaum never got the chance to tell him which cell Frank was in. The sheriff was watching the two of them too closely for that.

Coates and Mendelbaum went on. Aker waited until they disappeared into the store. Then he hurried toward the jail. He had slipped the knife up his sleeve before he left the store. Now he cut through a vacant lot on the south side of the courthouse, hoping no one would see him and tell Coates about it later, but knowing he had to take the chance. He circled the rear of the courthouse and stopped beside the back door of the jail.

The windows were high, the bars no more than an inch apart. Aker looked around for something on which to stand. The only thing available was the rain barrel, standing half full beneath a downspout coming off the roof of a nearby lean-to shed. Quickly he dumped it out on the ground. He rolled the barrel over beneath the nearest window. Climbing up, he peered through.

The inside of the jail was dark by comparison with the bright sunlight outside. It was hard to see and the close-set bars didn't make it any easier. He wondered if Frank would see him and be able to tell Coates who he was.

He was beginning to feel a little panicky when suddenly he saw movement inside the jail. The movement was that of Frank's white shirt and he saw that Frank was in the cell next to this one.

He got down and rolled the rain barrel beneath Frank's window. He got the knife out of his sleeve, climbed up and pushed it between the bars. He heard it clatter on the floor.

Swiftly he got down and rolled the rain barrel back where it belonged. He righted it. He knew it was doubtful if Coates would notice that it had been spilled. If he did notice, he would probably assume it was the work of boys.

Hurrying now, Aker circled the courthouse and came out into the street. Coates had not yet reappeared. Aker crossed the street, walked diagonally across the Plaza to the alley that ran behind his livery barn. He hurried along it, scared but relieved as well. Nothing that had been tried for getting rid of Frank had worked, but then everything tried so far had been crude and direct. Maybe something more subtle, like getting Frank to escape, would work where everything else had failed.

It was quiet inside the jail. The walls between it and the county offices adjoining were too thick to permit any noise to filter through. Frank therefore clearly heard the footsteps outside the back window and the rain barrel being overturned. He heard the scuffing sounds as it rolled beneath the window and someone climbed up.

He thought the face that appeared at the window was Aker's, but he could not be sure. The close-set bars obscured too much. The face disappeared and a few moments later reappeared at the window of Frank's own cell.

He flattened himself against the wall directly beneath the window, knowing it was possible that the man at the window would try killing him. But no shots were fired. A knife dropped through the window immediately above him, struck him on the shoulder, then clattered to the floor.

It was a wooden-handled butcher knife, new, the kind women used for cutting meat. Its blade was about eight inches long, and slightly curved. It was adequate for overcoming Coates. The point was sharp enough to penetrate his clothes and prick his skin. But he'd have to get Coates right up against the bars. He'd have to reach through and get the sheriff around the throat with one arm while he dug the knife against him with the other hand.

He crossed to his cot and hid the knife beneath the thin mattress. He sat down and stared thoughtfully at the bars.

He had no friends in Medicine Arrow, no friends who

would slip a knife to him and he doubted if Kate even knew he was under arrest. He was therefore forced to the conclusion that the knife had been dropped into his cell by one of his enemies. The face at the window had looked like Aker's, and probably had been.

But after lying to get him thrown in jail, why did they now want him to escape? Did they expect him to be killed while trying to overpower Coates? He admitted that was possible.

But supposing he made good his escape, and they must have considered the possibility, what had they planned for him? Were they waiting in concealed places outside the jail, prepared to riddle him with bullets as he emerged? That also was a possibility.

A third alternative was that they really wanted him to escape. They wanted him to get away. If he did, he would go as far from Medicine Arrow as he could and would never come back to it. That was probably what all of them wanted even more than they wanted him to die. They had consciences or the false conviction and execution of his father wouldn't have bothered them.

What lay in store for him once he overpowered Coates and escaped depended, he supposed, on who had slipped the knife into his cell. If it had been Keegle or Cozzins, then death surely waited for him outside in the street. If Mendelbaum, Aker, Sellers, Ferguson, and Thibault were behind it, then he would probably be permitted to get away.

He got up and began to pace restlessly back and forth. What did *he* really want to do, he asked himself. Did he want to remain in Medicine Arrow despite the hostility that had been shown him since his return. Or did he want to go away? Did he want to forget Medicine Arrow and his father's wrongful conviction and his own persecution at the hands of the jurymen who had convicted him?

And if he failed to act, what then? Conviction on the trumped-up theft charges was practically a certainty. He would go back to prison in Santa Fe, probably for five years this time.

Thought of that was what decided him. He retrieved the knife from beneath the mattress and slipped it inside his shirt where he could get his hands on it quickly and easily. Once more he began to pace the floor like a caged animal.

110

Chapter 18

FRANK did not have long to wait. He heard the key in the front door and a few moments later it swung open and Coates stepped inside.

He was grumbling disgustedly to himself. Frank wondered how he would get Coates close enough to overpower him. At mealtime it might be possible but he didn't want to wait that long.

His shoulder ached where Ford had shot him last night. And suddenly he knew how he could get Coates into the cell. He called, "Sheriff."

"What?"

"This shirt is too tight over that shoulder bandage and the damn thing aches like hell. Will you help me get it off or slit it or something so it won't put so much pressure on?"

"Sure." Coates came into the cell block and along the corridor to Frank's cell. It was obvious that he wasn't in the least afraid of Frank. He knew, thought Frank, that this robbery charge was a put-up job. There wasn't much he could do about it when a man like Mendelbaum swore out a complaint, but he didn't have to like it.

Coates turned his key in the lock and swung the door open leaving the key where it was. He crossed the cell to Frank.

Frank pretended to be fumbling with the buttons of the shirt. When Coates was close enough, he yanked out the knife and shoved it against the sheriff's slightly protruding paunch. He said softly, "Hold it! I'll shove it clear through you if you go for your gun!"

Coates froze. For several moments he didn't say anything while his breath sighed carefully in and out. At last he said, "Easy, Frank. I'm not going to put up a fight. But you're making a mistake. If somebody slipped you

111

that knife, you can bet they're waiting out there for you. You'll be dead before you go a block."

"Maybe not. Turn around, real slow."

The sheriff started to turn toward the right, but Frank said sharply, "Huh uh. To the left. I'll get the gun as you come around."

Coates obeyed. Frank slipped the sheriff's gun from its holster. He stepped away, tossing the knife out the door into the corridor, pointing the gun at Coates. "Drop the belt."

Coates unbuckled and dropped the belt. Frank said, "Now lie down on the cot."

Coates obeyed. Frank buckled on the belt, then went out of the cell, locked the door and pocketed the key. Coates said, "Frank—"

"Huh uh. Don't tell me it isn't smart to leave. You know better and so do I. They've got me backed into a corner and this is the only way out for me."

He didn't give Coates a chance to say anything else. He thought it likely that the sheriff would start yelling the minute he was out the door but that was a chance he'd have to take.

He stepped out onto the sun-washed gallery, blinking against the glare. There were a few people on the street. There were three Mexican women in the Plaza, talking animatedly, but nobody looked at him.

He shoved the gun into the holster. There were a couple of horses tied in front of the Treasurer's office. Frank stared up and down the street, looking on roofs and at passageways for the ambush. But he saw nobody and began to wonder if maybe he wasn't going to make it after all. He needed a horse desperately but he preferred to take one that would not immediately be missed.

The sheriff still had not yelled for help and a spare grin touched Frank's mouth. Maybe Coates hadn't taken a firm stand against Cozzins, Hapgood, Ford, and Keegle soon enough but it looked like he had taken a stand at last. He was going to give Frank a chance to lose himself before he raised a cry.

He stared longingly at the two horses tied next door, then turned and tramped through the vacant lot beside the jail to the alley behind. He headed uptown, knowing there would be less chance of running into someone there than if he went downtown.

Behind Doc Baker's office there was a small stable

where Doc kept his horse. Frank stuck his head in the door and saw Doc's buggy horse standing in a stall.

He hated to steal Doc's horse, but he couldn't be fussy now. There was a saddle hanging on the wall, an old, beat-up saddle that obviously hadn't been used for months.

Swiftly he exchanged the horse's halter for a bridle and swiftly he put blanket and saddle on his back. He hoped Doc wouldn't need the animal right away, but he supposed if Doc did need a horse he could get one quickly enough at the livery barn.

He led the horse outside and swung astride. He turned uptown. After he had gone two blocks he swung right and headed into the twisting alleyways of the Mexican section.

He meant to leave Medicine Arrow today and he knew he would not come back. Coates would get to keep the land. The town would be rid of him and the jurymen could stop being afraid.

But he couldn't leave without seeing Kate. He had to work out some way of communicating with her and he couldn't trust the mail. Not as long as Hank Thibault was Postmaster.

A few Mexican residents glanced incuriously at him as he rode toward Kate's. Most of them didn't even know who he was. Those who did weren't aware that he had been arrested and thrown in jail. He reached Kate's and tied Doc's horse. He opened the gate and went into the small courtyard.

Miguel was sweeping the gallery. He glanced up. Frank said, "I am looking for Senorita Kate."

"She is not here, Senor. She has gone to the bank."

"Can you go get her, Miguel, and bring her here? It is very important to me. It is also important that you tell no one that I am here."

"Si Senor." Miguel put down his broom and hurried out the gate. Frank led Doc's horse inside and closed the gate. He began to pace restlessly back and forth.

From Keegle's Gun Shop at the corner of the Plaza, the view of the courthouse was excellent. Nothing obscured that view but a single tree.

Keegle saw Frank Kailey walk into the jail, followed closely by Sheriff Coates and something about the way the two of them behaved told him that Frank was a prisoner. It was obvious even though Coates' gun was

113

holstered. Coates stayed far enough behind Kailey to get the gun out if it became necessary.

Frowning, Keegle wondered what it was all about. Had Coates arrested Frank for killing Sam Ford last night. Or was there something else?

For several minutes he paced back and forth, frowning puzzledly. He admitted that he was disappointed to see Frank placed under arrest. Whether he had realized it consciously or not, he had been planning to kill Frank. He had been planning a gun duel that would eliminate Frank once and for all and leave himself a hero in the eyes of the town.

Keegle put on his coat and hat, went out and locked the door behind him. He walked swiftly to the corner of Juarez Street, then turned toward Mendelbaum's. He went inside.

Sol was waiting on a woman customer. He took her money, made change and she left. Keegle said, "I just saw Coates take Frank to jail."

Mendelbaum nodded. "My store was robbed last night. Frank did it. Coates found the money in his room."

Keegle stared at him contemptuously. "Don't try to make me believe that. It's a put-up job, isn't it?"

Mendelbaum nodded sheepishly.

Keegle said, "That was stupid. I could have got rid of him for you."

"Like you and Cozzins and Ford did last night?"

Glancing out the window, Keegle saw the sheriff approaching. He said, "I'll see you later. Right now it might be just as well if Coates didn't see us together."

He hurried along the aisle and out the back door into the alley. Once more he headed uptown. He cut back into Juarez Street and returned to his shop.

He was beginning to feel his disappointment even more keenly than he had at first. Frowning, he tried to understand himself. He had put the gun away years ago when he came to Medicine Arrow after the fire in Wichita. He'd thought that all he wanted was to live in peace. He'd been tired of being afraid to turn his back on anyone. He'd been tired of the tough, bright-eyed, swaggering youngsters who were always trying to challenge him, hoping in a few fleeting seconds to assume the reputation he had built up over the years. He had even been tired of seeing men go down before his gun, tired of the sight of blood and lifeless eyes, tired of the awe his name inspired

114

and of the fawning admirers he encountered everywhere he went.

Now, suddenly, he realized he *had* missed all that. He had missed the excitement, the way his blood raced when he faced a man knowing that in split seconds one of them, or both, would die.

He'd meant to kill Frank. Without revealing his true identity, he had meant to recapture at least part of the old life by doing so. He held his hands out in front of him, palms up. The fingers were trembling. His heart was beating hard and fast. Damn Coates! Damn him anyway!

For a long time, he paced nervously back and forth. Then, unable to bear inactivity any longer, he went into the back room and began to assemble a revolver he had been working on.

His hands continued to tremble and he couldn't keep his thoughts on his work. All his mind could see was Frank Kailey standing in front of him. All he could feel was the old excitement as the seconds ticked away. . . .

Nervously he slammed the gun down on the bench. He went into the front of the store and withdrew a new Colt's single action .44 from the showcase. He spun the cylinder, cocked the hammer, tested the trigger pull. He got a belt and holster out and fitted the gun into it. He withdrew it several times, testing the ease with which it slipped out.

Unsatisfied, he got a bar of soap and soaped the inside of the holster slightly. Then he belted on the holstered gun and tied the bottom of the holster to his leg with a leather thong.

Time after time he drew, cocked, fired the empty gun. A casual onlooker wouldn't have noticed it but Keegle did. He was clumsy and slow. He was rusty. If he had to face a real gunman, he'd be shot before he got it out of the holster and the hammer cocked.

But maybe, he thought, that was just as well. He didn't want to appear *too* good. He didn't want to look like Jim Scull, who was dead, who wanted to stay that way. Besides, he didn't need much speed for Frank. Kailey had been in prison for two long years. He hadn't touched a gun in all that time. And he'd been no expert with a gun when he went away.

Wearing the holstered gun, Keegle walked to the front window again and stared broodingly at the courthouse across the Plaza. There was no use thinking about a gun

115

duel with Frank. Frank was in jail, charged with robbery. He'd be convicted and sent back to prison and that would be the end of it. He started to unbuckle the gun. He started to turn away.

Suddenly he stiffened. He stared across the Plaza unbelievingly. Frank Kailey had just come out of the door of the jail. And Frank was wearing a belt and holstering a gun, the sheriff's undoubtedly.

Frank stood there on the gallery a moment, looking longingly at two horses tied to the rail in front of the treasurer's office. Then he turned, hurried into the vacant lot next door and disappeared.

Then a wild elation sprang in Keegle. He chuckled to himself. Swiftly he got some .44 cartridges from a drawer and swiftly stuffed them into the cylinder of the gun. Holstering it, he went out and, at a swift walk, crossed the Plaza toward the courthouse.

In the vacant lot beside the jail, he paused momentarily, listening. Either Frank had knocked the sheriff out or killed him, or else the sheriff was keeping quiet, giving Frank a chance to get away. Keegle went on to the alley, where he stopped to glance up and down.

He saw Frank come out of the small stable behind Doc Baker's office, leading Doc's saddled buggy horse. Frank swung astride and headed uptown. He went about two blocks then turned right, heading into the Mexican section of town.

Keegle nodded imperceptibly. Frank was heading for Kate Guerrero's house, probably to tell her good-bye. Only Kate wasn't home. She had passed the gun shop earlier, heading for the bank.

He therefore probably had plenty of time. Frank would send Miguel to bring Kate home. There was only a small chance that he'd leave without seeing her. She was, after all, the only one in Medicine Arrow who had helped him since his return.

Keegle headed straight into the Mexican section, taking the most direct route to the Guerrero house. A block away from it, he saw Miguel hurrying along toward town. He nodded, pleased at the way things were turning out. Frank Kailey was waiting for Kate at the Guerrero house.

This was going to work out after all.

Chapter 19

KEEGLE concealed himself behind a low adobe wall directly across the narrow street from the Guerrero gate. He sat down, his back against the wall, and lighted a cigar. He looked indolent and relaxed, but was not. Every nerve in his body was taut, every muscle tense. In his mind was the old excitement, that heady exhilaration that had always come to him when a gunfight was imminent.

He realized suddenly that he should never have given up the gun. Not for a dull life in a dull town like this. There had been hardships connected with living by the gun. There had been times when he had been hunted like a wolf. But it *had* been living. Every moment of every day he had been *alive*.

He got up nervously and peered over the adobe wall. The Guerrero house dozed peacefully in the midmorning sun. A few flies buzzed around Keegle's head. A dog walked along the dusty, narrow street, saw him and began to bark.

Keegle ducked down again, cursing the dog irritably. He heard the gate squeak, and heard Frank Kailey speak soothingly to the dog. The barking stopped. The gate squeaked again and a few moments later when Keegle dared to look, the street was empty.

Now he settled down comfortably, knowing the squeaking gate would warn him if anyone entered or left the courtyard. He supposed he could have challenged and killed Frank a few moments before when he came out to investigate the barking of the dog. The reason he hadn't, he decided, was that Kailey's appearance in response to the dog's barking had caught him by surprise. Now he was glad he had been caught by surprise. When he killed Kailey he wanted witnesses who would say Kailey had gone for his gun first. Otherwise he might end up standing trial.

He waited another ten or fifteen minutes. At last he heard voices approaching. He did not raise his head until he heard the gate squeak. When he did, he saw Kate hurry through the gate, saw old Miguel, the Pueblo Indian, follow her. The gate squeaked shut again.

Frank would be leaving soon, he thought, and the tension within him increased. Unable any longer to tolerate sitting still, he got up and left the concealment of the wall. He began to pace nervously back and forth. A couple of times his hand reached for the grip of his gun as though to reassure himself that it still was there.

Strangely, the pacing did not relieve his nervousness. And there was something else—a vague uneasiness that was new to him. Was he actually afraid? He shook his head. He had never before been afraid and he wasn't now. What, then, caused his strange uneasiness?

Conscience? He scoffed at the thought contemptuously. But the uneasiness persisted and he was, at last, forced to admit that conscience was causing it. He was, whether he liked admitting it or not, waiting here to murder Frank. He was an assassin and it would be murder just as surely as if Frank had been unarmed. What good would Frank's gun be to him? He'd probably not even get it out before Keegle's bullet smashed into him.

That didn't change anything, he argued angrily. Frank *did* have a gun. He *did* know how to draw and fire it. He *was* a fugitive and he *had* broken out of jail. He might even have killed Ray Coates doing it.

Besides that, how many gunfighters bothered to worry about whether their opponent was as fast as they were? None that Keegle had ever known had ever given that particular aspect a thought. A gunfighter didn't remain alive by trying to equalize every fight in which he found himself.

Keegle practiced drawing his gun two or three times and at last nodded approvingly. He was rusty and out of practice but most of the old speed still was there. He could be as good as he had ever been within a month or two.

The two or three flies continued to buzz around his head. A hen cackled proudly in a nearby chicken coop, having laid an egg. From the direction of town, Keegle suddenly heard a strange, low-pitched murmuring sound. He frowned, and cocked his head, trying to hear it better and puzzled as to its source.

Suddenly he knew what it was. It was the sound made

by many people, all speaking or yelling at once. It became almost a low roar before Keegle was able to distinguish individual shouts.

Damn! Damn it anyway! Someone had discovered the sheriff locked up inside the jail. They had found Frank Kailey gone. They had organized a bunch of townspeople and they had guessed that Frank would probably come here.

He could imagine who the men were that had organized the mob. Cozzins undoubtedly was one. He had been in on beating Frank yesterday and he had been in on trying to murder him last night. But Cozzins wouldn't be the only one. Mendelbaum had falsely claimed he had been robbed. Aker had falsely testified he had seen Frank coming out of a back window of Mendelbaum's store. Sellers had to have been the one who had planted the supposedly stolen money in Frank Kailey's room. Those three would now be terrified. With Frank Kailey free, they would know he had an even stronger motive for wanting to dispose of them. They wouldn't be able to feel safe again until Frank was dead.

The noise of the approaching mob increased. The first of them rounded a corner and came toward him at a shambling run.

As he had expected, Cozzins was in the front. He was carrying a shotgun and he was yelling over his shoulder at those behind him to spread out and surround the Guerrero house.

A dozen or so more townsmen came into sight before Keegle saw the Sheriff. Coates was puffing and his face was red. He was yelling, trying to calm the mob, trying to gain control of it.

Oddly enough, Mendelbaum, Aker and Sellers seemed to be missing in the crowd. Keegle didn't exactly understand that at first, but then he did. One of them had undoubtedly slipped a weapon in to Frank, making it possible for him to overpower the sheriff and escape. But the three hadn't wanted Frank Kailey killed. They had planted false evidence so that he would be accused of robbery. They had engineered his escape. What they wanted was for him to flee with the robbery charge still hanging over him. That would insure that he would never again return to Medicine Arrow for to do so would mean that he would have to go to trial.

The mob surged close and Keegle was surrounded by its members. Most of them carried guns but a few carried

119

pitchforks and clubs. A kind of mob hysteria had infected them. Everybody in town knew about McCurdy's death. Everybody knew about Hapgood being killed by Frank Kailey yesterday. Everyone knew Sam Ford had been shot to death last night. It probably hadn't been very hard for Cozzins to inflame them once they found the sheriff locked up, once they discovered that Kailey had escaped.

Keegle felt a balked fury come over him and he suddenly realized how much he had been looking forward to challenging and killing Frank. And simultaneously he knew he wouldn't stay in Medicine Arrow as Hans Keegle any more. He would once again become Jim Scull. He would live the kind of life he now knew he had so sorely missed.

Coates touched his elbow. "Where did you come from?"

Keegle grinned. "Looks like everybody in town is here. How did Frank get away from you?"

"Somebody slipped a knife between the bars of his cell. He called to me to look at the bandage on his shoulder and when I unlocked the cell, he stuck that knife in my gut."

Keegle said, "Looks like he should have stayed in jail."

Coates peered closely at Keegle's face. "You seem to be enjoying this."

Keegle shrugged. "Excitement's scarce in a town like this."

Cozzins was yelling at the house. "Frank! Frank Kailey! We know you're there! Come out with your hands up and nothing will happen to you!"

Coates growled. "Like hell! If they don't riddle him the minute he comes out, they'll string him up from the nearest tree!"

He raised his own voice, "Stay in there, Frank! Don't come out until I disperse this Goddamned mob!"

Cozzins turned savagely on the sheriff. "What the hell's the matter with you? You sound like you was on *his* side. Maybe, by God, you *let* him escape!"

Coates said angrily, "You shut up, Cozzins, or I'm going to throw you in jail!"

"Maybe it's time the decent people in this town took things into their own hands. Then maybe we wouldn't have killers like Frank Kailey running around the streets."

Coates said disgustedly, "Like you and Sam Ford and Hapgood took things into your own hands yesterday? If you'd let Frank alone, Ford and Hapgood would still be alive."

Cozzins raised his voice again, "Frank! Kailey! Come out with your hands up and all that will happen will be that you go back to jail!"

Men in the crowd took up the cry, until there was bedlam in the street. There still had been no response from the house.

The mob surged toward the gates leading into the courtyard of the Guerrero house. Coates, swinging his revolver ruthlessly to clear a path, fought his way through them to the gate. He left behind him half a dozen men with bleeding heads but he reached it and put his back to it. He roared, "Goddamn it, get the hell out of here! Disperse, before some of you get killed! Nobody's going to drag Frank out of there and nobody's going to lay hands on him. Go home and I'll take him prisoner and put him back in jail!"

There was some grumbling among members of the crowd, but there was also a sullen withdrawal that might have resulted in dispersal of the mob had not Cozzins raised his voice, "He's lying! He ain't going to take Kailey prisoner! He's going to let him go! Did he arrest Frank yesterday after he beat Floyd Hapgood to death? Did he arrest him last night when he shot Sam Ford to death? Hell no, he didn't. He said Frank did it in self defense! Now he claims Frank's robbin' Mendelbaum's store was a put-up job. I tell you, if we want to get rid of Frank Kailey, we're going to have to do it by ourselves."

The mob, led by Cozzins, surged forward, pinning the sheriff tightly against the gate. Coates lashed out savagely and ruthlessly with his revolver barrel. A man went down under it, a second also went down. Keegle saw a club descend on the sheriff's head and the sheriff disappeared. The gate swung open and the mob surged over the prostrate body of the sheriff into the courtyard of the Guerrero house.

Almost instantly there was a burst of gunfire, whose source Keegle couldn't see. But the mob came backing hastily out of the gate and when they were clear of it, Keegle could see, in addition to the sheriff lying there, another man, whom he recognized as the postmaster Hank Thibault.

For the first time, Keegle believed what the other jurymen had said, that Frank Kailey had returned to Medicine Arrow for revenge. Why else would he have singled Hank

121

Thibault out of all the men who had surged in through the gate?

Thibault stirred and raised his head. He called on the men outside the gate for help, but none of them moved toward him. Thibault began to crawl, dragging a useless leg, his face contorted with pain and drenched with sweat. He reached the gate, crawled around the body of the sheriff and took refuge behind the wall.

Now members of the crowd moved to help him. Someone ran for Doc.

But for Coates lying in the gateway, the courtyard was empty. Keegle could see no movement in the windows of the house.

Earlier, there had been excitement in the crowd. They had been egged on by Cozzins but they hadn't been personally involved. Now they were. They had seen Thibault shot. The sheriff lay unconscious. Half a dozen of them had been bloodied by the sheriff's raking gunbarrel as he fought his way through them to the gate.

Their voices were angry now, sullen and angry and dangerous. They would get Frank Kailey out of the Guerrero house. One way or another, they would get him out.

Only they wouldn't shoot him now. They'd hang him. Already someone was yelling for a rope.

Chapter 20

FRANK, standing at one of the front windows of the Guerrero house, had fired instantly, almost without thinking, as the mob surged through. He had seen the sheriff go down as the weight of the mob burst open the gate. He knew that the door of the house would burst open the same way if he didn't turn them back.

But he only fired directly at them once, and when they had hastily withdrawn, he saw Hank Thibault lying in the courtyard. Thibault crawled back out painfully, dragging a shattered leg. Frank turned his head. "That will convince them I'm after revenge even if they weren't convinced before. But I didn't even see Thibault in that crowd. I just fired to turn them back."

Kate said, "You don't have to convince me, Frank."

He said, "I'm going out. I'm not going to subject you to what's likely to happen now."

"You are not going out! The sheriff is unconscious at the very least. He may be dead. That mob will tear you to pieces. You won't even get the kind of trial your father had."

"But—"

"But nothing. The walls of this house are thick. Bullets won't come through. I'm going to get all the guns and ammunition that we have. You just keep them outside that gate."

He grinned at her. Coates had finally taken a stand, he thought. Kate had taken a stand a long time ago. Two people of all those in town. But it was enough.

Kate hurried from the room. Her father sat in his chair on the far side of the room close to the fireplace. He seemed unaware of what was going on. Miguel stood close to the old man, trembling.

Frank peered out the window cautiously. Suddenly the mob surged through the gate again. Simultaneously, heads and rifles appeared at the top of the wall. Frank ducked to the floor as a volley ripped into the windows of the house. It shattered glass and sent it cascading to the floor. Bullets ripped through the heavy door, showering Frank with splinters. Dishes on the far side of the room shattered. Bullets flattened by their impact against the window glass, thudded into the fireplace.

Frank turned his head as a second volley smashed into the house hard on the heels of the first. Kate's father had slumped forward. His head sagged until his chin laid upon his chest. As Frank watched in horror, he toppled slowly from his chair and crashed limply to the floor.

Miguel knelt beside him. The second volley riddled Miguel and he fell across the old man's body, motionless and dead.

Frank got up and ran to the two, heedless of bullets still ripping through the windows into the house. Guerrero's chest was a mass of blood from half a dozen wounds. Miguel's throat was half torn away.

Fury raged through Frank. Kate came running into the room. Horror widened her eyes as she saw her father and Miguel, as she saw Frank standing over them. She carried a rifle, a shotgun, and an old flintlock pistol. Frank snatched the shotgun from her. He wanted to tell her how terribly sorry he was that he had brought this trouble to her. He wanted to hold her and comfort her, but there was no time for that now. He seized her by the arm and dragged her across the room. He shoved her down against the front wall, where adobe a foot and a half thick protected her.

He checked the shotgun's loads, checked the rifle similarly. He laid out the ammunition for both on the floor beside the window where he could get at it easily.

Shock was almost as strong in Frank as it was in Kate. Pale, trembling, she stared across the room at her father and at Miguel lying dead. Frank could feel only fury at the senselessness of it.

He'd done nothing more terrible since his return than defend himself. He'd intended no harm to anyone when he came back. He'd had no desire for revenge. But nobody had believed. And now five men lay dead. More would die before this day was done.

Desultory fire still ripped through the shattered windows, sometimes taking out a shard of glass or a partially shattered window frame. Frank said, "I'm going out."

He started toward the door, but Kate seized both his legs and held them desperately until she brought him down. "I've lost *them*. I'm not going to lose you too."

A can came crashing in through the window. Its contents gurgled out onto the floor. The smell of coal oil filled the room.

Frank started toward the can as another one came through another window across the room. And now, he heard windows in other parts of the house being smashed.

He couldn't see any chance that either he or Kate could now get out of this house alive. A torch came flying through the window. It landed in the spreading spot of spilled coal oil, which caught fire gradually. The fire spread until the whole spot was burning, sending up blinding, dense clouds of black oily smoke.

Raging now, Frank seized the shotgun, poked it through the window and fired blindly. He cocked the other hammer, and fired a second time.

In answer to the two bellowing shots, more bullets ripped into the house. More burning torches came crashing through the windows.

Frank had never really hated the town of Medicine Arrow before. It had been his home and he had wanted to come back and live in it. He had wanted to spend the rest of his life right here.

Not any more. Right now he hated the town, hated the people who lived in it. Two years ago they had been guilty of a wrong, but that could have been the end of it except that their guilt wouldn't let them forget. And now it had come to this.

He said furiously, "You stay right where you are. It will be safe for you to come out as soon as they have me. I'm not going to stay here and let you die too!"

Kate was weeping helplessly. "Frank, please!" But he disengaged himself from her clutching hands and, carrying only his revolver which he had reloaded, he started to pull open the door.

A shout outside the house stopped him. For an instant he stood frozen and unmoving, hardly daring to believe what he had heard.

It had been Keegle's voice outside, bellowing in order to be heard over the shouts and shots, over the crackling sound of mounting flames. Keegle roared, "He's getting away! The son-of-a-bitch is getting away! I just saw him running through that smoke at the back of the house!"

Frank literally held his breath. The firing had stopped.

The guns were silent. There were a few shouts, diminishing as the mob surged away pursuing a phantom they thought was Frank.

And suddenly it was quiet in the courtyard and in the narrow street beyond. Frank opened the door cautiously and peered out. No one was in sight except for Hans Keegle standing alone in the gate.

Frank turned and helped Kate to her feet. "It's all right now. It's all right. They're gone."

He pulled Kate out the door into the courtyard. He holstered his gun, returned and lifted Kate's father's frail body and carried him outside. He laid him carefully in the shade and went back for Miguel. Only then did he cross to where Keegle stood.

Beyond Keegle he could see the sheriff lying outside the gate. The sheriff's chest rose and fell regularly. There was a bloody gash on the top of his head. Beyond him lay Hank Thibault. Doc Baker was kneeling beside Thibault, bandaging a wound in Thibault's thigh. Everybody else had gone. Even those Frank had wounded with the shotgun had apparently been able to walk and had gone away with the mob.

Frank said, "I don't know why you did it, but thanks anyway. You saved my neck and you saved Kate's too."

For a moment Keegle stared at him, a half smile on his mouth, an unreadable expression in his eyes. He said, "Maybe I didn't want to see you torn to pieces by that mob. But I'm not going to let you get away. You're going back to jail."

Frank shook his head. "You're wrong. I'm not going back to jail. I'm getting out of this town and I'm getting out right now. Just stand aside."

Keegle didn't move. He said, "You'll have to go over my dead body, Frank. That's the only way." He was crouching slightly and his hand hung over the grips of his gun almost like a claw.

And now Frank understood. Keegle had only sent the mob away because he wanted Frank for himself. Keegle was something other than what he had always appeared to be. Frank had never seen him wear a gun the way he wore his gun today, low slung, with the holster tied just above the knee.

Keegle was a gunman, or he had been a gunman once. His expression said he was very sure of himself and not at all afraid. Confidence like that meant he knew exactly

Alive
with pleasure!
Newport

©Lorillard, U.S.A., 1976

Newport

20 CLASS A CIGARETTES

MENTHOL KINGS

18 mg. "tar", 1.2 mg. nicotine
av. per cigarette, FTC Report Dec. 1976.

Warning: The Surgeon General Has Determined
That Cigarette Smoking Is Dangerous to Your Health.

Regular: 5 mg. "tar", 0.4 mg. nicotine av. per cigarette, FTC Report Dec. 1976.
Menthol: 5 mg. "tar", 0.4 mg. nicotine av. per cigarette, by FTC Method.

True slashes tar in half!

Only

5

MGS. TAR

And a taste worth smoking.

how good he really was, knew as well that Frank was no match for him.

It was to be murder, then. The instant Frank touched his gun, Keegle's would come flashing out. It would be leveled and firing before Frank's had even cleared. Frank would be dead with several bullets in his chest before he could thumb the hammer back, before he could get off a shot.

He turned his head and glanced at Kate. She was kneeling beside her father. She was staring at Keegle as though she couldn't believe her eyes. But comprehension of what was happening was slowly beginning to dawn in her. And with the comprehension came horror and shock that held her frozen momentarily where she was.

Frank said, "And if I agree to go to jail?"

Keegle smiled. "I'm afraid I couldn't trust you now. I'm afraid that it's too late."

Frank's body tensed. In an instant now he'd try for the gun hanging at his side. It wouldn't do any good but he would try. And when he did, he'd feel the incredible, awful shock of Keegle's bullets tearing into him.

Kate screamed in a lost and terror-stricken voice, "Frank!" Instantly Frank flung himself violently to one side, his hand grabbing for his gun. He kept waiting for Keegle's bullets to tear into him, meanwhile trying desperately to get his own gun out so that he might at least get one bullet into Keegle before he died.

He heard shots roaring in his ears. A bullet threw a shower of dirt into his face, almost blinding him. Another grazed his thigh, burning like a red-hot iron. But another gun was firing too, even as Frank brought his own gun up. He found Keegle in the sights and began firing.

He stopped suddenly and let the gun sag to the ground. Keegle had staggered against the adobe wall and for a few seconds the wall supported him. Then he collapsed slowly forward. Blood stained his shirtfront and blood trickled from one corner of his mouth. He struck the ground with an audible thud.

Frank got slowly to his feet. He took a step toward the gate. He took another step, unable to understand why he felt no pain from Keegle's bullets, unable to understand why he could walk, why he was not dead.

Coates was up on one knee. A smoking revolver was in his hand. And now Frank Kailey understood. Coates had regained consciousness in time to prevent Keegle from murdering him. It was the sheriff's bullets that had brought Keegle down. He owed Coates his life.

Coates got up, wincing with the pain in his head. He walked through the gate to where Keegle lay. He turned Keegle over on his back. Keegle's eyes were open. He was still conscious, still alive, but going fast. He said haltingly, "You got me, didn't you? It wasn't him?"

Coates nodded. "It was me, not him." He was silent a moment and then he said, "You just couldn't give it up, could you? You liked the killin' too much to ever really give it up."

Keegle didn't reply. He was already dead. Coates got to his feet. He looked at Frank, and beyond him, at Kate. He said, "You can have your land. You can pay me the hundred and seventy-five dollars whenever it's handy. You can stay here just as long as you like and if anybody bothers you from now on, they'll have to answer to me. That was a long time coming, I'll admit, and I'm ashamed. But I'll stick to it."

Frank turned his head and looked at Kate. Beyond her the house was burning fiercely. The roof had caught and smoke poured from the windows and the door. Kate's glance held his tenaciously telling him all the things he had to know.

He turned back to the sheriff and shook his head. "We're going away, sheriff, just as soon as Kate's father and Miguel have had a decent burial. I couldn't live in this town now and I'm sure Kate feels the way I do. If you'll just quiet that mob and keep them off my back, I'll be out of town by this time tomorrow."

Coates seemed about to say something else but he changed his mind. "I'll send Burt Vigil for Mr. Guerrero and Miguel." He stared at Frank a moment more, then turned, went out the gate and disappeared.

Frank turned and took a step toward Kate. And suddenly she was running toward him. Tears streamed across her cheeks. He caught her and held her trembling body close as though he would never let her go.

MASSACRE
RIDGE

At eight in the evening, Jess Paddock stepped out into the bitter wind howling down out of the Bighorn Mountains half a dozen miles west of the fort. The post buildings and the eight-foot log stockade failed to break its sweep and Paddock had to lean into it as he walked. He passed the guardhouse and the unfinished post headquarters building and entered the sutler's store. He had just left a poker game in the NCO quarters at the east end of Laundress Row. His pockets were comfortably heavy with his winnings but his pleasure was tempered by memory of Sergeant O'Mara's fiercely scowling, reddened face. O'Mara was a poor loser and he had come close to accusing Paddock of cheating him.

The Sutler's store was as warm as any building at Fort Phil Kearny. It smelled of the pine sawdust on the floor, of whisky and cooking odors and of men. A bluish layer of tobacco smoke hung close to the ceiling, which consisted of rough-sawed pine boards laid over peeled pole ceiling joists. Jess Paddock crossed quickly to the bar.

A few enlisted men were here, those still having something left out of their pay. Five civilians had a poker game going at a table against the wall. The post sutler's agent, John Kinney, was behind the bar. Paddock said, "Whisky, John."

Kinney brought glass and bottle and Paddock poured his own. He drank it quickly, feeling still the chill of the bitter wind, and perhaps some uneasiness because of O'Mara's rage. Kinney asked, "Been playing poker, Jess?"

Paddock nodded, a rueful grin touching the corners of his mouth.

Kinney asked, "What are you grinning at? O'Mara?"

Paddock nodded. "He's a sorehead. He thinks he always ought to win."

"Don't laugh *him* off. He's mean and he's dangerous."

"I know."

Paddock poured himself another drink, but he slowly sipped this one. He was a big and broad-shouldered man, seeming even bigger in his heavy, sheepskin-lined winter coat. Warmed, he now unbuttoned it.

He wore a gray Confederate cavalry officer's hat with the insignia removed. His eyes were as gray as the hat. His brows were shaggy and his face was deeply seamed by years and weather and hardships unquestioningly endured. He had helped Jim Bridger guide Colonel Carrington's fort-building force to this place between the forks of Piney Creek. He had stayed when Bridger left. There was a reason why he stayed. She was a widow and she lived in the second hut on Laundress Row.

Kinney said, "There's something going on."

"What do you mean?"

"Colonel Carrington has had his officers over at his quarters for more'n an hour now."

"Maybe Fetterman and Brown have finally managed to talk him into an expedition against the Indians."

"Maybe. Most of the work on the fort is done. Everybody's out of the tents and the place is as secure as it will ever be."

Paddock said sourly, "And two thirds of the men are raw-assed recruits. None of them have fired a gun in months. The Sioux will eat them alive."

The door opened and Colonel Carrington's Negro servant, Black George, came in. He grinned when he saw Paddock and crossed the room to him. "The colonel, he wants to see you, suh."

Paddock downed his drink. He paid Kinney, nodded at George and, tugging at the brim of his hat and buttoning up his coat, followed him out into the darkness and the bitter wind.

The pair hurriedly crossed the snow-covered parade,

6

passed the uncompleted quarters intended for the post's commanding officer and entered one of the smaller temporary officers' quarters occupied by Colonel Carrington and his family.

The living room was filled with smoke. Carrington and his officers were seated around its sides. Carrington came forward and shook Paddock's hand. "Glad George found you, Jess. I want you to be in on this."

Paddock glanced around at the officers, nodding to them one by one. There was Fetterman, whose permanent rank was captain but who was usually addressed as colonel, his brevet rank during the war. There was Captain Tenedor Ten Eyck, Captain Powell, Captain Brown, Lieutenants Bingham, Wands and Grummond. The post surgeon, Dr. Hines, was not present.

Paddock faced Carrington again. The colonel said, "As you know, there has been considerable pressure upon me to take the field against the Indians. So far, I have resisted it because it has been my conviction that completion of the fort before winter set in was of the first priority. However, since most of the buildings are completed and the others nearing completion, I have decided that it might be time for a limited offensive against the Sioux."

Paddock waited expectantly. Carrington said, "We have discussed it thoroughly. Let me outline the plan for you." Quickly he outlined that he would send out a wood cutting detail in the morning as usual. When it was attacked, as it almost invariably was, a force of cavalry under Col. Fetterman and Lt. Bingham, would ride to its relief. They would pursue the Sioux along the Indians' usual escape route, over the Sullivant Hills into the valley of Big Piney Creek, thence over Lodge Trail Ridge and down into the valley of Peno Creek.

Carrington would, at the same time, lead a force of mounted infantry straight north along the Bozeman Trail, staying east of Lodge Trail Ridge. He would come into Peno Creek from the east, hopefully catching the Sioux between his force and that of Fetterman.

Finished, he asked, "What do you think?"

Paddock hesitated, glancing around the room. Some of the officers were eyeing him warily. Brown was

7

frowning, as was Fetterman. He said, "Might work, I guess, if all you got to contend with is the thirty or forty Indians that attack the wood detail."

Fetterman asked, "What do you mean by that?"

Paddock looked at him. "I mean that there are Sioux villages strung out along the Tongue River for nearly twenty miles. I've seen 'em myself. There must be several thousand fighting men in those villages, and no matter what else you might think of them, the Sioux are neither stupid nor cowardly."

Fetterman growled, "I could take a hundred men and ride through the whole damned Sioux nation."

Paddock didn't bother to answer him. Fetterman's eyes were glowing almost fanatically and his face was taut.

Carrington prodded, "What are you getting at, Jess?"

"If they've been baiting traps with their attacks on the wood detail . . ." Paddock stopped a moment. Then he asked, "Ever see coyotes lure a dog away from a farmyard, Colonel? They'll send in a bitch and she'll whine and bark until the dog starts after her. She'll head off across a ridge, an' every time the dog starts back, she'll stop and lure him on again. Soon's he gets over the ridge he finds the pack waitin' for him. They tear that foolish dog to bits."

Fetterman said disgustedly, "That's ridiculous. Do you really think they've been setting a trap for us out there every day?"

Paddock corrected, "I didn't say they had. I said 'if they have.' "

Carrington said, "We'll take a sufficient force. Fetterman, you take at least twenty-five men from Lt. Bingham's company. I'll take another twenty-five mounted infantrymen. Paddock, I'd like to have you accompany me."

Captain Brown muttered something that Paddock didn't hear. Carrington glanced sharply at Brown. "What did you say?"

Brown said, "I'd like to go along with Col. Fetterman."

Carrington nodded. He knew that wasn't what

Brown had said and so did Paddock. Paddock gave Brown a level glance that the captain met defiantly.

Carrington said, "I guess that's all then, gentlemen."

Immediately they rose and took their leave. Paddock went out into the bitter, driving wind and strode swiftly across the parade. The others took time to put on their greatcoats before venturing into the cold.

Light was shining through Molly Benedict's window. Paddock paused and stared at the beckoning square of light. It was only a little after half past eight. He turned and walked swiftly to the door. He knocked and a moment later the door opened.

Wind swirled in, stirring Molly Benedict's hair and skirt. She smiled and said, "Come in, Jess. Come in out of that awful wind. I think I have a little coffee left."

He went in, closing the door behind him. He removed his hat and unbuttoned his coat. "I won't stay. It's late."

"Stay for coffee. I was wishing you would come."

She was a strong and full-bodied woman in her early thirties. Her hair was dark, untouched with gray, and her face was high-cheekboned and smooth except for lines of good humor at the corners of her eyes. Her mouth was full and somehow sweet even when it held no smile. He had often felt sorry for her because of the way she had to work. He had seen her when she was very tired but he had yet to hear her complain. Her husband had been killed in a fight with another soldier at Fort Laramie. Without means of support and not wanting to return east, where she had no family anyway, she had come with Carrington's command as a laundress.

Paddock could remember the time, about a month ago, when he had asked her to marry him. She had studied him with an amused smile and had bluntly charged, "You just feel sorry for me."

He denied it, of course, but to himself he admitted she was right. He had been feeling sorry for her.

Still smiling, mocking him a little, she had said, "You're much too wild, Jess Paddock. I doubt I could tame you and I'm not sure I want to try."

Now he admitted he had felt somewhat relieved. She

turned from the stove, coffeepot in hand, and looked at him. "What are you grinning about?"

"I was thinking about the night I asked you to marry me. Have you changed your mind?"

She shook her head. "You could never stay in one place for very long."

He studied her deliberately until she blushed. "I think it might be fun to try."

She avoided his eyes as she filled his cup. She filled her own and sat down facing him. "Aren't you going to take off your coat?"

"It's late. I'm not going to stay."

Now it was her turn to study him. "Something's on your mind, isn't it? Do you want to tell me what it is?"

"Carrington's going to take the field against the Indians."

"When?"

"Tomorrow."

"Isn't that what everybody's been wanting him to do?"

He nodded.

"But it worries you. Why?"

He grinned. "You see too much in me."

"You needn't tell me if you don't want to."

"I don't mind. I just think that a lot of Carrington's officers, Fetterman particularly, fail to take the Sioux seriously."

"And you do."

"I do. This is their winter hunting ground. They have seen what happened to other tribes when they let the whites come in. They'll stand firm against this fort. They'll stand firm against the Bozeman Trail. And they can fight. When they want to, they can fight."

"But they have no guns."

"Not now they don't. But they have their lances and arrows and tomahawks. And sooner or later, they'll have guns as well. If they have to kill soldiers to get them."

He finished his coffee and got to his feet. Her face was now concerned as she asked, "You are going out with them?"

He nodded.

10

She came to him and took his hand. "Be careful, Jess."

He bent and kissed her lightly. There was, unexpectedly, a new expression in her eyes, a vulnerable look he had never seen in them before.

She reached up, put her arms around his neck and drew his head down toward her. She kissed him firmly on the mouth.

His arms went around her and tightened, but she pulled away. "Go now, Jess. See me tomorrow before you leave."

He stood there hesitating a moment, confused, his blood pounding in his head. Then he put on his hat and went out the door. He closed it softly behind him, remembering her face and the look he had seen so briefly in her eyes.

He knew he wanted her. But did he want her enough to stop the wild, free wandering which was all he had ever known? Frowning, he headed for his bachelor quarters on the northeast side of the quartermaster's corral.

CHAPTER **2**

Paddock's room was cold. He lighted his lamp, stirred the embers of the fire in his little potbellied stove and added several sticks of firewood. He stood close to the open door of the stove while the wood caught and only when it had did he close the stove and take off his coat.

His quarters consisted of a single twelve by twelve room built against the eight-foot log stockade that encircled the fort. The floor was of packed earth. The roof was close-laid poles over which dry prairie grass had been spread. Over that was a foot-thick layer of native clay. The log walls were chinked with the same clay and successfully kept out the wind. In the unlikely event that the Sioux attacked the fort, he had only to leap onto his roof from which position he could fire over the stockade at the attacking Indians.

The room warmed gradually. He could hear the wind whistling past the eaves. Intermittently it rattled the heavy plank door against its catch.

At nine-thirty, he added a couple of large pieces of firewood to the stove and removed his clothes down to his flannel underwear. He blew out his lamp, crawled into his blankets and pulled them up around his chin. He lay there, staring at the ceiling, listening to the wind for a while before he went to sleep.

He never knew exactly what awakened him. Some slight noise, perhaps, unusual enough to penetrate his sleep. He opened his eyes, lying quite still, listening. Instantly he knew someone was in his room. A faint glow of red came from the isinglass vent in the door of the stove. By this light he could see a bulky figure halfway between his bed and the door.

He heard the clink of coins and realized that whoever was in the room was going through his pants. He gathered his muscles and suddenly flung back his blankets and leaped from his bed. He reached the man in a couple of strides, striking him with a shoulder and encircling his thick body with his grappling arms.

The two, locked together, crashed against the door. Coins, dropped by the intruder, rattled against the log walls and rolled across the floor. The intruder cursed with startled surprise and tried to twist away.

He failed. Paddock hung on and the two struggled desperately, still locked together in a straining embrace. A heavily-booted foot came down on Paddock's bare one and he howled with pain. But he was angry now. He released the man, set himself and released a long, looping hard-clenched fist that caught the intruder on the cheekbone and sent him staggering against the stove.

It yielded with a crash, overturning and skidding across the earthen floor. It slammed against the far wall in a shower of sparks. The stovepipe came tumbling

12

down immediately afterward, making a racket that, Paddock thought, ought to wake the dead.

The intruder fell on a carpet of scattered coals from the upset stove. They burned through his pants and he uttered a roar of pain and rage. And suddenly Paddock knew it was squat, burly Sergeant O'Mara, who had so resented losing his money earlier tonight in the poker game.

Forgetting the coals that littered the floor, he rushed toward O'Mara, who was trying to get to his feet and at the same time beat out the smoldering places in his pants. Paddock stepped on a red-hot coal and let out a shout of pain. Ignoring O'Mara now for a moment, he raised his foot and slapped at the coal stuck to its sole.

O'Mara chose that instant to let loose with a hay-maker that must have started below his knees. It caught Paddock on the forehead and sent him crashing against the door. Stunned, he slid down into a sitting position in front of it. O'Mara tried to shove him aside so that he could open the door and escape, but Paddock locked his arms around the sergeant's knees and brought him tumbling to the floor.

The room was, by now, filled with smoke from the overturned stove. Paddock started to cough. The smoke burned his eyes and they streamed tears across his sooty cheeks. O'Mara was coughing too, but he was still frantically trying to get away.

Paddock felt a knife slash both his underwear and the muscles of his back and realized suddenly how deadly serious this had become. He released O'Mara's legs and plunged across the room toward his bed where his holstered revolver and belt hung from the bedpost.

Realizing what he was after O'Mara stopped, set himself and flung the knife. It thudded into the log wall a foot from Paddock's head. O'Mara followed, chopping at Paddock's head with his own hastily drawn service revolver.

Paddock yanked his gun from its holster and whirled, stepping on another coal as he did with the same foot he had burned before. It gave beneath his weight and he fell. At that instant O'Mara's gun blasted, its roar all but deafening in this small, enclosed area.

The bullet cleanly missed. On his back, still rolling, Paddock brought his gun to bear and fired.

He rolled onto a coal as the flash lighted the room and yelled again from the painful burn it made on his rump. He fought to his feet, thumbed back the hammer and roared, "Drop it you sonofabitch or I'll blow your goddam head off!"

O'Mara froze but he did not drop his gun. The door flung open and half a dozen men in their underwear crowded the opening.

O'Mara rushed them like a maddened bull. He bowled them aside like tenpins and disappeared into the darkness.

A couple of the men ran after him. Barefoot and wearing only their underwear, they soon turned back. Sentries began shouting excitedly from their platforms on the stockade.

The remaining men came crowding in. Paddock found the lamp, which was miraculously intact. He lighted it and stared around at the wreckage of his room.

Lieutenant Wands, apparently officer of the day, appeared in the doorway. "What's going on here? What's happening?"

Paddock knuckled his streaming eyes. He sat down on his bed and lifted his burned foot to stare at it. He said, "I woke up and found someone going through my pants."

"Who was it? Did you get a look at him?"

"Too dark and things were happening too damn fast."

Wands looked at his bleeding back, at the knife imbedded in the wall. He said, "I'll send Dr. Hines over to bandage up your back. Are you hurt anyplace else?"

Paddock shook his head. Wands left. The other men, all civilian teamsters, muttered their sympathy and backed out of the room.

Grumbling angrily, Paddock found a worn-out pair of gloves. He put them on and, walking carefully to avoid any more smoldering coals, righted the stove and put it back where it belonged. He put the sections of stovepipe together and connected it.

The room was icy now. With shaking hands, he laid another fire and lighted it. Shivering in his underwear, he stood close to the stove's open door until it began to throw off a little warmth.

Money was scattered from one end of the room to the other. His pants were smoldering. There were ashes and dead coals all over the floor. Muttering to himself, Paddock picked up his pants and pinched out the smoldering place. He gathered the money and put it back into his pants pockets. By the time he had finished, Dr. Hines was at the door.

The slash across Paddock's back, while painful, was not serious. The knife had not much more than cut through the skin. Dr. Hines put a compress over it, winding strips of bandage around Paddock's chest to make the compress stay in place.

He gave Paddock a small jar of salve for the burns. Finished, he sat down and looked at the mess the fight had made of the room. "I hear you won considerable from O'Mara tonight."

Paddock grinned at him.

"Couldn't have been O'Mara, could it?"

"If it was, he's got burns on his butt just like I have."

Hines grinned back at him. "Then all you got to make him do is show his butt."

"There'll be more important things to think about tomorrow."

"What do you mean by that?"

"The Colonel has planned an offensive action against the Sioux."

"Probably a good thing. They're getting pretty bold."

"They can afford to be."

"Fetterman says he can whip the whole Sioux nation with a hundred men."

"Fetterman is a fool."

"Maybe. But he's been pretty critical of Colonel Carrington. So have the other officers."

"I think Carrington's done a good job. He wasn't sent here to fight Indians. He was sent to build a fort and he's built it."

"He hasn't drilled the men the way he should. They're sloppy and the discipline is terrible. I patch men up every day, men cut with knives and men battered with fists. The sutler's store was broken into three times last week."

"The men have been working. They've been building instead of soldiering. It took three thousand foot-thick logs eleven feet long to build the stockade. A trench three feet deep and half a mile long had to be dug. And besides that they've built barracks and commissary buildings and warehouses and latrines and your hospital and officers' quarters and stables and God knows what else. There's been no time for drill. Carrington knew he had to get everybody out of the tents before the worst of the winter set in. He made it and I think he deserves more credit than anybody is giving him."

Hines stared at him. "That's quite an impassioned defense."

Paddock growled, "Somebody's got to defend the man. He won't defend himself."

"What do you think of the offensive he's planned for tomorrow?"

Paddock shrugged. "Fifty men against the thousands of Sioux out there?"

"You think they'll all get killed?"

"I think they could."

"Are you going?"

Paddock nodded.

Dr. Hines got to his feet. "Then you'd better get some sleep," he said. He went to the door, buttoned his heavy coat and turned the collar up. He stepped out into the bitter wind and Paddock closed the door after him.

He didn't feel like doing any more cleaning up tonight. He put a couple of thick chunks of wood into the stove and closed the damper partway so that they would burn longer. He put some salve on his burns, blew out the lamp and got into bed for the second time tonight.

16

He didn't think O'Mara would be back. But just in case, he withdrew his revolver from its holster and laid it on the floor beside his bed.

For a little while, pain in his back and in his burns kept him awake. But at last he slept, and he did not awake until the clear notes of reveille sounded outside on the parade.

CHAPTER 3

Immediately after breakfast, the wood train assembled in the quartermaster corral. Two teams of mules were hitched to each heavy wagon. Civilian teamsters drove and each was assigned a soldier who could fire at attacking Indians while the teamster handled the lines. All of the teamsters carried rifles, and most had revolvers as well.

The departure of the wood train was an almost daily occurrence and usually attracted little attention. Today however, a number of men climbed up onto the three-foot-high banquette that ran along the inside of the stockade in order to watch the fifteen wagon wood train as it slowly followed the wood road along the base of the Sullivant Hills.

Soon the sounds of hammers, sledges and saws, the fort's normal, daily noise, began. About twenty-five men of Lt. Bingham's cavalry company assembled on the parade, along with an equal number of infantry, hand-picked by Lt. Grummond for the day's sortie.

Jess Paddock left the teamsters' mess in the quartermaster corral and turned toward the parade. He overtook Molly Benedict coming from the creek, carrying two pails of water. He took them from her, noting that despite the cold morning air, her smooth forehead was beaded with perspiration.

17

He carried the water into her quarters where a large wash boiler was already steaming on the stove. He put the buckets down and turned to find her smiling up at him. "If you keep carrying water for me people are going to talk."

He grinned back. "Let 'em."

"What is this I hear about you? A fight in your room last night?"

He said, "Someone took a notion to go through my pants. I objected and he got away. There's no more to it than that."

Her expression lost its mockery. "Nothing more to it than that? I heard mention of a knife and of a deep cut across your back."

"It wasn't as bad as that. The cut was just a scratch. The surgeon bound it up."

"Do you still intend to go out with Colonel Carrington after the Indians?"

"Nothing to stop me. My back's a little sore is all."

She nodded skeptically and began to sort through a pile of laundry on the floor. Paddock left and continued his walk down the line of small log cabins that comprised Laundress Row.

Two enlisted men were coming out of one of the cabins that belonged to "Colored Susan," laundress for Company H, 2nd Battalion. They glanced guiltily at Paddock, then ducked their heads and hurried away.

Paddock grinned to himself, knowing that in all probability there would later be a report of the quartermaster storehouse being broken into sometime last night. Stolen articles would include dried fruit, flour, lard and other ingredients needed for baking pies. In addition to doing Company H's laundry, Colored Susan baked and sold pies to enlisted men, the pies being made from ingredients stolen from the quartermaster's stores. Susan also sold liquor, though it was not known where she obtained it. Probably it was smuggled to her by friendly teamsters from Fort Laramie.

Susan appeared in the doorway of her cabin and grinned cheerfully at Paddock as he passed. She was an ample woman with a face that was shiny and very

18

black. She called, "Anything I can do for you, Mistuh Paddock?"

Paddock returned her cheerful grin. Susan was loud, profane, sometimes obscene and with no more morals than an alley cat. She entertained soldiers in her cabin at night, both black soldiers and white. Paddock said, "Save me a pie, Susan. Apple."

"Good as done, Mistuh Paddock. You all goin' out with them soldiers after the Indians?"

He nodded.

"You watch your step, Mistuh Paddock. Them Indians remind me of a big ole cat playin' with a mouse. Standin' out there all day yellin', callin' the soldiers sonsabitches an' tellin' 'em to come out an' fight."

"I'll watch my step." He went on and came around the corner of the cavalry stables. He now could see the entire parade and the assembled troops. Susan had only echoed his own doubts about the sortie today but he knew that once having spoken his mind, there was nothing further he could do. Carrington had been painfully aware of the criticism among his junior officers of his failure to take the field against the Sioux. He had stubbornly resisted their demands as long as the necessary buildings within the fort's stockade were incomplete. Now he was acceding to them but Paddock suspected he was doing so unwillingly and against his better judgment.

Even now, Paddock could hear an Indian yelling outside the stockade. He walked to it and climbed to the banquette. The Indian was standing on the far side of Little Piney Creek, half hidden by high grass and brush. Paddock grinned because it was strange to hear an Indian speak English with a British accent. The Sioux must have learned his English from a Britisher, perhaps at one of the posts of the Hudson's Bay Company.

He climbed down, thinking that only the fort's artillery kept the Indians at a respectful distance. They feared it and knew what havoc it could cause with its cannister shot.

Among the infantry Lt. Grummond had assembled, he spotted O'Mara's burly figure and unruly shock of

19

reddish hair. He walked toward the line of troopers, his eyes steadily on O'Mara's face.

O'Mara saw him and scowled. Lt. Grummond dismissed the troopers, after telling them to be ready to assemble with horses and full combat equipment at a moment's notice.

Paddock intercepted O'Mara. He extended the knife to the sergeant, handle first. "I believe this is yours."

O'Mara took it without batting an eye. "I take it you didn't rat on me or I'd be in the guardhouse."

"What happened was between you and me."

O'Mara growled, "It ain't over, Bucko. You cheated me last night."

In the same conversational tone, Paddock said, "You know you can say that out here and get away with it. But you're a lying sonofabitch and a bushwhacker as well. Keep away from me. Next time you won't get off as easy as you did last night."

O'Mara's scowl deepened at the words. He turned and tramped toward the stables to saddle up a horse.

Paddock heard a voice at his elbow, recognizing it immediately as that of Lt. Grummond. "What was that all about?"

"Nothing, Lieutenant. A personal matter."

"Don't let it interfere."

"It won't."

Grummond hesitated. "You're going out with Colonel Carrington and me, aren't you?"

Paddock nodded.

"So is O'Mara. If he was the one in your room last night, I'd advise you to keep him in front of you."

Paddock liked the lieutenant and it showed in the way he met Grummond's glance. "I'll remember that, Lieutenant."

"Get your horse saddled. There is no way of telling when the attack on the wood detail will come."

"I'll be ready." He watched the lieutenant walk across the parade toward his quarters, then turned and headed for the stables to get his horse.

Paddock had two horses stabled here at Fort Phil Kearny. His riding horse was a sorrel, deepchested and longlegged, an animal that could outrun and outlast the best owned by the Sioux.

The other was a brown mare he used as a pack animal. He caught the sorrel out of the corral, led him to the stables and saddled him. He left the cinch loose and hung the bridle over the saddle horn, leaving the halter on. He gave the animal a couple of forks of hay. Leaving the stables, he walked to the stockade and climbed up onto the banquette so that he could look over the top.

The wood detail was out of sight behind a knoll about a mile and a half from the fort. No Indians were in sight.

He stared moodily at the landscape. Snow covered most of it, except for the south-facing slopes, some of which were now bare in spots.

Phil Kearny was backed up against Little Piney Creek just west of the junction of the two branches of the creek. The Bozeman Road ran south to north immediately west of the fort. It skirted the eastward end of the Sullivant Hills, skirted Lodge Trail Ridge on the east, climbed an unnamed bluff and descended into Peno Creek beyond. It was visible from the fort almost to the point where it climbed the unnamed bluff.

Death was commonplace, both at Fort Phil Kearny and along the Bozeman Trail. Hardly a wagon train reached the fort that had not been attacked by Indians. Hardly a party of travelers journeyed north along the Bozeman Trail who did not have to fight somewhere along the way. The Sioux had not attacked the fort itself, and probably would not, due to their fear of artillery. But they would attack everything else that moved.

Uneasiness stirred in Paddock's mind. He smelled a trap in the way the Indians attacked the wood details with such a monotonous sameness every day. He smelled a trap in the way they always withdrew the minute a relief force came in sight.

They always retreated along the same route, which, to Paddock, also suggested a trap. And if the cavalry did not pursue, they invariably halted and shouted taunts, in an attempt to draw them on.

21

Shaking his head, he got down and walked across the parade. The troops had been dismissed and had gone to their quarters. A few stood on the banquette staring in the direction the wood train had gone.

At eight, the sentries on the stockade were changed. The Corporal of the Guard marched his relief detail around the fort's perimeter. It was a sloppy, straggling performance. Glancing across the parade Paddock saw Fetterman and Brown watching, disgust evident in the way they stood.

Paddock let his glance rest curiously on Brown. The captain wore one revolver holstered in the customary manner on his right side. He wore a second thrust into his belt. Spurs dangled from the buttonholes of his coat. His hat was tilted rakishly. He stood with legs spread, trunk and head thrust forward aggressively.

Paddock had heard him say that he wanted to kill an Indian before he was transferred to Fort Laramie. Kill an Indian. *Any* Indian. He had been heard to say he preferred Red Cloud, but he wasn't going back without a scalp.

A murderous attitude for a regular army officer, Paddock thought. But it was only a manifestation of an attitude all too prevalent on the frontier—that Indians were not human. They were only some kind of wild prairie animal, whose pelts were to be sought as souvenirs.

Brown and Fetterman were two of a kind. Fetterman claimed he could ride through the whole Sioux nation with a hundred mounted men.

Shrugging lightly, Paddock headed for the sutler's store. Suddenly he wanted a drink. And suddenly he had the uneasy feeling that he should not go out with Carrington today.

At one o'clock, the picket on Pilot Hill, a mile and a half south of the fort, fired three rapid shots. At almost the same instant, one of the sentries shouted that a messenger was approaching from the direction of the Pinery.

The ponderous gates swung back, and the excited messenger, a private in H Company, rode through.

Carrington, Fetterman, Brown and several other officers had come from their quarters and stood at the edge of the parade looking toward the gates. Jess Paddock came from the sutler's store, a half-smoked cigar clamped between his teeth.

The messenger galloped across the parade and dismounted in front of the group of officers. He saluted and his words were clearly audible to Paddock all the way across the silent parade. "Indians have attacked the wood detail, sir. We were on our way back with our load of logs when . . ."

Paddock didn't hear the rest. A bugle called and men began pouring from the barracks at both ends of the parade. They ran toward the stables, and disappeared inside.

Paddock hurried past the guardhouse, also headed for the stables. He saw Molly Benedict come from her cabin, soapsuds to her elbows. She raised a hand to shield her eyes from the glare of the sky and he waved at her. Then he hurried on.

He collided with a man coming out of the stables, leading his horse at a run. He could hear firing now from the direction of the Pinery. The wagons of the wood train had undoubtedly been drawn into a hollow square. The men were fighting the Indians from beneath and behind them as they usually did.

The stable was a shambles, but he shouldered his way to the stall where he had left his horse. Quickly he exchanged the halter for the bridle and cinched the saddle down. He led the horse outside, mounted and trotted him to his quarters in the quartermaster corral. He went inside, got his rifle and revolver and came back out again.

The men were assembling raggedly on the parade. Nobody seemed to be making any effort to make them draw up into some kind of military formation.

Paddock spotted Col. Carrington and rode to him. The colonel was talking to Fetterman. "Go ahead, Colonel Fetterman. Relieve the wood train and pursue the Indians when they retreat."

Fetterman nodded. His face was pale and taut. There was excitement in his eyes. He galloped toward the

23

gate, waving his men on with a forward flung right arm. Lt. Bingham shouted excitedly, "Fo'ward, ho!"

The two dozen or so cavalrymen galloped after him, looking more like a mob of civilians than a detachment of cavalry. They thundered through the gates, which closed ponderously behind them.

Paddock sat his horse, waiting, while Col. Carrington looked over his mounted infantrymen. The feeling of uneasiness he had experienced earlier returned. It was as if he knew something was going to happen to him out there today. He shook the thought off irritably.

CHAPTER 4

From the back of his horse Paddock could see over the log stockade. He could see the wood road, stretching away emptily until it disappeared behind the knoll.

Captain Brown, in his unholy eagerness to kill an Indian, had not waited for Fetterman, Bingham and the cavalry to leave the fort. Without authorization, he had taken two mounted infantrymen and had galloped away as soon as the messenger arrived to report the wood train under attack. He and the two enlisted men were now nearly a mile from the fort, ahead of Fetterman and the cavalry by more than half a mile. As Paddock watched, they left the road and climbed the western slope of the Sullivant Hills to get a view of the besieged wood train beyond the knoll that hid it from the fort. They halted halfway up the slope and stared toward the west for several minutes. Then they charged their horses recklessly down the slope, taking the road again slightly ahead of Fetterman and the cavalry.

Colonel Carrington shouted, "Open the gates!"

24

The gates swung open. Carrington said, "Ride with me, Jess. You too, Lieutenant Grummond."

The three cantered out through the gate with the force of mounted infantrymen straggling along behind, some at a canter, some at a trot.

There was a rise between the two forks of Piney Creek, a kind of low ridge which was an extension of the Sullivant Hills. Cresting it, Paddock could see the wood train drawn up in a hollow square. The Indians were retreating, and Fetterman's force of cavalry was approaching at a full gallop. Between the wood train and the fort, Paddock could see another man galloping, rifle in hand. It looked like Wands but he could not be sure.

So far everything seemed to be proceeding according to plan in spite of the undisciplined excitement of both officers and enlisted men. Glancing behind, Paddock saw O'Mara staring at him malevolently, and he reminded himself that when the shooting started he had better keep O'Mara in front of him if possible.

Fetterman and the cavalry caught up with Brown and the two mounted infantrymen and left the road, pursuing the retreating Indians up over the Sullivant Hills along the escape route they always used. The wood train left its corralled position and continued once more toward the fort, traveling in two parallel columns as they always did so that forming the protective square would be quicker and easier.

Ahead of Paddock, Carrington and Lt. Grummond began to descend into the valley of Big Piney Creek, heading for the Bozeman Road crossing. There was a flurry of firing from Fetterman's direction, the reports sounding like exploding firecrackers.

They reached the crossing. Ice had formed on the water and it was impossible to tell how thick it was. Colonel Carrington tried to force his horse out onto it, but the horse balked, plunging and fighting for his head. Carrington cursed irritably and raked the animal with his spurs. Fighting, plunging, the horse finally took to the ice and promptly went to his haunches as his hind feet slipped and went out from under him.

Paddock grinned. Carrington, for all his age and

25

dignity, rode the horse like a cowboy riding a bucking bronc. He forced the horse, foot by foot, out onto the thin ice. When the horse finally went through, it was into three feet of swift-running, icy water. He snorted with the shock of it, reared and tried to unseat Carrington. Failing, he tried to turn around.

With a resigned curse, Carrington left the saddle and plunged into the water in which chunks of ice were floating now. Hauling on the reins, he waded for the other bank, breaking the ice ahead of him as he did. The horse followed docilely now, and Lt. Grummond rode in after him. Paddock's horse balked a little, but finally took the stream. The mounted infantrymen followed.

On the far bank, Carrington swung to his saddle again. Lt. Grummond said worriedly, "Hadn't you better go back to the fort, Colonel? You're soaking wet. You'll freeze to death."

Carrington, obviously out of sorts because of the cold, shook his head impatiently. "Let's get on with this," he insisted.

Leaving the Bozeman Road, he angled toward the west, climbing the eastern slope of Lodge Trail Ridge. Snow was deep here in the timber and the horses had to lunge through it. The troopers came behind in single file, staying in the trail broken by those ahead.

No Indians were now in sight, neither in force nor in small groups of pickets. There were only the pines, and the deep-drifted, crusted snow, and the sky filled with puffy clouds that speckled and dappled the sunlight over the land. Though it was only a little after one o'clock in the afternoon, the sun was well down in the sky, and Carrington's command rode in shadow most of the time.

Bearing west, Carrington finally crested Lodge Trail ridge about two and a half miles from the fort. Here he drew his horse to a halt and signalled the troops behind him to follow suit. The horses were sweating heavily from the climb and the deep snow they'd had to plow through, and they were breathing hard, their breath great clouds of steam in the frigid air.

Staring toward the northwest, searching for Fetter-

26

man and his men, Paddock spotted a group of thirty or forty Indians galloping their horses down the north slope of the Sullivant Hills into the valley of Big Piney Creek; not far behind them, perhaps a quarter mile, came Fetterman, Bingham, Brown and Wands at the head of their troop of cavalry. They were pushing hard, trying desperately to catch the fleeing Indians but not having much success. Their big cavalry horses were apparently winded by the long gallop from the fort while the small, wiry ponies of the Sioux were comparatively fresh.

It was an old and familiar story. The Sioux only fought when they wanted to and they never fought unless the odds were overwhelmingly in their favor. They'd elude Fetterman easily unless Carrington's force cut them off.

Carrington waved an arm and the command moved back to the right so that they would be hidden by the crest of the ridge. Nearly a mile ahead half a dozen Sioux pickets were retreating in front of them. All but three disappeared. The three stationed themselves on the highest point of the ridge, from there watching the troops advance.

Reaching a high point on the north edge of the ridge some minutes later, Paddock looked down and saw a bunch of Indians hidden in a deep ravine. He pointed them out to Carrington who counted them aloud. Thirty-two. They were apparently waiting for Fetterman's command to pass below them. Plainly visible on the Bozeman Road to the right of the ravine were four pickets.

There was now a look of concern on Carrington's face. He was shivering visibly and his teeth were chattering from the cold. Standing in his stirrups, he waved his little command forward, spurring and forcing his horse to a gallop now. They thundered up the crest of the ridge toward the high point where the Indian pickets were, now perhaps half a mile away. Ahead, like quail flushed from underbrush, Indians came out of hiding and retreated, just out of effective rifle range.

Paddock realized that Carrington was afraid that Fetterman, in his eagerness, might get ahead of him, thus spoiling the plan worked out the night before. Reaching the high point from which the three Sioux pickets had retreated, they could look down into the valley of the west fork of Peno Creek. Several groups of Indians were galloping toward the east, closely followed by Fetterman's troop of cavalry. They were, perhaps, a mile away.

It was impossible to count the enemy at this distance, but Paddock's estimate ranged from a hundred to a hundred and fifty. To see Fetterman chasing that many Indians was a good bit like watching a mouse chasing a cat and Paddock couldn't help smiling to himself. Carrington's command had halted for a moment to let the horses blow.

Gunfire suddenly erupted in the valley as the Indians stopped running and turned to fight. From ravines to north and south, other small groups of Indians poured, to reinforce those already on the valley floor.

Carrington stood in his stirrups and waved an arm, shouting, "Forward! Ho!" Immediately he forced his horse to gallop, despite the scattered timber, brush and occasional rocks upon the slope. Lt. Grummond dropped back, ranging along the line of galloping troopers to see that none of them fell behind. Paddock kept pace with the Colonel, who, in the hope of letting Fetterman know he was coming, drew his service revolver and fired a couple of shots into the air.

The shots may or may not have been heard by Fetterman but some of the Indians turned their heads to look at this unexpected force galloping toward them from their flank. Uncertain, perhaps, as to how large a force it really was and suspecting they could see only part of it, they retreated toward the east, breaking off the engagement with Fetterman.

Fetterman's cavalry immediately pursued them on across the valley of the west fork of Peno Creek and, once more fearing Fetterman's cavalry might get ahead of him and thus spoil the plan, Carrington turned and headed across a saddle toward the east fork of Peno Creek, obviously intending to descend into it and follow it north to the point where it flowed into Peno Creek.

28

To Paddock he shouted, "Stay here, Jess, and watch which way Fetterman goes. I think they'll lead him down into Peno Creek, and if they do, I'll be to their rear."

Paddock nodded and angled his horse away from the galloping command. He caught a glimpse of Sergeant O'Mara's face as the man thundered past and he thought the sergeant looked disappointed at seeing him stay behind.

As for himself, he was relieved, because he'd been able to figure no way he could keep O'Mara in front of him when the shooting began. Fascinated, he watched the battle going on below.

The Indians, more than a hundred strong, had now all but surrounded Fetterman's little force of cavalry. Ringing in a horseshoe formation, they were closing in.

Fetterman's men were still moving stubbornly forward and as they did, the horseshoe of Indians retreated toward the east. But instead of turning north down the valley of the west fork, they retreated toward the top of a low ridge dividing the two tributaries and halfway up forced Fetterman and his men to stop.

Still uncertain as to which way Fetterman would finally go, Paddock remained watching. The pressure from the Indian horseshoe increased. Arrows rained among Fetterman's cavalry. Gunfire, ragged and undisciplined, crackled on the little ridge. Fetterman's cavalry began to give way, to retreat, despite the shouted and angry exhortations of their officers to stand fast and stop the Indian advance. Paddock could see Fetterman standing in his stirrups, waving his revolver, shouting angrily at his men.

Suddenly and unexpectedly, about half of the force of cavalry broke away from the others and galloped toward the rear, out of the open end of the horseshoe that was closing so fast. Paddock could hear the shouts of Fetterman faintly, but the fleeing cavalrymen did not heed.

It was not an ordered retreat; it was a rout. It was panic, outright cowardice, and it left the remaining cavalrymen at the mercy of the surrounding Indians. Appalled, Paddock watched as the fleeing troopers, led by Lt. Bingham, managed their escape from the horseshoe, then turned and veered east toward where Paddock sat his horse, toward the place they had seen Carrington only a few minutes earlier.

Seeing half their enemy fleeing, the Indians suddenly began to scream fiercely and redoubled their efforts to panic the remaining cavalrymen. Recklessly they rode in closer, to a range where their arrows and lances would be more accurate.

Fetterman, Brown, and Wands ordered the remaining men to dismount and coolly waited for the Sioux to reach point-black range. When the Indians did, a murderous volley crackled and half a dozen Indians fell. A second volley killed three or four more. After that, Lt. Wands' repeating rifle brought down at least one more. Shocked at their sudden losses, the Indians precipitantly drew back out of range.

Paddock had seen enough. Carrington would want to know about this development as soon as possible: he would immediately change his plan of battle and ride to Fetterman's relief.

Bingham and the fleeing cavalrymen were less than half a mile away as Paddock put his horse into a gallop, descended into the west fork and thundered up the ridge beyond along the trail left by Carrington and his men. Glancing to his left, he saw Lt. Bingham's white and frightened face. Bingham turned to follow him, understanding, perhaps, that Paddock would lead him to Carrington.

Bingham and his men were galloping their horses recklessly; but now, instead of heading straight toward Paddock, they were angling toward what appeared to be his destination, a small spur between two upper branches of the east fork of Peno Creek. It appeared to Paddock that they would reach the spot at about the same time he did, or perhaps a little ahead of him.

Bingham's army career was at an end. If he wasn't court-martialed for cowardice, he would at least be forced to resign.

But Paddock knew what had happened was the natural and inevitable consequence of leading untrained recruits into battle against an overwhelmingly superior force. Probably two-thirds of the men involved in this action today had never fired at another man, nor been fired upon before.

Paddock's premonition of the night before seemed now to have been justified. But he got no satisfaction out of being right. He only hoped Carrington and his men could get back to Fetterman before it was too late.

CHAPTER 5

There was a pocket of timber halfway up the slope of the saddle that separated the two forks of north Peno Creek. Bingham and his defecting cavalrymen were about a quarter mile west and riding as if the devil were in pursuit.

Suddenly, out of the timber ahead of Paddock, half a dozen Indians rode. They spotted him and immediately changed their heading and came galloping toward him.

Paddock veered east, sinking his spurs into his horse's sides. The surprised animal immediately began to run, and Paddock raked him again with the spurs, leaning low over his withers as the Indians, now less than a hundred yards away, began loosing their arrows at him.

The range was too great for accuracy, and few of the arrows reached him. The Indians began slowly to fall behind. As they did, Paddock circled gradually back toward the north so that he could rejoin Carrington. He had no wish to be caught out here alone by any large body of Indians. Cut off, his guns would be of little use before he was overwhelmed by the Sioux.

Reaching a high point of land, he could see Carrington's command ahead, strung out, with the stragglers almost a quarter mile behind the main body of the command. Carrington now encountered the group of men who had deserted Fetterman with Lt. Bingham, and who had gotten ahead of him. He passed them and went on.

Bingham's defecting cavalry seemed to be demoralized. They had dismounted and were huddled together in a shallow ravine, their horses held so that they served as a bulwark against attack. Paddock had seen Carrington wave an arm and shout, ordering the men to mount and follow him, but they had not obeyed. They remained in the ravine. Bingham was nowhere in sight.

Paddock experienced a sudden and disquieting uneasiness. The way Carrington's men were strung out, they were extremely vulnerable to a flanking attack if any large body of Indians happened to be in the vicinity. The dismounted and demoralized cavalrymen were also vulnerable, having no officer to rally them and tell them what to do.

Paddock spurred his horse again. He could see up the long slope leading east. He spotted Lt. Bingham and Lt. Grummond now, together with three enlisted men, galloping their mounts through the scattered timber that covered the ridge, hotly pursuing about thirty Indians.

One Indian's horse lagged and Bingham leveled his revolver and fired at him. Paddock could see the puff of powdersmoke. The horse went to his knees and then collapsed. The Indian, thrown clear, scrambled to his feet and fled up the slope afoot.

Bingham galloped after him excitedly. He leveled his pistol again but this time no smoke billowed from its muzzle. Bingham threw it away disgustedly and drew his sword, afterward cutting viciously at the fleeing Sioux with it whenever he drew close enough.

The remaining Indians, reinforced by others who had ridden over the ridge from the east, now stopped, turned and charged back down toward Grummond and the others. Grummond and the enlisted men, seeing that they would be overrun, veered left along the side of the slope.

For some reason Lt. Bingham did not follow the other four. He rode straight into the oncoming wave of Indians, savagely cutting at them with his sword. He was almost immediately surrounded and overwhelmed. He disappeared from the back of his horse into the milling group of Indians.

Paddock felt a chill run along his spine. He knew what Bingham's fate would be. He was doomed and if he was allowed to die quickly he would be a lucky man. His body, when it was found, would be filled with arrows shot into it after it was stripped, and it would be mutilated beyond belief. The Sioux knew how to hate. The white man's fort was a cancer they could not cut away because of the white man's artillery. So their hatred showed itself whenever they managed to catch a white man helpless and alone.

But Bingham's inner torment prior to death must have been worse than anything the Sioux could do to him. A military man, he had turned and run from the enemy. He had abandoned comrades to what he believed to be certain death. Worse, he had led inexperienced recruits in a humiliating rout when he should have given them an example of courage and steadiness.

His self-hatred must have been intolerable. And when from the bottom of the shallow ravine, he had seen Carrington, Grummond and the others approaching, he must have grasped desperately at the fleeting chance to redeem himself. Recklessly he had called to Grummond and three enlisted men to follow him, and had charged toward the Bozeman Road in pursuit of twenty-five or thirty Indians threatening Carrington's flank.

There was no time for Paddock to further consider Lt. Bingham's fate. Carrington was still trying to reach the valley of Peno Creek ahead of Fetterman, whom he still believed was pursuing fleeing Indians down its course. Paddock could see Carrington's stragglers ahead, and looked for O'Mara specifically, without being able to pick him out.

Galloping, he passed the huddled cavalrymen. To them he roared, "Lieutenant Bingham's dead. You will be too if you don't follow me!"

He didn't wait to see if they would comply or not. He thundered away in the direction Carrington had gone. He wondered whether Fetterman's force had been

33

overrun and he wondered what was ahead of Carrington.

He pounded past a group of a dozen or so stragglers from Carrington's command. He shouted, "For God's sake, close up!" as he heard firing ahead. He knew what these men did not, that Fetterman was pinned down by over a hundred Indians, that there could be as many as a hundred engaging Carrington and the few who had kept up with him.

Coming out of a scattering of timber, Paddock glimpsed Carrington and half a dozen men ahead. They had reached a bend from which point they could look down into the valley of Peno Creek. Not seeing Fetterman, the colonel had turned and looked back uncertainly in the direction he had come. He saw Paddock galloping toward him. At the same instant, between fifty and a hundred Indians charged him from the slope on his left. Their arrows literally filled the air, some falling short, some falling in the midst of the pitifully small body of men.

Paddock saw O'Mara with this group. Private McGuire fell with his horse on top of him. An Indian galloped in, knife in hand, to finish him and secure his scalp. Carrington roared an order at his men to dismount and fight on foot. Kneeling, he himself knocked the scalp-hungry Indian from his horse with a single shot.

The Indians charged again. Paddock reached Carrington's little group while the screaming horde was less than a hundred yards away. Carrington shouted, "Hold your fire! Wait until you can empty a saddle with every shot!"

At fifty feet, the troopers' ragged volley rolled out and three Indians were driven from their horses' backs. The rest, screaming furiously, veered away, after loosing their arrows at the soldiers kneeling on the ground.

In the lull following, Paddock shouted at Carrington, "Fetterman is pinned down back there, Colonel, and half his men have deserted him! He won't be coming down Peno Creek!"

He could see in Carrington a sudden fear that this sortie against the Sioux was about to turn into a major disaster. His command was widely scattered and surrounded by howling, bloodthirsty Indians that outnumbered them ten to one. If he did not quickly regroup his forces, disaster was inevitable.

Carrington glanced around, worried but not panicking. He stared at the high ground on the right, at the ridge along which ran the Bozeman Road. It offered not only a commanding height, but an easy route back to the fort. He shouted, "Prepare to mount!" and almost immediately afterward, "Mount!"

The troopers swung to their saddles. Carrington waved an arm toward the ridge on the right. "Forward! Ho!"

He led the men across the shallow valley and began the ascent through scattered timber toward the crest of the ridge. To Paddock he shouted, "Go back and bring the stragglers! O'Mara, go with him!"

Paddock held his horse still a few moments, giving O'Mara time to reach him. O'Mara scowled briefly but the situation was too desperate for personal animosity and the scowl did not remain. Side by side the pair galloped up the ravine, yelling at the stragglers to close up, to bear right and rejoin the colonel on the slope.

One group of about a dozen men galloped their horses and rejoined Carrington before he and his men had much more than started up the slope. The Indians, readying themselves for another charge, changed their minds when they saw Carrington's group strengthened. Howling their disappointment, they retreated eastward down the valley of Peno Creek.

Paddock and O'Mara located the last of the stragglers and, shortly afterward, the group of cavalrymen who had deserted Fetterman. Both shouted at the men to get on up the ridge and join Carrington. The men, galvanized at last by specific orders, mounted their horses and galloped them up the slope toward Carrington's men.

Paddock said, "I'm going to find Fetterman."

O'Mara nodded, saying, "And I'm going to see that those bastards get where they're going this time." He spurred away and followed the group of cavalrymen.

Paddock swung his horse westward, now climbing

35

the ridge that separated the two forks of the narrow creek. At the top, he encountered Fetterman with about a dozen men. The man looked harassed and worried. When he saw Paddock, he shouted, "Where's Carrington?"

Paddock pointed toward his rear, "He wants you to join him at the top of that ridge."

In a more normal tone of voice Fetterman asked, "Where's Bingham, and where are the men he had with him?"

"Bingham's dead. The men he had with him are all right. Last I saw of them they were heading up that slope with Sergeant O'Mara herding them along."

"How was Bingham killed?"

Fetterman now was riding at Paddock's side. Both men held their horses to a steady trot. The cavalrymen followed along, occasionally glancing worriedly toward the rear. They'd had about all the fighting they wanted for today, Paddock thought. Even Fetterman seemed subdued.

Paddock said, "Colonel, Bingham panicked and I guess he was sorry afterward. He tried to redeem himself. He and Lieutenant Grummond and three men charged up that slope into about thirty or forty Indians, to protect Colonel Carrington's flank. When more Indians came over the ridge, Grummond and the three men went back down but Bingham charged right on up into the middle of them."

"Has his body been found?"

"Nobody's had time to look for it, Colonel. But I don't guess it'll be very hard to find."

Fetterman said, "If he'd stood fast, we'd have been all right."

Paddock didn't answer. But he was thinking that Bingham's panic hadn't been entirely his fault. He had simply been too green to cope with full-scale combat.

36

Fetterman's little force straggled up the slope to join Carrington at the top of the ridge. The wagon ruts of the Bozeman Road were visible in places where the snow had melted or blown away. Carrington, until being told by Fetterman, had not known that Lt. Bingham was dead. Now, he ordered the men to spread out and move eastward to search for the lieutenant's body.

The command had no sooner left the crest of the ridge when Lt. Grummond and two of the three who had been with him came galloping up out of a timbered ravine.

Grummond was flushed and his eyes were narrowed with anger. He rode to Col. Carrington and halted in front of him. His words were loud and intemperate as he furiously asked Carrington whether he was a fool or a coward for failing to come to his and Lt. Bingham's aid.

Paddock didn't hear Carrington's reply, because his voice was not as loud as Lt. Grummond's had been. He was surprised that Carrington bothered to answer at all. Most commanding officers, addressed that way by a subordinate, would have immediately placed the offending subordinate under arrest.

Paddock was beginning to feel considerable sympathy for Carrington. The man had mounted this offensive against his better judgment because of pressure from his junior officers. His reluctance to take the field against overwhelmingly superior numbers and with untrained recruits had been vindicated by the happenings today. Yet now he was being accused of cowardice, or at the very least of being stupid when the real blame rested on Lt. Bingham's foolish compulsion to redeem himself. Carrington hadn't even seen what happened, either to Bingham or to Grummond and the other three.

Jess Paddock rode his horse to the two officers. He was as angry as Lt. Grummond was, but in him it only showed as narrowed eyes and a mouth that was compressed. He said thinly, "Lieutenant, you and Bingham left the colonel's command without his knowledge and without orders. I saw what happened to you but the colonel did not. How could he possibly ride to your rescue when he didn't even know you were in trouble? If there is a fool here today, I would say that it was you."

Grummond's face turned an even deeper red. For several moments he was too furious to speak. Before he could, Carrington interrupted, his normally even voice touched with anger at last. "That will be all, gentlemen! We are out here to fight Indians, not to argue among ourselves. Lieutenant Grummond, rejoin your men!"

Scowling, Grummond turned his horse and rode away. He returned almost immediately. "Sergeant Bower is back there, sir, with an arrow in him and with his skull split open by a tomahawk." His tone of voice was accusatory, as if Carrington was personally responsible.

Carrington said sharply, "Then take some men and get back to him. Don't leave him lying there." He turned to Paddock. "Ride back to the fort, Jess, and have an ambulance sent out—with a sufficient escort to protect it from attack."

Paddock nodded. "Right, Colonel." He whirled his horse and galloped away toward the fort.

Riding along the road, the going was easy and he made good time. He covered the four miles in less than half an hour.

The gates swung open as he approached. Brevet Major Powell, commanding in Col. Carrington's absence, met him just inside the gate. "What happened, Jess?"

"Long story, Major. But Lieutenant Bingham is dead and Sergeant Bower probably is too. The colonel

38

wants an ambulance sent out, along with a large enough escort to protect it from attack."

"Where is the colonel now?"

"Four miles north on the Bozeman Road."

Powell turned and spoke to a private, who immediately turned and sprinted across the parade toward the stables. Paddock said, "I'm going back, Major. Any message for Colonel Carrington?"

"Just that the ambulance is on its way."

Paddock turned his horse and rode back toward the north. He knew he should have taken time to get a fresh horse. But he'd been afraid that if he did, he'd be ordered to accompany the ambulance.

When he reached the place he'd left Carrington, he found about a dozen men squatting in a clump of trees. Bower's body lay nearby, covered with a tarpaulin. Paddock asked a corporal, "Where is Colonel Carrington?"

The man gestured toward the east. "Still huntin' fer Lieutenant Bingham over on that ridge."

Paddock nodded and took the descending slope leading toward the east. He could see a thin line of blue-clad troopers about a mile away, working their way up toward the top of a low ridge.

His horse was covered with sweat despite the chill. He wondered suddenly how Carrington had stood it, being out here in the cold, soaking wet all afternoon. But Carrington hadn't said a word about being uncomfortable.

He caught up with the line of troopers just as one of them shouted, "Colonel! Here he is!"

Immediately, all the troopers rode toward the sound. Paddock reached there slightly ahead of Carrington. Half a dozen troopers were gathered in a circle around the body, staring down, their faces pale with shock.

The body lay face down over a dead and rotted stump surrounded by heavy brush. It had been stripped naked and from it protruded over fifty arrows. Some of them must have been shot into him before his death, because blood had trickled from the wounds. Others had apparently been shot into him after death, in a frenzy of hatred and excitement.

Paddock glanced at Colonel Carrington. The man's face was white and his eyes were narrowed with pain that seemed almost physical. He said, "Wrap him in blankets and load him on a horse. Let's get back to the top of the ridge."

Wrapping Bingham's body in blankets with that many arrows sticking into him was difficult, but the men managed it. They tied the blankets in place by winding rope around the lieutenant's body. Four of them hoisted him across the saddle of a horse and tied him down. The little cavalcade headed west toward the Bozeman Road on the spine of the ridge.

As they crested the slope and rode out of the timber, Paddock heard the creak of wagon wheels and saw the ambulance approaching from the direction of the fort.

The vehicle turned around and the bodies of Bower and Bingham were loaded into it. The wounded also were permitted to ride. Saddles and gear from horses that had been killed were loaded into the ambulance with them. The command headed back toward the fort. The sun had already set and it was getting dark.

It was a grim column of soldiers that filed back down the road toward the fort. The expedition against the Indians had been a dismal failure. A few Indians had been killed, but not enough so that the survivors would feel defeated or even chastised. Worse, the Sioux had seen the United States Army break and run, and the knowledge that they could force the white soldiers to turn tail would make them even more arrogant than they had been before.

It was almost seven o'clock before the straggling command reached the fort. The gates swung open. First through was Colonel Carrington, followed by Paddock, Brown and Fetterman. The ambulance came next and behind the ambulance came Dr. Hines, followed by Lieutenants Grummond and Wands.

The ambulance turned immediately after entering the gate and headed straight for the post hospital. There was no attempt made to draw the command into line for proper dismissal. The men simply scattered once they were through the gate, each to take care of his own horse and then to head for his barracks mess for supper.

Paddock suddenly realized how tired he was. Surprisingly, he glimpsed a white and familiar face among those lined up on both sides of the gate and immediately rode to her. He dismounted, startled at her intensity as Molly ran to him and threw her arms around his neck.

She hugged him hard for a moment and when she finally drew back she left his cheek wet with her tears. Jess said, "Here! Here! There's nothing to cry about!"

"Nothing to cry about? You've been out there six hours and we've heard shooting all that time and no word sent back to the post and you say there's nothing to cry about?"

Jess grinned and gathered her into his arms again. He held her tightly until she stopped crying. Then, with an arm around her he walked her across the cold and wind-swept parade toward the beckoning lights beyond. He said, "I could eat a horse."

"I've got some Irish stew."

"Sounds good." He squeezed her appreciatively.

There was noise already coming from the sutler's store, as the men who had money began celebrating their safe return.

Paddock saw Carrington give his horse to an enlisted man and then walk toward his quarters across the dark parade. Against the snow that covered the parade, he made a slumped and dejected silhouette. Paddock watched until the door of his quarters closed after him.

Molly was silent all the way to her door. There was a lamp burning inside and the room was warm. The delicious smell of stew and of coffee filled the air. She found a bottle of whisky and a glass and brought them to him. He grinned. "You're just going to have to marry me, Molly Benedict."

She poured him a stiff drink and corked the bottle, "You're just hungry now."

He shook his head. "I mean it. I want to take you back to Fort Laramie with the next escort that heads out of here." He was remembering the premonition he'd had this morning, the uneasiness he'd felt last night.

She was studying him, her face still pale, her eyes concerned. "Something's the matter. What is it?"

He said, "That was a disaster out there today. It's a miracle the whole command wasn't wiped out to a man. Worst of all, Lieutenant Bingham and about a dozen men ran, and now that the Indians know they can make white soldiers run, they'll be more cocky than they ever were before."

"The colonel won't try anything like that again, will he? After the experience he had today?"

"I wouldn't bet on it. Brown is still breathing fire and Grummond is mad as a hornet because Carrington didn't come to his rescue when Lieutenant Bingham was killed."

"Why didn't the colonel rescue him?"

"He didn't even know Grummond and Bingham were under attack." He grinned ruefully. "As a matter of fact, they weren't. They were *chasing* the Indians. The Indians just stopped, turned around and began to chase *them* instead."

"Poor Lieutenant Bingham. He was so young."

Paddock nodded. "He was a good officer. All he needed was time and experience. He just lost his head. There must have been over a hundred screeching Indians around Bingham's cavalry and he'd never seen anything like that before. Then, after it was over, he was so ashamed that he tried to redeem himself by making a reckless attack on some Indians coming over the ridge from the east."

Molly shuddered. "Was it . . . was it quick?" she asked.

He nodded. "I saw him go down. It was quick all right."

She put a plate of stew in front of him and brought coffee immediately afterward. He finished the whisky and began to eat. Molly said, "There won't be another escort going out of here for at least three weeks."

"Then you'll go with me?"

She nodded. "I'll go with you."

He got up, crossed the room and took her into his

42

arms. Holding her, he admitted that he was still uneasy in spite of his decision to take Molly with him and leave.

He tried to put his doubts out of his mind. Molly had promised to marry him. They could put Fort Phil Kearny behind them. Jess had money enough to buy a good ranch in Kansas or Colorado Territory and enough to stock it.

They could raise a family ... Then why did that damned core of uneasiness linger in the back of his mind?

CHAPTER 7

On the following morning the entire garrison of Fort Phil Kearny, and most of the civilians, assembled on the parade for funeral services. The bodies of Lieutenant Bingham and Sergeant Bower lay in flag-draped pine caskets, made during the night by the carpenters. The caskets had been placed side by side in an ambulance and the canvas sides rolled up to make them visible.

Carrington stood in the cold wind, which whipped his coat around his legs, and read as loudly as he could from the heavy Bible. After that, the regimental band played the Funeral March, and when the last notes had died away, Lt. Wands, in command of the burial detail, shouted, "Forward—Ho!"

Wands led out through the gate, followed by four troopers. The ambulance, drawn by a team of black mules, came next, and behind that rode the remainder of the escort. Behind the escort came another wagon, this one loaded with shovels, picks, black powder, and enough men to dig the graves quickly so that, with luck, the detail could be back in the fort before the Indians could mount an attack.

Jess Paddock rode behind the wagon. There was no particular reason for him to accompany this small detail but he wanted to ride to the top of Pilot Hill. He was curious as to what the Indians were doing and how many of them were still around.

The procession crossed Little Piney Creek and followed the two-track road to the cemetery. Paddock saw no Indians.

At the cemetery, Lt. Wands selected two gravesites and marked them out with his foot. He, the men of the escort, and the two wagons drew away and the workmen began to dig.

They first scraped snow and loose dirt from the graves. When they struck frozen ground, they brought star drills and sledges from the wagon and began to drill. They went down until they struck thawed ground and then poured black powder into the holes. Caps and fuses were next, and then earth to seal the holes. No more than one fuse was lighted at a time and there were eight in all. Each explosion made a dull thump and flung only a small geyser of dirt into the air. But afterward, the earth was cracked sufficiently so that the men could, with their picks, take out the fractured chunks.

Working swiftly in short shifts, the men had the two graves dug in less than an hour. Meanwhile Paddock had ridden his horse to the top of Pilot Hill. From there he stared out over the bleak winter landscape, at the near slopes of the Sullivant Hills, at the slope of Lodge Trail Ridge beyond, and along the Bozeman Road west of it. Still he saw no Indians.

They must be having a powwow, he thought, going over the happenings of yesterday in their councils, and planning what their next move would be.

The Sioux would be enormously elated. They had defeated the hated whites. They had routed Bingham and a dozen of his men. They had made Fetterman retreat and they had killed two white soldiers, one of them an officer.

44

They still might fear the fort's artillery. But no longer would they fear the men.

Paddock started down off Pilot Hill. The picket, standing atop the platform built for his use called, "Mr. Paddock?"

Jess turned his head. The man pointed to the northwest. Half a dozen mounted Sioux were sitting their horses on the top of Lodge Trail Ridge. They had just ridden into sight and were silhouetted against the sky.

Even at this great distance, he could make out their elaborate feathered headdresses. Chiefs and Medicine Men, he thought. Red Cloud might be one of them.

Scarcely had he glimpsed the chiefs on the ridge when a rifle cracked below. Paddock immediately put his horse into a gallop down the side of Pilot Hill. Behind him, the picket cocked his weapon and stared around nervously.

Smoke had billowed out of some heavy brush about a hundred yards from the burial party. It had probably come from one of the muzzle-loading Springfields captured by the Indians yesterday, Paddock thought.

He reached the burial party. They were just now lowering the caskets into the graves by ropes, glancing over their shoulders nervously in the direction of the shot.

An arrow, arching high, came from the same direction and stuck in the canvas cover of the ambulance. Lt. Wands shouted, "Take cover behind the wagons!"

The men did so quickly. The caskets were already in the graves which a couple of men were filling, glancing fearfully every now and then toward the brush from which the shots had come.

Paddock reached Lt. Wands who was still sitting his horse. He said, "Give me half a dozen men, Lieutenant. There can't be more than two or three in there."

Wands nodded. Paddock said, "Anyone that wants to, come along."

Several men left the shelter of the wagons and ran for their horses. Paddock galloped toward the brush, the others following. He was almost instantly rewarded by seeing three Indians running ahead of him. They

45

reached their horses, tied in the brush thirty or forty feet away, vaulted to their backs and thundered away. Paddock pulled his horse to a halt at about the spot from which the Indians had fired earlier. He yelled, "No use, boys!"

Turning, he trotted back to the burial party, the others following reluctantly. The graves were now almost filled. Three men were working on each one. Wands said, "I wonder how many guns they got yesterday."

"Check the men that went along. See if they all have theirs."

Wands chuckled shortly. "Those that lost their guns probably broke into the quartermaster storehouse last night and replaced them."

"I saw Bingham throw a pistol away. He must have lost the other one earlier because he had been carrying two. And the Indians must have captured Bower's rifle when they killed him. They have those three at least."

The earth was now carefully mounded over the two fresh graves. One of the men took two white crosses from the wagon. On one was Lt. Bingham's name. On the other was that of Sgt. Bower. The man pushed them into the loose earth at the heads of the graves.

Lt. Wands shouted, "Let's go back." He rode toward the fort with Paddock riding at his side. The ambulance and wagon followed and the escort and workmen brought up the rear. There were no more shots and no Indians visible.

Halfway to the fort, Paddock asked, "Do you think Colonel Carrington will try going after the Indians again?"

Wands shrugged. Then he turned his head and grinned ruefully. "The pressure won't let up, that's sure. Brown and Fetterman haven't changed. Fetterman blames what happened on Carrington. He thinks that if Carrington had done what he was supposed to, everything would have turned out differently. And maybe so."

Paddock said, "I was with Carrington. He was afraid Fetterman was going to get ahead of him. By the time the Indians stopped you, he couldn't see you any more.

Besides that, he thought you were going to drive the Indians down the valley of Peno Creek. Instead, they came over the saddle between the two upper forks."

Lieutenant Wands shrugged. "It's over now. And hindsight is always a hell of a lot better than foresight, isn't it?"

The burial party entered the fort and Wands dismissed the men. Paddock headed for the stables. Even now, with the sun up, the wind was cold and raw. He wondered wryly if the wind ever stopped blowing here.

Nearing the stables, he heard someone call to him. Turning, he saw Lt. Grummond hurriedly crossing the parade.

Walking, leading his horse, Paddock turned back. He met Grummond near the magazine, a half buried building near the middle of the parade with a painted tin hip roof. Grummond said, "I want to talk to you."

Paddock nodded. "Talk away."

"What the hell was the big idea of jumping me in front of the colonel yesterday?"

Paddock moved away toward the bandstand in the center of the parade. Grummond followed Both men got out of the wind in the lee of the bandstand before Paddock answered. "Lieutenant, maybe I was out of line." Paddock liked Grummond and he didn't want to quarrel with him. He *had* been out of line in interfering between the commanding officer and a subordinate.

"You're damned right you got out of line." Grummond's face was red. He had come out here looking for a quarrel and he seemed balked by Paddock's refusal to enter into one.

He glared at Paddock a moment more. "I'll ask you to remember, mister, that you're only a *civilian*. You have no right. Stay out of things you don't understand."

Paddock felt his own temper stir. He said, "I understand well enough. I held the rank of major in the Confederate Army during the war. You were wrong, Lieutenant. Cut it any way you like, you still were wrong."

"Wrong? God damn it, he left us to shift for our-

47

selves! We went up there to protect his flank and he left us to shift for ourselves!"

Paddock stared steadily at him, his eyes now smoldering. "Lieutenant, I hate to call a man a liar. But are you real damn sure that was what you and Bingham were trying to do? Bingham had just tucked his tail between his legs and run away. He must have been sick with shame. To make it worse, he went off and left the men who had run away with him. So he was out to redeem himself, no matter what he had to do to accomplish it. He didn't give a damn about Carrington's right flank. All he wanted was to prove to himself and to everybody else that he wasn't a coward, no matter what it took."

Grummond, his flush fading, asked, "What's so wrong with that? If you saw any action during the war you must know how he felt."

"I know."

"Then why condemn the man?"

"Hell, I'm not condemning him. I'm just saying that you had no more thought about Carrington's flank than Bingham did. You knew how Bingham felt and you wanted to help him vindicate himself. You took three enlisted men along and now one of them is dead."

All the color had faded from Grummond's face. "And you think Bower's death is my fault?"

"I'm not trying to blame anything on anyone. You're the one that laid it all on Carrington. You blamed him for Bingham's and Bower's death because he didn't come to your aid. But how the hell could he, when he didn't even know you were on that slope? There was timber between Carrington and you. I only saw you because I was over on the ridge opposite."

Grummond said savagely, "Damn it, Paddock—"

Paddock interrupted. "Lieutenant, Carrington was sent out here to build a fort. He's not a combat officer. Even so, I think he did pretty well yesterday. I was with him. Fetterman thinks he didn't do what he was supposed to, but Fetterman is wrong. The colonel was afraid Fetterman was going to get ahead of him and that would have been disastrous. Carrington kept bearing right to keep that from happening. It wasn't his

48

fault the Indians retreated over the ridge between the two upper forks of Peno Creek instead of down the main valley the way they were supposed to. It wasn't his fault that Bingham took half Fetterman's men and ran away. That slowed Fetterman and ruined the whole plan."

Grummond glared at him. The wind was rising and even here in the lee of the bandstand it cut through and chilled both men.

There didn't seem to be much more to say. Paddock didn't want Grummond's enmity. He said, "I'm sorry, Lieutenant. I don't want to quarrel with you."

"You should have thought of that yesterday." Grummond stared coldly at him for several moments. There was more he obviously wanted to say, but he didn't go on. Suddenly turning on his heel, he stalked away.

Paddock watched him go regretfully. Then, shrugging helplessly, he led his horse toward the stables across the snowcovered, wind-swept parade.

He was glad he was leaving soon. The dissension inside this isolated outpost could only worsen as time went on. There would be more instances of insubordination involving both officers and men. And if those instances occurred outside the stockade, they could easily turn out more disastrously than had the expedition yesterday.

They were a tiny nucleus of whites surrounded by thousands of hostile, warlike Sioux who wanted nothing more than to exterminate them all. One small mistake in judgment might be all it would take to give the Sioux their opportunity.

CHAPTER 8

Jess Paddock unsaddled his horse and put him into his stall. He gave him some hay, then stepped out into the cold wind again. Low clouds were scudding along overhead, their dark undersides brushing the crest of Lodge Trail Ridge. Paddock wondered if it was going to snow. It didn't feel like it, but the low clouds could be an indication of a new storm blowing in.

He hesitated for a moment in front of the stables, then turned and crossed the parade toward Col. Carrington's quarters on the western side. A steady hammering filled the air. Outside the fort, the sawmill screeched as the saw bit into a frozen log.

Paddock knocked on Carrington's door and was admitted by the colonel himself. He went in, quickly pulling the door closed behind him. The room was warm from a cast-iron potbellied stove. He removed his hat.

He said, "Colonel, I'm going to be leaving with the first escort that heads back to Fort Laramie."

Carrington frowned slightly. "I hope your decision has nothing to do with what happened yesterday."

Paddock shook his head. "It hasn't. Molly Benedict is going with me. We're going to be married."

Carrington's frown disappeared. He grinned and extended his hand. "Congratulations. Mrs. Benedict is a fine woman, indeed."

"I expect it'll be a couple of weeks before there will be an escort. In the meantime, Colonel, I'm available to help in any way I can."

Carrington nodded. "Good. I may want you to make a scout or two for me. I want no repetition of what happened yesterday." He studied Paddock narrowly. "How have *you* assessed our failure yesterday?"

Paddock grinned. "Simple, Colonel. Too many Indians."

"There was more to it than that."

"Yes sir. Green, untrained men. Inexperience. Failure to properly respect the capabilities of the Sioux."

"Fetterman thinks I let him down."

Paddock said, "You didn't let anybody down. You were trying to stay ahead of Fetterman so he wouldn't get ahead of you. Nobody could foresee that Bingham would take half of Fetterman's men and run away."

Carrington frowned. "I don't much like that way of describing it. He . . ."

"He vindicated himself?" Paddock suggested, shrugging. "At what cost, Colonel? Bower paid for Bingham's anxiety to redeem himself."

"Aren't you being a little hard on him? He paid with his own life too, you know."

"I know. And I'm not being hard on him. Not half as hard as he was on himself. He committed suicide, Colonel. You know it and I know it. And he took Bower along with him."

Carrington shuddered slightly. "Damned red-skinned barbarians! I wonder how long he lived after—"

"Not long, Colonel. Not more'n a minute or two."

"A minute or two can be a lifetime. I just wish I had a thousand men I could take out against them."

Paddock smiled wryly. "Don't blame the Indians too much, Colonel. They see us here and they know we're going to stay and that more will follow until they've been driven from their lands the way all the other tribes have."

Carrington said, "You like them, don't you, Jess?"

"Can't help it. I've known some of them. They really aren't barbarians, and they have a way of life a man can't help envying sometimes."

"Well, the fort is almost finished now and I'm going to start drilling the men every day. If it comes to a fight again, I want them to be more ready than they were yesterday."

Paddock nodded. "A good idea. But don't let the Indians draw you into anything against your will. They will also have learned something from what happened yesterday."

He opened the door and stepped quickly out into the bitter wind, closing it behind him as he did. Head down, he crossed the parade. As he went past the NCO quarters, someone yelled at him. He turned his head and saw O'Mara standing in the door.

A kind of wariness came to him. He felt it as tension in his arms and legs and in the way his heart speeded up. If O'Mara wanted a fight . . .

He approached the man and O'Mara called, "We're

51

havin' a little game tonight, Bucko. We figure you owe us the chance to get our money back."

Paddock nodded. "I'll be there. Right after supper?"

O'Mara nodded. He was not scowling and there was a speculative quality about his glance. Paddock studied him curiously from a dozen feet away.

This was a different man from the one who had lost so heavily in the game day before yesterday. The action yesterday must have relaxed him, Paddock thought.

He turned back, and continued along the wind-swept street toward his quarters beyond in the quartermaster corral. He went in and immediately crossed to the stove and stirred the ashes, afterward adding a couple of sticks of firewood.

Frowning, he puzzled about the change in Sergeant O'Mara. He had credited the action yesterday with bringing about the change in the man, but was it really the fight that had been responsible? Wasn't it possible that O'Mara had rigged tonight's game so that he could win?

He shook his head. It didn't matter. If O'Mara wanted his money back badly enough to rig the game, then Paddock was willing to give it back.

He put O'Mara and the game resolutely out of his mind. He thought instead of Carrington and he couldn't help wondering if Carrington was going to let his junior officers push him into mounting another offensive against the Sioux. The colonel had wished aloud that he had a thousand men to lead against the Indians.

That was about what it would take to beat them, thought Paddock ruefully. A thousand seasoned men, and howitzers, repeating rifles instead of the single-shot Springfields with which most of the men were armed, and an unlimited quantity of ammunition. Only superior armament could overcome the numerical superiority of the Indians, who were, in addition, fighting for their homeland against an invader who, they knew, would take it all from them if he could.

Carrington obviously felt badly about the deaths of Bingham and Bower and he was smarting under Grummond's accusation of cowardice. Feeling as he did, he might be tempted to do something he ordinarily would not do.

Paddock stood close to the stove, trying to rid himself of the chill that lingered in his spine. He began to sweat beneath his heavy coat, but the chill did not go away. He removed his coat and began to pace angrily back and forth. He was getting to be a damned old woman, he told himself. He was making things up in his mind. Nothing was going to happen here at Fort Phil Kearny. The stockade was strong, the howitzers ready day and night.

He stopped and stared out the streaked window. He glimpsed movement and saw Molly Benedict, with two buckets, walking along in the direction of the water gate. Grabbing his coat and shrugging into it, he hurried after her.

She wore her own heavy coat, its collar turned up against the biting wind. She had a scarf tied over her head. Paddock took the buckets out of her hands.

The wind was now so strong it snatched her words away. She caught his arm and they walked together, heads down, diagonally across the quartermaster corral to the water gate. There was a sentry at the gate which stood open enough to permit a person to pass through.

Paddock went through and filled the buckets in the stream. Rocks had been used to create a fill so that those wanting water could get it without wetting their feet. Carrying the buckets, Paddock came back through the gate. Molly asked, "Did you tell the Colonel that we were going to leave?"

He nodded.

"And?"

Paddock grinned. "He congratulated me. Said you were a fine woman. A fine woman indeed is what he said. I think you have an admirer."

She did not answer him because by now they had left the shelter of the stockade and were exposed to the full sweep of the wind again.

Hurrying, they reached her tiny cabin. Colored Susan, just coming out of her own hut farther up the line, called with good-natured mockery, "Y'all kin car-

53

ry water for me, Mistuh Paddock, if you through with hers."

"You're a big girl, Susan. Carry your own," he shouted back.

He put the buckets down inside while Molly closed the door. Turning, removing the scarf from her head, she asked, "Did the Colonel say when there would be an escort to Fort Laramie?"

Paddock shook his head. "He doesn't know. It will depend on when the supply train gets through to us. It's supposed to arrive before Christmas."

She nodded, her eyes studying him worriedly. He could see that the two deaths yesterday had disturbed her, frightened her. She said, "The time's so short. Nothing's going to happen, is it, Jess?"

He leaned down and kissed her lightly on the nose. "Nothing's going to happen."

"Then get yourself out of here and let me do my work."

Paddock left, grinning to himself at her sudden change of tone.

At six-thirty, Paddock opened the door of the NCO quarters and stepped inside. The game was already in progress at a table about halfway between the two potbellied stoves. There were four men in the game and perhaps half a dozen onlookers.

Paddock took off his coat and laid it on a bench. He sat down opposite O'Mara. He knew what he was going to do but he doubted if even that would do any good. Furthermore, he wasn't sure how much he could lose to O'Mara without letting the sergeant and the other players know he was doing it deliberately. If O'Mara so much as suspected he was losing on purpose it would be worse than if he won.

O'Mara's face was already flushed from the excitement of the game. Paddock put his money on the table in front of him. Part of it consisted of well-worn greenbacks and yellowbacks, part of it gold coin. The four finished the hand they had been playing and the deal passed to O'Mara.

Paddock accepted his five cards and looked at them. He raised his glance and let it rest on O'Mara's face.

O'Mara was a different man from the sullen, morosely brooding one of two nights before. And Paddock suddenly understood something that had not previously occurred to him. O'Mara, along with all the other troopers at Fort Phil Kearny, needed more than building, than work, to keep up their morale.

They needed action—the kind they'd had yesterday. In its absence they needed drill, long hours of it every day. These men weren't carpenters. They were soldiers and they needed to keep busy at their trade.

Paddock threw down three cards, called the bet and drew three more. He had drawn another eight, which gave him three.

O'Mara was studying him. Paddock tried to look disgusted. He threw down his hand.

The other players stayed. O'Mara won the pot.

The deal passed to Lance Corporal Kelly. He dealt the cards deftly. Paddock looked wryly at the ones he now held, and couldn't help grinning to himself. When a man wanted to lose, it seemed to be damned near impossible. He had two pair, queens and tens.

The dealer called for openers, and Paddock put a dollar into the pot. They'd know he had jacks or better, but they wouldn't know he had a second pair.

Two dropped out. The other two stayed, O'Mara one of them. Paddock checked the bet.

O'Mara bet five dollars and put a gold piece into the pot. Paddock folded; the other player called. Again O'Mara won the pot.

Paddock wasn't foolish enough to think that letting O'Mara win his money back would end the trouble between him and the sergeant. O'Mara was quarrelsome and unforgiving and his army record was one long chronicle of drunkenness, brawling and insubordination. He had made sergeant and been broken back half a dozen times. He was no stranger to the inside of the guardhouse. His nose had been broken and flattened and he was missing several of his teeth. His ears were twisted and misshapen as a result of repeated blows.

But Paddock also knew that he would be gone in less than a month. If he could placate O'Mara that long, he might not have to fight the man again.

CHAPTER 9

Paddock won despite his trying not to win. He knew he couldn't fold every time without arousing suspicion. He had to play a few of the hands dealt to him. And it seemed that every time he decided to play a hand, he held the winning one.

O'Mara's temper steadily grew worse. He glared at Paddock every time Paddock bet. At last, around ten o'clock, Paddock had enough. He raked his winnings into his hat and rose to go.

O'Mara growled, "Quittin' winners again, Bucko?"

Angrily Paddock slammed the hat back down on the table. He said, "All right. One hand. For everything in the hat."

"Count it."

Paddock dumped the hat out on the table and counted the money. There was a little over fifty-seven dollars. O'Mara counted what money he had left in front of him. He borrowed several dollars from the man on his right, more from the man beyond. Another sergeant, who was not in the game, loaned him the rest. O'Mara counted it and pushed the money into the center of the table.

Paddock knew this was a hand he didn't dare win. He said, "Wait a minute. I said one hand. I didn't say showdown."

O'Mara shrugged and pulled his money back. One of the other men shuffled the cards and Paddock cut. The man dealt and Paddock picked up his cards. He had

56

three aces, a five and a four. He looked questioningly at O'Mara.

O'Mara pushed a five-dollar gold piece into the center of the table. Paddock called it. He discarded two of the aces, keeping the third one, a four and a five. He drew two cards and looked at them. One was an ace.

He looked at O'Mara. "Bet 'em."

Even though they were playing only one hand, O'Mara hesitated a fraction of an instant. He had opened and had drawn three cards, so Paddock knew he had at least a pair of Jacks. He could have no more than a pair of kings. His hesitation now betrayed him. His draw had not bettered his hand.

He shoved another five into the pot. Paddock said, "We're playing one hand for the pile. Bet it all."

O'Mara nodded and shoved what money was left in front of him into the pot. Paddock let his breath sigh slowly out. O'Mara couldn't have three of a kind. He wouldn't have hesitated about betting if he had. He could have a second pair, but Paddock didn't think so. He himself probably had the winning hand and he didn't dare turn it up.

He shoved his own money out into the pot and looked at O'Mara. "You're called. What've you got?"

O'Mara turned over a pair of kings. Paddock slammed his own hand face down on top of the deck. He said disgustedly, "I thought you had jacks. I had queens myself."

He hoped nobody would look at his cards. He reached disgustedly for the deck to shuffle, but O'Mara beat him to it. He flipped over the top five cards.

Paddock got to his feet, thinking, "Here it comes!"

O'Mara's face lost color, and then turned a dark and angry red. He scowled at Paddock. Quickly he flipped the cards back over and began to shuffle them.

Paddock glanced at the faces of the other men, wondering if they had seen the cards. He thought they had but they didn't say anything. Nor did O'Mara.

Paddock met the sergeant's glance steadily. He glanced down at the pot, wondering if O'Mara would refuse it or pick it up. O'Mara raked it over the edge of the table into his hat.

Paddock grunted, "Good-night," and shrugged into his coat.

One or two of the men answered him. O'Mara did not. He just glared at Paddock malevolently.

Paddock tramped disgustedly out into the night. He had tried to better things between O'Mara and himself and he'd only made them worse. O'Mara might have forgiven him for losing deliberately, if it had remained between the two of them. It hadn't. The others who had been in the game had to have seen the cards O'Mara turned over. They knew Paddock had lost deliberately and they knew why.

He went into his quarters, lighted the lamp and angrily slammed the door. He built up the fire and began to pace nervously back and forth.

He supposed that when a man is determined to quarrel, there is not much that can be done short of accommodating him. He would have to fight O'Mara. Sooner or later, out behind the stables, he'd have to fight the sergeant in a bruising marathon that couldn't end until one or both of them lay unconscious on the ground. Or until one was dead.

Finally, nervous and knowing he wouldn't sleep unless he did, he got a brown bottle out of a drawer and poured a glass half full. He gulped the whisky then took off his shirt, pants and boots. He blew out the lamp and got into bed. He placed his revolver within reach of his hand on the floor, even though he doubted if O'Mara would show up again. O'Mara had the money and unless he was bent on outright murder there'd be no point in his coming here.

He hadn't expected to sleep but he did. He didn't stir until reveille sounded out on the cold, wind-swept parade.

He had his breakfast in the teamster's mess as usual, then went out and walked toward the parade. He did not see Molly Benedict.

As he reached the corner of the stables, the bugler sounded Officers' Call. Immediately thereafter, Lt. Wands, who was apparently Officer of the Day, crossed the parade toward him. The sun was up this morning and was welcome even though it gave off little warmth.

Wands said, "Colonel Carrington wants to see you in his quarters, Jess."

"What's up?"

"A rehash of what happened day before yesterday, I suppose. He's got to file a report."

Wands didn't say it, but Paddock knew what he was thinking. Carrington wanted to word his report in such a way that it would not later be challenged by his officers.

Collar up around his ears against the bitter wind, Paddock followed Wands across the parade to Carrington's small log house. Other officers were leaving their own quarters in response to the bugle call. Paddock followed Grummond in, and Fetterman came in immediately behind, closely followed by Capt. Brown.

Carrington nodded pleasantly enough to Paddock, but he seemed worried and preoccupied. It was clear he felt the hostility of his junior officers, whose greetings were correct and nothing more.

When everybody had arrived, the colonel said, "I am writing my report of the engagement day before yesterday. I want your thoughts on what happened and I want to know why you think we failed in what we tried to do." He looked at Fetterman, who seemed subdued. "Colonel?"

Fetterman shook his head. Captain Brown jumped to his feet. "Colonel, there were several reasons why we failed. I doubt if they're important now. What is important is that the Sioux whipped us and, except for luck, would have whipped us worse. We can't let that go unchallenged, Colonel. If we do, we're finished here."

Carrington asked drily, "And what would you suggest, Captain Brown?"

"They need to be taught a lesson, Colonel. They need to be taught that we can whip them any time we please."

"You're suggesting another expedition against the Indians?"

Brown's eyes glowed and he got to his feet. "Exactly. Let me take sixty of the civilians, Colonel. Sixty with revolvers and repeating rifles. And give me forty mounted troopers with repeating rifles. By the Lord,

59

Colonel, we'll show those Sioux a thing or two. We'll ride to the Tongue River and burn their villages and scatter their pony herds. And I promise you, Colonel, they'll not bother this fort again."

Carrington glanced at the younger officers. "Lieutenant Wands?"

"I'll be proud to go along with Captain Brown, sir."

"Fetterman?"

Fetterman's lethargy seemed less. He said, "Glad to go, Colonel, if you authorize the expedition."

Paddock stared closely at Fetterman. He thought he knew why Fetterman seemed so subdued. Fetterman had, day before yesterday, stared defeat and death squarely in the face and the experience had shaken him. He had been so sure, Paddock thought, that he could ride through the whole Sioux nation with a hundred men. But that had been before he saw the thousands of howling Indians out there in the hills. Now he was not so sure.

His confidence would return, of course. He was a professional soldier. Carrington looked at Capt. Ten Eyck. "Captain?"

Ten Eyck asked wryly, "Are you going to authorize such an expedition, sir, or are you just sounding us out?"

Carrington showed him the faintest of smiles. "Sounding you out, Captain. I'm not going to authorize such an expedition. At least not now."

Brown's face had reddened. He said, "Colonel, you can't be serious! Those dirty-blanket Indians have beaten us. If we don't get out and avenge that defeat, they'll be coming over the stockade next."

Carrington asked, "Did you see how many of those 'dirty-blanket Indians' there were?"

"Am I to gather from that, Colonel, that you are afraid?"

It was Carrington's turn to flush. His eyes glowed with anger. Paddock had never seen him so furious. "Captain, are you accusing me of cowardice?"

Brown never got a chance to reply. Lt. Grummond broke in intemperately, "Colonel, why didn't you attack the Indians' rear day before yesterday according to the

60

plan? And when you saw Lieutenant Bingham and me and the three men we took with us to protect your flank engaged, why didn't you come to our aid?"

Carrington's face lost some of its angry color. He was trying hard to maintain his control. He said, "Lieutenant, I didn't attack the Indians' rear because I never got an opportunity. The last I saw of Fetterman, he was chasing the Indians and I was afraid he was going so fast he'd get ahead of me and I'd never get the chance to attack the Indians' rear. I didn't know Fetterman got pinned down when Bingham and his cavalry ran away."

"Then why didn't you support Lieutenant Bingham and myself when we were attacked trying to protect your flank?"

"Because I knew nothing about it. I gave you no orders, Lieutenant Grummond, to attack Indians on my flank. I couldn't see you and I had no way of knowing you were under attack."

Carrington was still angry, and the accusation of cowardice obviously still rankled him. Paddock wondered how many commanding officers would tolerate this kind of abuse from their junior officers.

Perhaps it was Carrington's own uncertainty as to his qualifications that kept him from ruthlessly asserting his authority. He was not a combat officer. His war service had been behind a desk.

Grummond subsided into angry grumbling. Carrington looked challengingly around the room. "Anybody else got anything to say?"

Paddock said, "I'd like to put in my two cents worth. The way I see it, Bingham made the biggest mistake the other day. You can't retreat from Indians, Colonel. The minute you do they're all over you. When Bingham broke and ran, it gave the Sioux the encouragement they needed. I think we're lucky we came out of it as well as we did. The whole command could have been wiped out if the Indians had been organized better than they were."

Carrington nodded. "Thank you, Mr. Paddock."

None of the other officers commented on what Paddock had said. Most of them looked irritated because he'd had the temerity to speak at all.

Carrington said, "All right, gentlemen, the subject is closed. I will write my report and send it in. I want no more discussion of what happened day before yesterday."

He glanced challengingly around the room. Then he said, "There will be some changes made, so that something worse won't happen sometime in the future. First, all troops will be drilled daily. There will be both close order drill and mounted drill. I would like to authorize target practice for every man. That is impossible because we have too little ammunition here to use it up practicing. But I want a perpetual state of readiness maintained. Cavalry mounts will be saddled every morning and left saddled all day in case it is necessary for us to leave the fort and rescue the wood train again. Cinches will be kept loose and bits out so that the horses can eat and drink. Is that clear, gentlemen?"

The response was less than respectful and consisted mostly of surly grumbling. Carrington caught Paddock's eye and the slightest of grins touched the corners of his mouth. He said, "Then that's all, gentlemen. But before you go, let me stress one thing. Disobedience of my orders will result in court-martial for the guilty, be they officers or enlisted men."

The resentful grumbling was even more audible than before as the officers filed out into the cold.

Paddock watched them go, hat in hand, waiting his turn to go out the door. Carrington stopped him before he could. "I've got a funny feeling, Jess."

"About what, Colonel?"

"About this fort. About what may happen if we're not careful. That's an insubordinate bunch if ever I saw one."

Jess said, "Nothing's going to happen, Colonel. Just don't let them talk you into anything."

He stepped out into the cold, cramming his hat down on his head. He had reassured the colonel but he didn't feel reassured himself. Carrington's junior officers *were* insubordinate. And in their rebellion might lie the seeds of disaster for everyone.

62

The days dragged past. It did not storm, but neither did it thaw. The wind blew ferociously, drifting the snow that still lay unmelted on the parade. It whistled endlessly around the eaves of the buildings, chilling anyone who ventured out. Occasionally the sun broke through the clouds but it had no warmth and never got more than halfway up the sky.

On the parade, the troops drilled, the commands of their sergeants audible in every corner of the fort. Cavalry horses trotted and galloped. Their riders practiced repeatedly the command to dismount and fight on foot, and the shout, "Horse holders!" became a familiar one.

Jess saw Molly at least once a day, sometimes more. It became routine for him to carry her buckets to the water gate every morning and fill them for her. It became as routine for him to have coffee with her each night just before Taps sounded on the parade.

His uneasiness remained. The ingredients of trouble all were present here at Kearny. Boredom. Isolation. The ever-present menace of the horde of hostile Indians outside the stockade. The insubordinate junior officers inside.

And in spite of all the drill, drinking and brawling among the men was as prevalent as before. Colored Susan did a thriving business in contraband whisky, particularly among the NCOs who had more money to spend on it than the privates did. The guardhouse held twice the number of occupants its design called for and more were being sentenced to it every day.

Sergeant O'Mara hardly seemed to draw a sober breath. Twice within a week he fought another NCO in back of the stables, both times beating the other unmercifully. Every time he saw Paddock he scowled and met Paddock's glance with malevolent promise. Paddock knew that sooner or later the sergeant would force him into a fight.

It finally happened on the morning of the 17th of December. Paddock was walking past the NCO quarters with Molly, carrying the last load of water, when O'Mara, unshaven and red-eyed, came out of his quarters and stood on the walk, not a dozen yards away. His voice was loud and its challenge was unmistakable. "Well now, how is it you're goin' to be paid for all that work, Bucko?"

Paddock glanced at O'Mara, then at Molly Benedict. Her face was very pale. She said, "It is all right, Jess. He is only baiting you."

"I know. But it's not all right." He put the buckets down and walked to O'Mara. Molly hurriedly picked them up and went on with them.

Paddock said, "I wondered when you'd get around to it. Do you want it here and now, or do you want it behind the stables later on?"

O'Mara grinned. "The stables, Bucko. I don't want to be interrupted when I go to work on you."

Paddock nodded. "This afternoon?"

"Two o'clock. The men'll be drillin' on the parade an' it'll not be so likely the officers will hear."

Paddock nodded. He turned and walked away. Molly had disappeared into her cabin but when he approached, she opened the door for him. Her face was worried. "Jess, you're not going to fight him?"

"No way out of it. If I was to back away, he'd make life miserable for both of us."

"He's vicious. He'll kill you if he can."

He knew her husband had been killed in just such a fight at Fort Laramie. He said, "I can handle him."

"Are you so sure you can? My husband thought he could handle the man he fought with too. But he couldn't handle a pitchfork driven into his chest. And it didn't help that the man who did it was sentenced to twenty years."

64

Paddock said, "Molly, I can't get out of it. There's no way. But I'll be careful."

She stared at him exasperatedly, hands on her shapely hips. "Why is pride so important to a man?"

Paddock grinned, shrugging slightly as he did. "Nature of the critter, I suppose. But without it, a man's not much."

"When is it to be?"

"This afternoon. At two o'clock."

"I could go to Colonel Carrington. I could have it stopped."

"But you won't."

"How do you know I won't?"

His smile faded. "Don't do it, Molly. Don't interfere."

"Should I let you get yourself killed rolling around in stable dirt? Is that what you want from me?" Tears were very close behind her eyes and her chin was trembling.

Paddock crossed the room and took her in his arms. She began to cry, softly, almost silently. He said, "Molly, it will be all right."

She pulled angrily away. "Damn you. Oh damn you, Jess Paddock, for being such a stubborn mule!" She turned her back to him and busied herself at the stove. He could see her shoulders shaking.

He wanted to comfort her but knew that he could not. He opened the door and stepped out into the wind, closing it quickly behind him.

He hesitated a moment on the stoop, then strode rapidly away. He could feel a kind of emptiness in his stomach. It was always this way just before a fight, whether the fight be one with fists or a more serious duel with guns. Today it seemed even worse, perhaps because he knew the unpredictability of the man he was to fight. O'Mara was not above using a pitchfork if he could lay his hands on one. Or an ax. Or a singletree.

But the waiting would be the worst part of it. It now was only half past eight and the fight was to be at two. Six hours of waiting. Six hours, while tension grew each minute until by the time the fight began it would be almost intolerable.

For a while, he paced nervously back and forth inside his room. Unable to stand the confinement any more, he went out, walked along the frozen street until he came to the parade. He stood watching the troopers drill until the wind had chilled him to the bone. He looked at his watch. It was still not ten o'clock.

He went into the sutler's store and drank a beer. He idly watched a poker game between four civilians for a while. He went back and had another beer. Returning, he got into the game and it diverted him until noon, though he neither won nor lost.

He walked to the teamsters' mess. Everybody seemed to know about the fight and Paddock wondered curiously how the news had managed to get around so fast. He had told no one and Molly certainly hadn't. O'Mara must have spread the word. He grinned at a teamster named Larabee and asked, "What are the odds by now?"

The man grinned back. "Five to three on O'Mara, Jess."

Paddock pulled out three ten-dollar gold pieces. "Get me some of that. And take my advice. Bet some yourself."

"You think you can take him, Jess? He's tough and he's mean as hell."

"I can take him, Larabee. Go lay that bet."

Larabee left. Paddock knew he would bet the thirty dollars against O'Mara but he couldn't be sure Larabee would place any of his own money the same way.

He ate sparingly. Afterward he took a rapid turn around the perimeter of the fort. When he finished he was breathing faster and he was sweating a little underneath his coat. The fight would start fast and he wanted to be warmed up when it did.

It was half past one when he reached the appointed place. It was a large area, bounded on the northwest by the cavalry stables, on the southwest by a row of incomplete NCO quarters, used in the interim as cavalry barracks and on the remaining two sides by a secondary stockade. In all, the area was a hundred and fifty by three hundred feet, but not all of that was open space. Wagons, buckboards, buggies and ambulances were drawn up against the stockade on the southeast side. A tackroom and saddler's workshop took up a corner near the partially constructed NCO quarters.

Forty or fifty men, both troopers and civilians, were waiting for the fight to start. Paddock saw several bets change hands. One man seemed to be booking bets from all comers. He held a thick wad of paper money in one hand, a bag of gold in the other. Beside him stood a man with pencil and paper, recording the bets he made.

All the men present studied Paddock speculatively, and he grinned faintly to himself. O'Mara was already here, stripped to the waist, the upper half of his red-flannel underwear drooping below his waist, the sleeves tied behind his back. O'Mara's chest was like a barrel and was covered with a thick mat of rust-colored hair. Even his back had hair on it.

He was dancing around in a circle, feinting with his fists at an imaginary foe. Paddock handed his hat to a trooper standing nearby and followed it with his coat. He did not strip as O'Mara had. He said, "Let's get on with it."

O'Mara bared his teeth. He said, "Anything goes, Bucko."

Paddock shrugged. He had no idea how he was going to fight this man. He'd have to wait and see what O'Mara's style of fighting was.

O'Mara didn't make him wait very long. Lowering his head, he came charging across the cleared area. His arms were outstretched, grappling for Paddock, who stepped aside at the last moment and brought both hands, clasped together to make a single outsized fist, down on the back of O'Mara's neck with all the force he could command. O'Mara made no sound. He pitched forward, his face skidding on the manure-covered, frozen ground. He groaned, and rolled, and fought to his hands and knees, looking over his shoulder and up at Paddock who was approaching to administer a kick while he still was down.

Before Paddock reached him, he pushed himself to hands and knees and then to his feet. The arrogance was gone now from his face, replaced by wariness. He stood, swaying slightly, playing for time to let the effects of Paddock's blow wear off.

Paddock bored in, slamming a fist into O'Mara's gut. O'Mara doubled with the force of it, but as he staggered forward, he caught Paddock around the waist with both arms before Paddock could retreat. Bending his thick body forward, he tightened the grip of his short and powerful arms until Paddock, bent backward like a bow, felt ribs and spine crack, and cried out involuntarily with the pain of it.

He tried to twist, but O'Mara's grip was too powerful. The breath of the man was strong and hot against his face, reeking of the rot-gut whisky Colored Susan sold. O'Mara was chuckling triumphantly, as if the fight was already won.

Paddock let himself fall backward by kicking his feet free of the ground. Both men crashed down. Falling, Paddock brought a knee slamming up into O'Mara's groin and felt the sergeant's grip loosen slightly. The knee expelled a grunt of pain from him. Paddock twisted violently. He did not succeed in breaking O'Mara's terrible grip, but he turned inside it, so that his back was to the sergeant. Grabbing both O'Mara's hands now with his own, he flung himself to one side at the same time dragging O'Mara's clasped hands across the rough and hard-frozen ground.

Skin peeled from O'Mara's knuckles, leaving them bleeding and raw. He released Paddock, and Paddock rolled clear, coming to his feet as O'Mara swung a long, looping right that caught him squarely on the side of the head.

Stunned, he retreated, covering with elbows and forearms. O'Mara bored in recklessly. When O'Mara was open, Paddock stopped, set himself, and buried a fist in O'Mara's bulging belly, driving another painful grunt of breath from him.

He was angered now, angered enough to stand flat-footed and trade punches with the sergeant. Slugging savagely, taking as much as he gave, he soon had a torn ear, a flattened nose, a swelling eye and a badly bruised and bleeding mouth.

Both men breathed rapidly, blowing out a huge

cloud of steam with each breath exhaled. Paddock's head was ringing from O'Mara's blows but the sergeant seemed unaffected by the ones he had landed and Paddock knew O'Mara was going to outlast him if he continued to fight this way. He stepped back, ducking and weaving and relying on footwork to keep him from getting hit.

O'Mara growled, "Fight, ye sonofabitch."

Paddock didn't waste breath on a reply. He heard someone in the crowd yell, "Two to one on O'Mara, lads!" and thought ruefully that he must be getting the worst of it or the odds wouldn't have changed that much. O'Mara rushed at him and now he waited until the man was less than half a dozen feet away before he plunged ahead. His fist caught O'Mara squarely on the nose and it burst like a tomato, showering blood on both Paddock and O'Mara as it did.

Stopped and bloodied, eyes streaming, hurt at last, O'Mara let out a bellow and charged. Paddock stepped aside, once more slamming down both clasped hands on the back of O'Mara's neck as he went past. Once more, O'Mara skidded face down in the frozen manure, only stopping after he had plunged into and scattered a part of the crowd.

His head slammed into a broken singletree, half-buried in the frozen ground. Stunned, he fought to his hands and knees. Seizing the half-buried singletree, he wrenched it loose and rose with it grasped solidly in both his hands. Frozen clods still clung to it. O'Mara growled, "Now, ye sonofabitch, I'll bust yer head like a rotten punkin."

Paddock waited, balanced lightly on the balls of his feet. A quick glance around had revealed nothing that might even the odds. O'Mara came on, and, half a dozen feet away, set himself to swing the singletree.

Paddock saw it start and knew if it struck him, it would break bones wherever it happened to land. Ready for it, he ducked as it started, too late for O'Mara to change the direction of its swing.

It whistled overhead, less than an inch away, and Paddock straightened immediately. The momentum of the club swung O'Mara halfway around. Paddock closed with him and seized the singletree as it completed its circle. He wrenched it out of O'Mara's hands and poised to strike.

Something stopped him. It wasn't gallantry and it wasn't a conviction that the singletree was unfair. It was, instead, both the knowledge that he could kill O'Mara with the thing and the further knowledge that beating O'Mara this way wouldn't solve anything. Stepping back, he flung it into the air, over the heads of the crowd and beyond, where O'Mara couldn't get his hands on it again. He turned and faced O'Mara, prepared now to do this the hard way, prepared to stand toe to toe and slug it out with the other man.

O'Mara came boring in, surprised, but as willing as Paddock was.

Time lost meaning and became a blur of weariness and pain. Paddock slugged until he couldn't raise his hands, until each breath was a red hot flame searing his lungs and throat. He sank to his knees, dimly aware that O'Mara was also on his knees but still he swung his fists, though each blow now took half a minute to start and land.

His head whirled and he felt himself falling and he thought dimly that he had lost the fight. But no more blows landed and somewhere he could hear someone groaning and after a while a bucket of icy water was thrown directly into his face.

Gasping and choking but partially revived, he struggled to his hands and knees. O'Mara lay on his back, gasping like a fish out of water. Men helped him to his feet and others helped Paddock up and he heard someone shout, "All bets are off! It ended in a draw!"

With a man supporting him on each side, he let himself be led away toward his quarters. Someone gave him a bottle and he drank, his smashed lips burning like fire as he did. He fell back on his bed and suddenly he knew no more.

When Paddock awoke, it was to look into Molly Benedict's eyes. She was sitting beside his bed, gently bathing the lacerations on his face with a warm, wet cloth. Seeing he was awake, she said spiritedly, "Well, I am glad to see you are alive."

A lamp was burning and he realized he had been unconscious all afternoon. Molly's voice had betrayed impatience, but her glance, resting on his face, was soft. He asked, "What time is it?"

"Ten o'clock."

"And I've been asleep all that time?"

"You have."

For an instant there was silence. At last she asked, "What did it prove? If the stories I have heard are true, neither of you won. So what was the use of it?"

He grinned. "I guess women find something like that hard to understand." His grin widened and his scabbed, split lips hurt as a result. "But then there are one or two things about women that men find equally hard to understand."

A reluctant smile touched her mouth. "All right. Anyway, it's over. Do you want something to eat?"

He nodded.

"I have some soup simmering on the stove over at my place. Do you want to come over, or do you want me to bring it here?"

He said, "Give me ten minutes to change my clothes."

She got to her feet, hesitated a moment, then put on her coat and went out the door. Paddock struggled to his feet, feeling the ache in every muscle, in every bone. Wincing with each movement, he took off his shirt, boots and pants. He found clean clothes and put them on. Shrugging painfully into his coat and cramming on his hat, he went out into the everlasting wind.

Head down, he hurried to Molly's door. She opened it at his knock and he went inside.

The soup smelled delicious and he realized he was ravenous. Eating was difficult because of his smashed mouth, but he put away two bowls of soup and several pieces of bread. Finished, he thanked her and went back to his own room. This time he stripped to his underwear before getting into bed. He was almost instantly asleep and did not even stir at reveille. A loud knocking on his door roused him about an hour afterward.

It was Col. Carrington's servant, Black George. Paddock stood shivering in the icy wind blowing through the open doorway and asked, "What is it, George?"

"Colonel Carrington say he want to see you, suh. Soon's you kin make it. It's impo'tant, the colonel says."

"All right. I'll be there in twenty minutes or so."

"Yessuh." George hurried away and Paddock closed the door.

Moving still hurt him but not as much as it had the night before. Quickly he washed and shaved and tugged on his coat. Putting on his hat, he hurried out.

Molly was carrying her own water this morning. She was just entering her house with the last two buckets. He waved to her but he didn't stop to talk.

Carrington was waiting. Paddock closed the door behind him and crossed the room to put his back to the glowing stove. Carrington looked at his bruised and lacerated face for several moments before he asked, "How do you feel?"

"I'll live."

Carrington nodded, by his nod dismissing the subject. "I'd like you to make a scout." He grinned faintly. "There is always the chance I'll be pressured into going out again."

"When do you want me to go?"

"Today. Tonight. Whenever you think it's fairly safe."

Paddock said, "It'd be suicide to go out of here in daylight. They've got pickets watching every move we make. But I could go out tonight and stay out all day tomorrow and come in again tomorrow night."

"All right."

"What do you want to know?"

"How many Indians there are now in the vicinity of the fort. What they're doing and what they're planning, if you can tell. If they're going to attack the fort, I'd like to know ahead of time. If they're just waiting for us to come out, I want to know that too."

Paddock nodded. Carrington said, "I need that information, Paddock, so don't do anything foolish."

Paddock shook his head. "I won't."

"How will you keep from getting caught?"

"Why, I'll wear moccasins and go out afoot. I'll find me a high point before dawn and hole up there for the day. I won't move until it gets dark again."

"All right, Jess. Good luck."

Paddock went out the door. He intended to sleep all day if he could. He'd be awake all night tonight and all day tomorrow. Head down, he hurried toward his quarters, deciding on the way that he wouldn't tell Molly what he was going to do. There was no use worrying her and he couldn't change what he had to do.

He waited that night until after ten o'clock. He kissed Molly lightly at her door and heard it close behind him. He hurried to his own quarters then and put on the moccasins he kept for just such an eventuality as this.

At the sutler's store he got a sack of grub. He got a plug of chewing tobacco but left his pipe behind, knowing its smell could get him killed.

Armed with rifle and revolver and plenty of ammunition for both, he left the fort by climbing the banquette and vaulting over the top of the stockade. He didn't want to risk the squeak the gates made opening.

Outside the stockade, he crouched a moment, listening. All he could hear was the endless whistling of the wind. Slowly and soundlessly, he edged along the stockade until he came to the bed of Little Piney Creek.

Following this and staying hidden in the brush, he worked his way down to the point where the two creek branches joined.

He hated getting wet but he knew there was no help for it. He crouched silently in the brush for a while, listening. Deciding it was safe, he removed his moccasins and pants. Carrying them he waded out into the icy water, breaking the crust of ice ahead of him with one hand. He was shivering violently from the cold when he reached the other side and his teeth were chattering.

He squeezed as much of the water out of his lower underwear as he could, then put on his pants and moccasins. After that he moved out briskly along the rutted Bozeman Road.

He trotted for about a mile before his feet and legs felt warm again. Drawing off to the side of the road and down the slope into a clump of pines, he waited silently, watching the road in the direction of the fort.

He did not have to wait long. Two Indians came trotting up the road. They stopped not a dozen yards away and conversed briefly in the Dakota tongue. After that they went on, but more slowly and cautiously than before.

They had seen him, or heard him, he thought, trotting up the Bozeman Road trying to take the chill out of his legs and feet. But they weren't sure who he was or even that he wasn't another Indian and they'd give up the pursuit when they failed to find any trace of him.

He stayed where he was, crouched and silent, for almost an hour before he dared to move again. His legs were still damp, and they had chilled and turned stiff with the inactivity. He hoped they'd be thoroughly dry before daylight came because after that he wouldn't dare to move around at all.

Finally, deciding the two Indians had gone back to their camp, he climbed cautiously up to the road. He did not stay on it, however, deciding it was less safe than the hillside since the Indians were prone to use it going back and forth. Instead, he moved down onto the northern slope of Lodge Trail Ridge.

There were times when traveling silently was impossible. Crossing patches of crusted snow, his feet made what seemed like thunderous crunching sounds breaking through. In complete darkness, his feet snapped twigs and occasionally dislodged rocks.

He stopped every hundred yards or so to listen intently and sometimes he halted unexpectedly, trying to catch the sounds of someone following. He heard nothing but the endless sighing of the wind in the pines and the muted roar of Big Piney Creek far below.

There was little danger in traveling this slope of Lodge Trail Ridge, he thought. No pickets would be stationed here because from here the fort wasn't visible. Indians not on picket duty would be in camp, probably sleeping because the hour was very late.

At last, nearly four hours after leaving the fort, he reached a high point on Lodge Trail Ridge that he remembered from the other day. From it he knew the fort was visible. He could also see into the valley of Big Piney Creek, and beyond the northern tip of the Sullivant Hills, into the drainage of Little Piney Creek, where the wood road was.

Looking the other way, north, he would be able to see a long stretch of the valley of Peno Creek.

There was a jumble of rocks here at the crest of Lodge Trail Ridge, but instead of concealing himself in them he chose to climb a thick pine, knowing that the Indians were likely to make use, at some time tomorrow, of this high vantage point. Indians were no more likely to look up into nearby trees than white men were and he judged it to be the safest place.

He climbed about two-thirds of the way to the top, and here found a branch about three inches thick upon which he could comfortably sit. A lower branch made an excellent place for him to put his feet. He felt exposed and vulnerable and he knew that if one of the Indians happened to spot him, there would be no chance to escape. They'd shoot him out of the tree the way a hunter shoots a lion his dogs have treed.

Leaning against the trunk, his rifle across his knees, he closed his eyes and tried to sleep.

But sleep eluded him. His body still ached from the pounding O'Mara had given him the day before yesterday. His underwear was still damp from wading across the creek and the wind, up here in the trees, was cold and had an unbroken sweep for miles.

Dawn came finally, gray and cheerless and even colder than the night had been. Faintly he heard the clear notes of the bugle at the fort calling reveille.

It was a long time before he saw anything. Then it was a deer, picking its way daintily up the slope toward him. The deer passed beneath his tree and went on.

A bluejay lit on a branch below him, saw him and flew away again with a raucous squawk. Paddock pulled out his watch. It was nine o'clock. He glanced toward the fort and saw the gates swing open. The wood train came rolling out, its wagons looking like toys at this distance. He counted them. There were fourteen. They headed northwest along the wood road and shortly disappeared behind the Sullivant Hills.

Now he swept the horizons carefully with his glance. A file of Indians came up the valley of the west fork of Peno Creek. There were, he guessed, several hundred of them. More came riding over the ridge from the east fork of Peno Creek. They grouped on the relatively flat valley floor, some galloping back and forth, yelling and making imaginary passes at an imaginary enemy. They seemed to be waiting for something and at last Paddock saw what it was. A chief, accompanied by several others, probably lesser chiefs or medicine men, came up the valley and as soon as he reached them, they clustered around to listen to what he had to say.

He harangued them for a long time, gesturing as he talked. Paddock could neither hear his voice nor tell what the gestures meant, but shortly a group of fifty or sixty detached themselves from the others and galloped away over the divide separating the Peno Creek drainage from that of Big Piney Creek. He glimpsed them again going over the Sullivant Hills and he understood that they were heading for the Pinery to attack the wood train that had left the fort earlier.

Now the ominous meaning of the Indian gathering became plain to him. The Indians had done something Indians rarely do. They had formulated a battle plan.

They had laid a trap and baited it with the fifty or sixty who had gone to attack the wood train from the fort.

There was nothing Paddock could do but watch. More Indians kept trickling over the ridge and up out of the valley of Peno Creek, until Paddock judged there must be well over a thousand down there in all. Suddenly they split, about half of them retiring back down into the valley of Peno Creek, the other half moving in a body east, over the saddle separating the two forks of Peno Creek and beyond, past the Bozeman Road and into the heavily wooded hills beyond.

Paddock stared, fascinated. All the Indians had now disappeared and he strained his ears, waiting for the sound of gunfire from the direction of the Pinery. For an instant he debated trying to get back to the fort, but he knew it would be no use. By the time he reached it, this drama would have played itself out to its inevitable, tragic end.

CHAPTER **12**

Paddock scanned the landscape in all directions. Not an Indian was in sight. The wind still blew briskly toward him out of the northwest, from the direction of the Pinery. Although the distance was almost three miles, the sound of gunfire carried clearly, if faintly to his ears. The Sioux had attacked the wood detail.

He fixed his eyes on the fort. He was too far away to clearly see what was going on inside the log stockade, but once he thought he caught the faint notes of a bugle call and, fifteen minutes after hearing the first gunfire, he saw the gates swing wide.

A column of cavalry rode out at a swift canter and headed along the wood road toward the Pinery. In minutes they had disappeared behind the Sullivant Hills.

Paddock realized he was shivering, and it was not entirely from the cold. He would soon know if the commander of the relief column was going to take the Indians' bait.

He did not have long to wait. The fifty or sixty Indians who had been dispatched to attack the wood train suddenly appeared on the crest of the Sullivant Hills, riding at a gallop as though pursued.

Paddock muttered to himself, "No! Don't do it! Don't follow them!" He was sure Col. Carrington would have given the commander of the relief column specific orders not to pursue the Indians over the Sullivant Hills and if the commander did pursue, it would be in direct disobedience of those orders. But Paddock also knew Brown's and Fetterman's eagerness, and he knew that both believed in the adage that disobedience of orders was never punished if distinction was achieved.

He realized suddenly that he was holding his breath. He let it exhale but he did not take his eyes off the crest of the Sullivant Hills where the relief column would appear if its commander had decided to pursue the Indians.

Several minutes passed. Paddock slowly relaxed. By now, the fleeing Indians had reached the valley of Big Piney Creek and were splashing across the stream. They had slowed their horses to a walk. On the east side of Big Piney Creek, they stopped and their horses milled uncertainly as their riders stared back in the direction they had come.

Paddock grinned with his relief. He watched the Sioux braves ride up the side of Lodge Trail Ridge and thence down into the valley of the west fork of Peno Creek, following the route taken by Fetterman's cavalry on December 6th. They climbed the saddle separating the two forks and halted there again.

Now the two concealed forces of Indians came suddenly into sight. Like a swarm of ants they came riding from right and left to join the decoy force on the little ridge. They milled around for fifteen or twenty minutes, listening to their chiefs, before they rode slowly away down into the valley of Peno Creek and disappeared.

The trap had failed. Whoever had been in command of the force sent out to relieve the wood detail had obeyed his orders and done no more than drive the Indians off. Paddock looked back toward the fort and saw the wagons of the wood detail, accompanied by the troop of cavalry, come into sight from behind the Sullivant Hills. They reached the fort and entered it and the gates swung shut behind them.

Paddock dragged his watch from his pocket. It was only eleven o'clock. The whole operation had taken less than two hours. He'd have to remain here until dark but he already had the information Col. Carrington had sent him out to get. The Sioux had no intention of facing the artillery in a direct attack upon the fort. Their strategy was to lure a column of cavalry into their trap. The white soldiers might have learned something from their encounter with the Sioux December 6th, but the Sioux had also learned.

He got some dry biscuits and cooked meat from his grub sack and ate, afterward drinking water from his canteen. No sooner had he finished than he heard the sounds of horses approaching.

He froze and a few moments later saw two Indians come riding to the top of the ridge from the north. They were conversing in their own language. They dismounted, tied their horses and took up a position in the rocks below Paddock's tree.

He cursed sourly to himself. He doubted if they'd look up and discover him but their presence would mean he didn't dare to sleep. It would also mean he'd have to spend the rest of the day virtually motionless so that he wouldn't give himself away.

The Indians were watching the fort, but occasionally they would glance toward the Sullivant Hills as though expecting soldiers to appear suddenly at their crest.

The minutes and the hours dragged. Briefly the sun came out and then it went behind the clouds again. In mid-afternoon, the wind picked up, swaying the pine in which Paddock sat.

It was almost dusk when the Indians finally mounted their horses and rode away. Paddock remained where he was until full dark. Then, stiffly and carefully, he climbed down from his lofty perch.

He was chilled to the bone. He staggered and nearly fell when he tried to walk. Grumbling inwardly, he headed for the fort. It had been a long, hard night, and a longer, harder day. But he had the information he had been sent out to get.

He traveled with extreme care, knowing well the temptation to hurry when heading back. He stayed clear of the Bozeman Road, and once heard horses traveling on it. When he reached Big Piney Creek, he waded across at the same place he had crossed last night without bothering, this time, to remove his moccasins and pants.

Reaching the fort, he called to the sentry nearest the gate, "Open up, trooper. It's Paddock and I'm cold."

The gate swung open enough to permit his passage. He went in and headed for his quarters immediately. He lighted the lamp and, shivering, got out of his wet clothes and put dry ones on. The room was icy, having had no fire in it since yesterday. He built one and lighted it, then got a bottle of whisky and took a drink. Standing as close to the stove as he could, he took another, and another still.

The room was slow to warm, and Paddock stayed beside the stove until his pants began to scorch. Then he turned and scorched the other side. After that he took another drink, then left and headed for Colonel Carrington's house to make his report. He hoped Carrington would be alone, for he was in no mood to be scoffed at by Fetterman and Brown—and he was sure they would scoff at the conclusions he had reached.

Carrington was alone, except for his wife and Black George, both of whom left the room as soon as Paddock was admitted. Carrington looked at him and asked, "What did you find out?"

"Well, first of all, I don't think they're going to attack the fort."

"How do you know that?"

Paddock grinned. "Colonel, I watched them bait and

set a trap. There were over a thousand of them. They sent fifty or so to attack the wood train and the rest of them split into two forces. One went down into the valley of Peno Creek and the other crossed the Bozeman Road. They stayed out of sight until the decoy force reached the saddle between the two forks of Peno Creek. If your relief force had followed the decoys, they'd have been cut off and slaughtered to a man. By the way, who did you send out to relieve the wood train?"

"Captain Powell. And I gave him explicit orders not to pursue the Indians over Lodge Trail Ridge."

Paddock grinned. "Good thing it wasn't Fetterman."

"Fetterman has never disobeyed his orders, Jess."

"That don't mean he won't. Well, anyway, I haven't closed my eyes for a day and a night and I'm damn near froze. I'm going to bed."

He stopped by Molly Benedict's house on the way to his own and told her where he had been. She looked at him exasperatedly but she didn't say anything about his having left without telling her. He hurried back to his own quarters and crawled into bed immediately. He did not awake until he heard reveille.

On that day, December 20th, Col. Carrington decided to do something he had been considering for a long, long time. Every time the wood detail went out, it had to cross Big Piney Creek to get to the Pinery. Crossing, it was always extremely vulnerable to attack by the Indians. Today Carrington was going to build a bridge.

He left the fort about ten o'clock with a dozen wagons and forty or fifty men, half of whom were soldiers to protect the workmen while they cut the timber and built the bridge. Paddock went along, more out of curiosity than anything: would the detail be attacked this time?

At the crossing, Carrington sent a guarded wood-cutting detail into the woods while he remained at the bridge site to supervise the building of rock supports for the stringers in the center of the stream. Paddock sat his horse and smoked his pipe and waited for the Sioux.

Oddly, they did not appear. Once, he saw three pickets on the top of Lodge Trail Ridge, but they soon disappeared.

Carrington was a natural engineer, he thought, as he watched the work progress, and it was obvious that the colonel liked this kind of work. First he had a rock piling built in the middle of the stream. It was eighteen feet long and about six feet wide. The rocks were contained by logs set upright like a stockade in the stream-bed. Because they could not be sunk very deeply into the rocky stream-bed they were held tight by chains passing all the way around them. Filled with rock, the enclosure made a solid base for the stringers that would support the bridge. These were logs slightly more than twenty-five feet long and a foot and a half thick at their base. They were skidded out into the stream with teams. The big ends, on both banks, were laid into trenches. The smaller ends were then lifted up onto the rock piling. In all, there were six supporting stringers, which should, Paddock thought, make a solid bridge.

Now workmen started from both banks and hewed the topsides of the stringers flat. As soon as this was completed, the three-inch sawed bridge planks were laid and nailed down with ten-inch spikes.

Paddock kept looking around for a sign of Indians, but he saw none. When the bridge was almost finished, and the sun low in the western sky, Carrington walked to where he sat. "Where are the Indians?"

Paddock shrugged. "Damned if I know where they are. Maybe they didn't figure we'd be out again today and they made no plans for it."

"Those three saw us here. They had time to go back for the others."

"I've been thinking that's what they did. But I guess I was wrong. They'd have been here by now."

"You couldn't have been mistaken about that trap?"

Paddock shook his head. "Not a chance, Colonel. Not a chance."

It was nearly dusk when the bridge was finished. The

wagons rolled back toward the fort, with Paddock and Carrington riding behind. The bridge would take an hour off the wood train's time each day, half an hour going, half an hour coming back. Carrington was content and pleased with what had been accomplished.

But Paddock continued to watch the skyline, looking for the Sioux. He couldn't believe they had passed up this chance today after being disappointed yesterday. He wondered if disappointment and failure had started them to quarreling among themselves. He certainly hoped so—but he doubted it.

CHAPTER 13

It was now December 20th, and Paddock knew the supply train might arrive at any time. It would remain at the fort a day or two and would then return to Fort Laramie, under heavy escort. Among the soldiers and civilians who were also leaving, would go Paddock and Molly Benedict, as would Captain Brown, who was being transferred to Fort Laramie.

But for some reason, the imminence of the supply train's arrival failed to erase the worried look in Molly's eyes. Nor did Paddock's uneasiness disappear.

He left her house early that evening because he could see that she was tired, and he was thinking he would be glad when she could leave the heavy work she was doing here. He made his way thoughtfully to the sutler's store for pipe tobacco and a drink.

As he reached it, the door to Col. Carrington's house across the parade opened and he saw an officer step outside and come hurrying across the dark parade.

Paddock packed his pipe with the last of the tobacco in his pouch and lighted it, cupping the flame of the match against the wind. When the officer reached him he saw that it was Captain Brown. "Evening, Jess."

"Good-evening, Captain. It looks like another windy night."

"The damn wind never stops blowing here. If it was up to me, I'd say give it all back to the Indians."

Paddock said, "I'll buy you a drink."

"Thank you." Brown preceded him into the sutler's store and crossed to the bar. In the light, Paddock could see that he carried his customary two pistols and wore his spurs. Brown caught the direction of Paddock's glance and smiled a little selfconsciously. "I'm going back to Laramie in a day or two and I want to be ready if the chance comes to go out and get myself an Indian scalp."

Paddock ordered a bottle and glasses and pushed the bottle toward Brown. Brown poured himself half a glass and passed the bottle back. He said, "It doesn't look like we're going to get another chance at the Indians before we leave, does it?"

Paddock grinned. "That will suit me. That will suit me fine."

Brown frowned, then with an effort forced a smile instead. "We will have to fight them eventually. There is not room here for both the Indians and the whites."

It was apparent to Paddock that Brown was trying to be agreeable. He poured himself a drink and raised his glass. "Your health, Captain."

Brown clinked his glass against Paddock's and both men drank. Brown said, "I take it you do not approve of our presence here."

Paddock said easily, "It's not my business to approve or disapprove, Captain. What's happening is inevitable. Sooner or later we'll have it all, no matter how we get it or what we have to do."

Brown frowned again, then changed the subject suddenly, saying, "My congratulations on your coming marriage to Mrs. Benedict."

"Thank you."

"What will you do? No more scouting I would suppose."

Paddock smiled and shook his head. "A ranch, I guess. I could never live in town."

Brown finished his drink. "Thank you, Jess. Goodnight." He turned and left the sutler's store.

Paddock looked at Kinney. "Some pipe tobacco, John. Ridgewood."

Kinney got him a package. Paddock dumped the tobacco into his pouch and put the empty wrapping on the bar. He didn't want to leave. He realized that he didn't want to be alone and wondered why.

He paid for his tobacco and the drinks, told Kinney good night and left. Molly's house was dark.

He built up the fire in his own quarters and went to bed. His last thoughts were to wonder when the supply train would arrive, and why he had so dreaded, tonight, to leave the sutler's store and be alone.

The next day, December 21st, dawned clear and cold. While it still blew, the wind was not as strong as usual. The fort awakened to its daily business. Paddock carried Molly's water for her from the creek. After that, he climbed up on the banquette and stared southward along the Bozeman Road, wondering how far away the supply train was.

At ten, Carrington ordered the wood train out but, perhaps mindful of what Paddock had seen on scout, ordered a strong escort to accompany it, under the command of Corporal LeGrow. Counting soldiers and civilians, there were about ninety men.

The wagons creaked out the gate and headed for the Pinery. Paddock watched until they disappeared behind the knoll.

At eleven the picket on Pilot Hill signalled that the wagons were under attack by a large party of Indians and immediately the bugle sounded and troops began to assemble on the parade.

Frowning, Paddock watched, thinking of what he had seen from the tree on top of Lodge Trail Ridge. He saw a couple of Indian pickets ride into sight on Lodge Trail Ridge, dismount and sit down to watch the fort.

On the north side of Big Piney Creek four more Indians suddenly appeared and these began to shout epithets and obscenities at the soldiers inside the fort. Carrington, obviously annoyed, ordered three shots fired at them from a twelve-pound howitzer. The piece roared, flushing out about twenty more Indians from the road crossing when the shot exploded nearby. These and the other four fled northward, taking up positions near the first two on the slope of Lodge Trail Ridge, well out of range of the howitzers.

Col. Carrington roared, "Captain Powell!"

Powell mounted the horse that an orderly had just brought to him and rode to where Carrington stood on the banquette. He saluted perfunctorily. Carrington said, "You will take fifty men, Captain, and relieve the wood train."

Powell again gave his perfunctory salute and rode away. Fetterman, also mounted, rode now to Carrington.

He saluted more briskly than the other, and Paddock heard him say, "Colonel Carrington, I claim seniority over Captain Powell. Let me take out the relief force, sir. I would think it was my right, particularly since Powell went out with it the other day."

Carrington stared at him doubtfully. Paddock could tell that the colonel was reluctant and knew exactly why. Carrington doubted Fetterman's reliability. He was afraid Fetterman, in his eagerness to whip the Indians, would disobey orders and ride away on his own.

At last Carrington nodded reluctantly. Fetterman grinned, saluted smartly and said, "Thank you, sir."

Carrington said, "Select your own command."

Fetterman rode out onto the parade, past the men assembled there. Paddock thought, "Oh hell," and ran for the stable to get his horse. Until now, he'd thought this was going to be routine and with Powell in command it would have been routine. But with Fetterman...

He glimpsed Molly standing on her stoop, shading her eyes with an upraised hand. He ran into the stables and quickly saddled up his horse. He rode back out to the parade.

Fetterman was in the process of selecting his command. Sitting his horse in front of his own Company A, he picked out twenty-one men by name. Moving on, he called out the names of nine more men from Company C, six of Company E and thirteen of Company H. All four companies belonged to the 18th Infantry. The men selected fell out, and reformed farther out on the parade in front of Colonel Fetterman's quarters, a force of fifty, counting Fetterman himself.

The guard was just being mounted and turned over to Lt. Wands, who was officer of the day.

Carrington beckoned to Fetterman and Fetterman rode once more to where he stood. There was an eagerness, or perhaps an impatience about him that was noticeable.

Curious, Paddock rode his horse closer to Carrington. Carrington was talking to Fetterman and Paddock caught the last of what he said. "Support the wood train. Relieve it and report to me. Do not engage or pursue Indians at its expense. Under no circumstances pursue over the ridge, as per map in your possession." The wording of Carrington's orders was excessively formal and Paddock understood that was so because Carrington suspected Fetterman might be tempted to disobey.

Fetterman's horse, as though his rider's excitement was contagious, was prancing, pulling at the bit, trying to rear. Fetterman rode back to his troops and sat for a moment looking them over, every inch the commander of cavalry, thought Paddock wryly to himself. Then, turning his horse and raising an arm, he waved the column forward and his shout, "Fo'ward, ho!" reached every corner of the fort.

Paddock glanced at Colonel Carrington. The post commander was frowning, and it was plain he understood Fetterman's thoughts just as well as Paddock had. Fetterman was going out for glory, going out to prove once and for all that he and Brown were right, Carrington wrong.

Paddock called, "Want me to go with him, Colonel?"

Carrington shook his head. "I may need you later, Jess," he said, and this was a betrayal of his anxiety that Fetterman would disregard the orders just given him. To Fetterman, as he rode past at the head of his troops, Carrington called, "I'll send some cavalry after you as soon as they're ready."

Fetterman acknowledged what he had said and, at a trot, led his command on out through the gate. Paddock wondered where Brown was. He had made a point of being ready in case of just such an eventuality as this and now he was nowhere to be seen.

Staring after Fetterman's command, the uneasiness he had felt so often over the past couple of weeks returned. The 18th Infantry was equipped with obsolete muzzle-loading Springfield rifles. Against the thousands of Indians Paddock knew were waiting for them, they would be virtually helpless. Fifty men, fifty shots. It took several minutes for the troopers to reload the Springfields and the Sioux would not be idle then.

There was considerable shouting on the parade as the cavalry began to form ranks there. Captain Brown came trotting from the stables mounted on Jimmy Carrington's spotted pony Calico, which he had apparently borrowed from the boy. Two civilian employees, Jim Wheatley and Ike Fisher, armed with repeating Henry rifles, joined the cavalry, obviously hoping they would be allowed to go along.

Paddock breathed a little easier when he saw the rifles the cavalrymen were carrying. They were Spencers, seven shot repeaters that had been taken from the Regimental Band a few days earlier and given to them instead.

Lt. Wands, officer of the day, strode swiftly to Carrington. Saluting, he said, "Colonel, Lieutenant Grummond would like to know who is taking out the cavalry."

Carrington smiled but his eyes remained concerned. "I take it Grummond would like to go."

"Yes, *sir*."

"Then tell him to go ahead, but to report to me before he leaves. And tell him his orders are to join Colonel Fetterman, report to and receive all his orders from Colonel Fetterman. Also he is to tell Colonel Fetterman to remember that his orders were to go out and relieve the wood train, bring it back if necessary, or if he thought best, take the train to the woods and later bring it back. Under no circumstances is he to cross the bluff in pursuit of Indians."

Wands saluted again. "Yes, sir. I will relay those orders to him." He walked quickly away and rejoined Grummond on the far side of the parade.

There were twenty-seven men in the cavalry company, which was Company C, of the Second Cavalry. With Grummond, Brown, Wheatley and Fisher, the total came to thirty-one. With Fetterman and his forty-nine, it made eighty-one men in all. Paddock said, "Want me to go with this bunch, Colonel?" The colonel answered him this time with only an abrupt shake of his head.

He had no faith in Grummond either, Paddock thought, and he was holding Paddock back to carry direct orders to the two commanders if it became apparent they were disobeying the ones he had given them when they left the fort.

Lt. Grummond waved his arm, gave the command to move and cantered out of the fort, with Captain Brown riding beside him on Calico, with Fisher and Wheatley riding just behind. The ponderous gates swung shut and Paddock rode his horse closer to the stockade so that he could better see over the top of it.

He stared in disbelief. Carrington had been justified in thinking his orders would be disobeyed. The colonel suddenly roared at Grummond, just outside the fort. He ran swiftly along the banquette and climbed to the sentry's platform. Grummond halted his command and rode back, halting just below the platform where the Colonel stood.

Carrington repeated the orders he had given Grummond earlier through Lieutenant Wands, and asked if he understood them thoroughly. Grummond nodded somewhat irritably and said he did. He turned and rejoined his command and they galloped after Col. Fetterman. Carrington watched, scowling angrily.

It was obvious, almost from the time that Col. Fetterman left the fort with his fifty mounted infantrymen, that he had no intention whatever of obeying the orders given him by Col. Carrington. The wood train was corralled and fighting the Indians a couple of miles due west of the fort on the south side of the Sullivant Hills. Fetterman headed due north instead of west, straight toward the eastern end of Lodge Trail Ridge, which Carrington had told him specifically not to cross.

Carrington's anger over this deliberate disobedience was just as obvious. His face was red, his eyes narrowed and angry. Paddock rode closer to him and asked, "Want me to try and catch him, Colonel? If he's headed for the wood train, he's sure as hell going at it by a roundabout way."

Carrington hesitated an instant. Then he shook his head. "No. Grummond will catch up and remind him of his orders. He'll turn back."

Paddock didn't say anything but he was thinking that Grummond wasn't much better than Fetterman as far as obeying orders was concerned. And by the time Carrington found out that neither Fetterman nor Grummond intended to turn back, it would be too late for a messenger to reach them from the fort.

Carrington's eyes were fixed on Fetterman's little force. It had reached Big Piney Creek. There was still time, Paddock thought, for Fetterman to obey the orders given him. He could turn west along the south side of Big Piney Creek and come over the Sullivant Hills behind the Indians.

But Fetterman did not turn. His command splashed across the ice-bordered creek and started up the near

90

slope of Lodge Trail Ridge. Carrington's orders to Fetterman had been "under no circumstances are you to pursue Indians over the ridge"—over Lodge Trail Ridge. Technically, then, Fetterman was not disobeying that part of the orders given him. He was not pursuing anything.

Grummond's cavalry troop, galloping in an effort to catch up, finally caught Fetterman's force just beyond the Big Piney crossing. Both commands halted a moment, and Paddock could see Grummond and Fetterman conferring. Carrington's face had relaxed somewhat as if he anticipated that both commands would now turn back.

But neither did. Instead, they moved on up the slope of Lodge Trail Ridge. Paddock saw Fetterman wave his hand and the command spread out to left and right as skirmishers as if action with the Indians was imminent.

Carrington said, "Damn!" and turned his head to look at Jess. "At least they're not riding into the Indian trap. Maybe they'll actually be able to come around behind the Indians."

Paddock said, "Won't do 'em any good. A thousand Indians are waiting out there and Fetterman has eighty men. I don't care what side he hits 'em from, eighty men can't beat a thousand."

They still could hear firing from the direction of the besieged wood train. Carrington turned suddenly and yelled, "Lieutenant Wands!"

Wands, who had borrowed a horse somewhere, came trotting to where Carrington stood on the sentry platform. "Yes, sir?"

"Find Dr. Hines. There may be casualties at the wood train and if Fetterman isn't going to relieve it, Hines had better go out there and take care of them."

Lt. Wands asked, "Are you going to send another force to relieve the wood train? Do you want me to get them ready?"

Carrington shook his head. "Not right now. I want to wait and see what Fetterman and Grummond do. Just get Dr. Hines, and a few volunteers to go with him. Three or four will do."

Wands trotted his horse away across the parade toward the post hospital.

Carrington looked at Paddock. "Do you mind going along with Hines?"

"No, Colonel. I'll go." Paddock glanced across the parade toward the post hospital and saw Dr. Hines and his orderly come hurrying out. Hines was carrying his black leather bag. Wands yelled at a couple of mounted infantrymen and they broke out of their formation on the parade and brought their horses to Hines and his orderly. Another man, a civilian named Portugee Phillips, joined the two, as did Sergeant O'Mara. The four came riding across the parade toward Carrington.

It was the first time Paddock had seen O'Mara since the fight and he watched the sergeant warily. Surprisingly, O'Mara grinned at him. "Howdy, Bucko. You goin' along with the surgeon too?"

Paddock nodded, frowning slightly because O'Mara's sudden change of attitude puzzled him. Maybe the fight had cleared the air, he thought. Maybe by slugging it out with O'Mara until both were on the verge of unconsciousness, he had earned the burly sergeant's respect, something he would probably have been unable to do in any other way.

He shrugged slightly, accepting the change in the man even though he didn't entirely understand it. Briefly he studied O'Mara, trying to decide if the sergeant's new attitude toward him was genuine or feigned. He decided O'Mara was much too direct to feign anything like that.

Carrington said, "Doctor, I want you to ride out to the wood train and treat any wounded they may have. After that is done, Paddock will guide you to Fetterman and Grummond and you are to stay with them."

Hines nodded. "All right, Colonel." He turned his head and looked at the men with him. "Ready?"

Paddock nodded, and Hines headed toward the gate. Carrington was still on the sentry platform, a very worried look upon his face.

The massive gates swung open and the little group rode through. Hines rode in front with Paddock.

O'Mara and the doctor's orderly rode immediately behind, followed by Phillips, the civilian.

They were no more than fifty yards from the gate when they heard galloping hoofs behind. Turning his head, Paddock saw Lt. Matson and an infantry private overtaking them. Hines halted long enough for the pair to catch up and then went on. Half a mile farther along the road they overtook a wagon in which were two civilian employees of the quartermaster depot. These had apparently left the fort while everybody's attention was on the troops being readied on the parade. What they had in mind and what they thought they could accomplish was a mystery.

Hines slowed enough for the men with the wagon to keep up. He obviously did not want to leave them behind, alone and exposed to attack by lurking Indians.

Paddock had not seen an Indian since leaving the fort and he was beginning to feel uneasy about it. O'Mara, as though echoing his thoughts, said, "Bejesus, where are all the redskins, Bucko? It's like they'd vanished into the air."

Paddock could no longer hear the sounds of firing from the direction of the corraled wood train. They rounded the knoll that hid the train from the fort and saw it suddenly ahead of them. It was breaking its protective square and heading once more toward the Pinery. There still was not an Indian in sight.

Paddock's mild uneasiness had now changed to deep concern. The fact that the Indians had so suddenly and precipitantly withdrawn could only mean that a trap had indeed been set for Fetterman. As soon as he had left the fort and headed for Lodge Trail Ridge, the Indians must have broken off the engagement with the corraled wood train.

He turned his head. "Want me to ride ahead and see if they've got any casualties, Dr. Hines?"

Hines nodded. Paddock dug spurs into his horse's sides and the animal galloped eagerly along the rutted road, which now began to climb the divide between the two branches of Piney Creek. O'Mara, surprisingly, joined him before he had gone a hundred yards.

The wood train was more than a mile ahead and had almost reached the bridge Carrington had built across Big Piney Creek before Paddock and O'Mara were able to catch up with it. Corporal LeGrow was riding in the rear wagon and O'Mara yelled at him, "You got any casualties, Corporal?"

LeGrow shook his head. "Nothin' serious. One of the teamsters got an arrow through his shoulder, but I pulled it out. He's still drivin' to keep from gettin' stiff."

"You don't need the doctor then?"

"Hell no. We're goin' on to the Pinery to get a load of logs."

O'Mara nodded and stopped his horse. The two watched the wood train cross the bridge. It wound up the steep and twisting road into the pines. O'Mara said, "Bucko, it looks like Colonel Fetterman has bit off more than he can chew."

Paddock had been thinking the same thing. He cocked his head and listened intently for the sound of firing from the direction Fetterman had gone. All he heard was the murmur of the stream and the wind whispering through the pines. He said, "Let's get back to Dr. Hines."

He did not gallop his horse going back because he knew that before he returned to the fort he might need every bit of strength and stamina the horse possessed. He was becoming increasingly uneasy about Fetterman and his eighty men, and the silence was anything but reassuring. The Indians were probably only waiting until Fetterman's men got far enough away from the fort so that rescue was impossible.

O'Mara asked, "You don't think Fetterman is going to try attacking their villages on the Tongue, do you? I've heard him say he could ride through the whole Sioux nation with a hundred men."

Paddock didn't know. Fetterman had certainly headed away from the fort as if he knew exactly where he was going. He said, "I don't think even Fetterman could be that stupid. Fifty of his men are armed with those damned muzzle-loading Springfields."

"Then where the hell *has* he gone? If he intended to

94

circle around and hit the bucks that was attackin' the wood train, he'd have been here by now."

Involuntarily Paddock glanced up toward the crest of the Sullivant Hills. He saw no movement there.

Fetterman had disobeyed his orders. He had gone over Lodge Trail Ridge, taking Grummond along with him. He'd never had any intention of coming to the wood train's relief, and that fact must be plain to Col. Carrington by now. Paddock wondered what Carrington would do. Would he send out another force to relieve Fetterman? Or would he wait to see if Fetterman made it safely back?

Shrugging fatalistically, he kicked his horse into a trot, and ten minutes later reached Dr. Hines and the other men. He said, "They only have one casualty, Doctor, a man with an arrow through his shoulder. Corporal LeGrow pulled it out and he says the man is driving to keep it from getting stiff."

"Then they don't need me."

"No. I guess we'd better see if we can find Colonel Fetterman."

Hines nodded. He turned to the men in the wagon. "Take your choice. Drive on and join the wood train or go back to the fort. We're heading over the hill and we can't take you along."

The driver, his face bearded and seamed, said, "We'll join the wood train, I reckon."

Hines nodded, and looked at Lt. Matson and the infantryman. "You can come along or go back to the fort."

Matson said, "We'll stay with you."

"Then let's get on with it. Paddock, lead the way."

Paddock put his horse up the steep slope, heading for a narrow ravine between two rounded hills. The others spurred their horses after his, the animals lunging because of the steepness of the trail.

And now, so faintly he could not be sure of it, Paddock thought he heard firing from ahead.

CHAPTER **15**

At this moment, they were about three miles from the fort. Looking east, Paddock could see it, but the distance was too great to make out individual figures inside its walls. He wondered if Carrington had done anything about sending a relief force after Fetterman. He doubted it. Fetterman had eighty men and there were ninety with the wood train. Carrington could not have much more than two hundred left at the fort. He would think twice about sending any substantial force to Fetterman's relief because doing so would leave the fort itself dangerously undermanned.

Halfway up the south side of the Sullivant Hills, Paddock halted to let the horses blow. They fidgeted, tossing their heads and rattling their bits. Paddock kept an ear cocked toward the north, listening for the sounds of firing. This time he was sure he heard it even though the distance was considerable and even though two ridges lay between him and Fetterman's men. Dr. Hines said, "That's gunfire all right. No doubt of it."

Paddock nodded. The horses' breathing was more regular now and he touched spurs to his horse's sides. The animal lunged on up the steep slope toward the top of the ridge.

Reaching it, Paddock halted again. The firing was now very distinct but Fetterman's force was nowhere to be seen. The sounds seemed to be coming from a spot perhaps two and a half miles to the northeast. Paddock urged his horse down the northern side of the Sullivant Hills toward Big Piney Creek in the valley below. The going was treacherous and several times his horse slid on his haunches. When he reached the bottom, his legs were trembling.

96

The others slid their horses down behind Paddock and halted beside him. Here, Big Piney Creek ran narrow and deep and very swift, its banks steep and overgrown with brush and trees. Hines said, "Let's go downstream a ways and see if we can't find a better place to cross."

Paddock nodded. He put his horse into a trot, paralleling Big Piney Creek. There was no advantage in trying to cross it here. Doing so would neither save time nor shorten greatly the distance to Fetterman and his men. They still would have to cross Lodge Trail Ridge, descend into a ravine, and climb the ridge beyond. If they followed Big Piney Creek to the regular crossing of the Bozeman Road, they could then follow the road north on an easy grade, gaining time and saving the horses as well.

O'Mara ranged his horse up beside Paddock's. There was worry in the sergeant's eyes. "What do you think, Bucko? You think Fetterman's in trouble?"

Paddock nodded. "There are at least a thousand Indians out there and maybe more."

O'Mara said, "He claimed he could ride through them with a hundred men. Looks like he's got his chance."

"Don't like him much, do you?"

O'Mara looked surprised. Frowning, he thought about it and finally said, "I guess I don't, now you mention it. To him, them troopers are only tools. And that damned Brown is worse. He's so hot to have an Indian scalp he'd sacrifice his own mother to get one. No, I guess I ain't got much use for either one of 'em."

The firing continued as they rode. Paddock kept watch for a crossing but did not find one until they reached the place where the Bozeman Road crossed the creek.

By now, the hills to the north were swarming with Indians. They galloped back and forth with seeming aimlessness, like ants in an anthill that has been disturbed. Hines stared northward worriedly. "What do you think, Jess? Can we get through?"

Hines continued to stare north along the climbing course of the Bozeman Road. At last he said, "Fetterman is probably surrounded, and if he is, we haven't got a chance of reaching him. At least not without reinforcements."

Paddock nodded. "You may be right. Why don't you and Lt. Matson go back to the fort and get more men? Fetterman likely needs help more than he needs you."

Hines nodded and turned to go. Looking back he said, "You sounded like you weren't going along with us. What are *you* going to do?"

"Fetterman's force may still be intact. I thought I'd try reaching him to tell him Carrington wants him to turn back. Maybe it's not too late. There's still a lot of firing over there and we know the Indians don't have many guns. So most of Fetterman's men must still be all right."

Hines touched heels to his horse's sides and the animal trotted away. Lt. Matson and the infantryman fell in behind, as did Phillips, the civilian. O'Mara hesitated. He looked after the doctor, then back to Paddock. At last he asked, "Mind if I go with you?"

Paddock shook his head. "I don't mind, but you might lose your hair."

"You think you're any better than me?"

Paddock said, "Oh Christ, let's don't start that again."

O'Mara grinned unexpectedly.

Paddock studied the man with something like regret. He knew that his decision to try reaching Fetterman had been brash and ill-considered. There was little chance they could reach Fetterman and even if they did, little chance that Fetterman, having initially disobeyed Carrington's orders, would now heed them and turn back to the fort. But he'd stuck his neck out and he had to go through with it.

He stared up the Bozeman Road once more. He could, at any given time, count thirty or forty Indians galloping back and forth across it near the top of the ridge. He wondered how far Fetterman and Brown had gone before the Indians had pinned them down. The firing now seemed to be stationary. Fetterman's infantry and Grummond's cavalry must have taken cover on some hillside and be fighting it out even though com-

98

pletely surrounded by the Indians. Still, Fetterman and Brown had successfully fought their way through several hundred Indians on December 6th. If Hines brought out a relief force Fetterman still might be extricated from the situation with little loss.

He beckoned to O'Mara, then ascended through the timber on the east side of the ridge. This way, perhaps they could avoid discovery at least until they were a quarter to a half mile away. It was slower going but the Bozeman Road was too open and exposed.

Behind him, O'Mara said, "I must be crazy for offering to go with you."

Paddock grinned. "And I'm crazy for going."

"Do you really think we can get through?"

Paddock shook his head. "No. I never did think we could."

"Then what the hell are we doing here?"

"I want to find out how much trouble Fetterman is in. I want to be able to tell Colonel Carrington how many men are going to be needed to get him out of it."

O'Mara looked relieved. "Well, I'm glad you're not going to try riding through all them howlin' devils. How close do you think we'll have to get?"

Paddock shrugged. "Close enough to see what's going on."

A mile from the creek, Paddock drew rein in a thick grove of pines. They were closer to the firing now, which had continued unabated. If there had been any doubt before about the seriousness of Fetterman's predicament, none remained. He had apparently been pinned down at least half an hour, maybe longer. His men were fighting for their lives.

Conscious that little time now remained, Paddock spurred his horse suddenly, and recklessly climbed to the Bozeman Road on the spine of the ridge. Pounding along beside him, O'Mara yelled, "Have you lost your mind? What are you trying to do?"

"Find out what's going on before it's too late. They must be getting low on ammunition. They've been firing for more than half an hour now."

O'Mara looked at him and shook his head. He dropped back a little but he kept pace. Paddock reached a spot near the crest of the ridge and from here could see far enough ahead to grasp the scope of the Indian attack.

Involuntarily he pulled his horse to a halt. It was hard to estimate a rapidly moving, close-packed body of Indians, but it looked to him as though there must be twice as many involved in this attack on Fetterman as he had seen rehearsing their trap several days before. He and O'Mara did not seem to have been spotted, even though they now were less than half a mile from the nearest Indians. O'Mara yelled, "For Christ's sake, let's get back to the fort. Fetterman needs help and needs it bad."

Paddock yelled, "You go on back. Tell Carrington to send out some men. And some artillery. That's what it'll take to scatter that bunch."

O'Mara shook his head. "I'm not going back until you do, Bucko."

"Don't be a fool!"

O'Mara grinned. "You mean don't be like you?" Paddock shrugged. He touched his horse's sides with his spurs and the animal, seemingly infected with his rider's excitement, pounded up the rutted, narrow road.

CHAPTER 16

Not long afterward, Paddock and O'Mara reached a high point from which they could clearly see ahead. Now, for the first time, Paddock saw the blue uniforms of Fetterman's infantrymen and those of Grummond's cavalry, half a mile ahead.

It was obvious that Fetterman's command had been spread out as skirmishers but under the unrelenting pressure of the howling, circling Indians, the skirmishers farthest out had been forced back in toward the center of the line.

Slow progress by both commands had led Paddock to believe the racket of firing was stationary while actually it was not. Both Fetterman and Grummond had apparently continued to move in much the same way Fetterman had on December 6th, slowly, almost inch by inch through the ever closing circle of Indians.

Mindful of the experience on December 4th, when Bingham had lost his head and retreated from that pressure, Fetterman had made no attempt to turn back or retreat toward the fort, but instead had continued stubbornly to go ahead. Whether that was right or not was problematical. Retreating would have given the Indians the idea that they had the white soldiers on the run. Continuing to advance when there was no place to go might turn out to be as disastrous as the first course would have been.

Quite obviously, Fetterman was holding his men together only by the sheer force of his own will. They were firing raggedly, and, with the ancient muzzle-loading Springfields, were forced after each shot to stop, to ram home a charge, to follow it with a ball, and then, before they could fire again, to affix a cap. The whole reloading process could not be done, even by an expert, in less than a minute and none of Fetterman's men were expert. Reloading usually took from three to five minutes and during that time the soldier was helpless, unable to defend himself.

There were some casualties, but from this distance it was hard to tell how many or how serious they were. Fetterman's men would be reluctant to leave their dead behind because they knew how horribly the bodies would be mutilated by the Indians. Paddock supposed some of those being dragged or carried along with the command were already dead.

He thought Fetterman must know that he was doomed. The men must also know. Looking beyond Fetterman's command, he could see Grummond's cavalry. Like Fetterman's men, they had dismounted to fight on foot, turning the horses over to horse holders. The horses were in the center of the circle they had formed, the cavalrymen forming its perimeter. They were better able to keep the Indians at a distance with their repeating Spencers and seemed in no immediate danger.

Silently, Paddock exhorted Grummond to turn back and help Fetterman. The colonel was in dire need right now of more firepower, firepower that could be supplied by Grummond's cavalry. But Grummond apparently was not aware of Fetterman's need and made no attempt to return and help him out.

He saw a man fall on Fetterman's right flank, and another, and another still, and so close was the horde of Indians that their bodies could not be recovered by their comrades before they were swarmed over by the Sioux. Uniforms were snatched off, to reappear almost at once on the bodies of the Indians, a hat on one, a tunic on another, a pair of trousers on a third. A glimpse through the milling Indians showed Paddock a gleam of white, which must have been the naked body of one of the dead infantrymen.

He realized that he had been watching in a kind of a daze. He turned his head and looked at Sergeant O'Mara. He wondered if his own face was as white as O'Mara's was. He yelled, "Get back to the fort. Tell the colonel what's going on."

"What are you going to do?"

"I'm going to try and reach Grummond. If he doesn't get back to Fetterman and help him out, Fetterman's men are dead."

"You can't get through that bunch of Indians!"

"I'm going to try."

"You're a damned fool!"

"Probably. Get going. Tell Carrington to get some howitzers out here as fast as he can."

O'Mara shook his head. "Dr. Hines has already told him that. I'm going with you, Bucko. If you're going to make a jackass out of yourself, then I'd just as well do it too."

Paddock didn't have time to argue the point with him. Besides, he knew O'Mara probably was right. Hines and Lt. Matson had gone back to the fort earlier. A relief force should already be on its way and

Col. Carrington would not have to be told to send artillery along. It was the only thing the Indians feared.

He dug spurs into his horse's sides and the startled animal leaped ahead. He couldn't help thinking about Molly Benedict and for an instant he could see, in his mind, her white face looking at him from the crowd beside the stockade gate. He remembered the way her lips had been parted and the terror in her eyes. And he wondered if he would ever see her again.

He leaned low over his horse's withers, drawing his revolver as he did. He could hear the thunder of O'Mara's horse pounding along behind. Fetterman's men seemed to have come to a halt. The last of the skirmishers had joined the main command, which now was huddled so closely together that Paddock wondered how they could even fight.

He thought savagely, "Spread out, you damn fools! Spread out and take cover! You're just making it easy for them to kill you off!"

But the men of Fetterman's command were thoroughly demoralized by the awful pressure of the Indians. And they knew there was no way of getting out of this alive. The fort was miles away and more than a thousand Indians barred their way to it. They knew death was very close.

Paddock could no longer see Fetterman. He wondered if the colonel had been killed. Perhaps he had. It would explain the thorough demoralization of his men.

Now, less than a quarter mile separated Paddock and O'Mara from Fetterman's mauled command. And suddenly, for the first time, they were spotted by the Indians.

The howling quieted. A couple of hundred of the Indians nearest them halted their ponies and milled about uncertainly, staring down the road past Paddock and O'Mara as though they believed they were the vanguard of a relief force from the fort. But when they saw no soldiers coming on behind the pair, they began to howl again, even louder than before. A body of at least two hundred detached itself from the others and came galloping down the Bozeman Road straight toward the two.

O'Mara yelled, "Holy Christ! We'll never get through now."

Paddock knew there had probably never been the slightest chance of getting through. It had been a foolish idea and now they could just as well give it up.

He glanced past the rapidly approaching Indians, beyond Fetterman's huddled command, to that of Grummond farther on which still seemed to be intact, but would not be long. As soon as the Indians had killed the last of Fetterman's command, they would turn to Grummond's and annihilate it too. He caught a glimpse of a spotted horse. Jimmy Carrington's horse, he thought, the one Brown had borrowed so that he could go after the Indian scalp he had talked so much about.

He hauled his horse in so abruptly that the animal reared, pawing the air and fighting for his head. O'Mara's horse came to a stiff-legged halt immediately behind, then whirled and began to buck. The sergeant stayed with him for half a dozen jumps, fighting to yank up his head, cursing savagely all the while. Then suddenly O'Mara sailed off, striking the dirt of the road with a thud and skidding half a dozen feet.

Paddock didn't even look at him. He spurred, and reined his horse hard over toward O'Mara's, now galloping down through the thick timber on the east side of the ridge.

Almost immediately he realized that he couldn't overtake the horse in time to return him to O'Mara before he was overrun by Indians. He therefore abandoned his attempt to catch the horse and returned at a gallop to where O'Mara lay.

The fall had driven the air from O'Mara's lungs. He lay on his side in a crouched position, fighting desperately for breath. Paddock roared, "O'Mara! Get up behind me! Quick!"

O'Mara glanced up, his face dirty and almost green. His eyes showed his agony. It was with a superhuman effort that he fought to his hands and knees.

The Sioux were closer now and their howls made O'Mara turn his head. The Indians were galloping along the crest of the ridge about ten abreast, a solid wall of barbaric fury the sight of which brought O'Mara stumbling to his feet. He caught Paddock's saddle horn and slammed a foot into the stirrup Paddock gave to him. The horse was already running as he hit its back behind Paddock's saddle. He held on by putting his arms around Paddock while he continued to fight desperately for breath.

An arrow whistled past Paddock's head and struck the road a dozen feet ahead. Another scratched the horse's rump, bringing blood but falling to the road.

The pain made the horse run even faster than before. But he was carrying double weight and could not possibly outrun the Indians. It was only a matter of time before they got close enough to knock both Paddock and O'Mara out of the saddle.

Paddock heard the solid thump of the arrow that struck Sergeant O'Mara in the back. And he felt the way O'Mara's arms tightened briefly before they fell away.

O'Mara sagged to the right, dead weight, and Paddock half turned in the saddle, holding him, keeping him from falling off. Immediately ahead there was a cluster of rocks beside the road. He turned slightly, reining in. The horse showed its side to the pursuing Indians, and took an arrow in the neck.

He went down, throwing both Paddock and O'Mara neatly over his head. Rolling and skidding in a cloud of dust, the pair, with O'Mara wholly limp, rolled into the shelter of the rocks. The horse somersaulted once and then lay still, forming a bulwark between Paddock and the Indians, who now were hauling their horses to a halt and milling in confusion less than thirty yards away.

Paddock's revolver still was in his hand. He fired carefully, and with three shots knocked three Indians from their saddles. The others split to right and left, bent on encircling the rocks. He took advantage of the brief respite to look at O'Mara and to grasp his wrist. There was no pulse and O'Mara's chest was still. The arrow must have pierced his heart and killed him instantly.

Turning, Paddock fired twice more, then crouched

105

behind his horse and replaced the spent cylinder with a loaded one. Arrows thudded into the horse and into the ground immediately behind. They made an unmistakable twanging sound as they left the bow, and an equally unmistakable thud as they struck.

Paddock yanked his rifle from the saddle boot and laid it beside him against the time when the revolver would be empty again.

He thought, "God damn it, I'm not going to get out of this," and reared up to fire at two Indians, running toward him half crouched, one carrying a knife, the other a tomahawk. He killed the one with the knife with a bullet in the chest and, firing hastily, broke the leg of the second one.

Behind them, three more Indians came galloping, intending to run him down or flush him out for the other Indians, now ranged on both sides and behind the cluster of rocks.

Paddock rammed his revolver back into its holster and snatched up his rifle before he leaped aside. He set himself and, standing spread-legged, swung the rifle like a club.

It struck the nearest Indian in the chest, forcing an explosive grunt out of him, driving him backward over his horse's rump. The horse, confused and terrified, reared and turned, pawing the air over Paddock's head. Paddock had a quick glimpse of the painted faces of the other two Indians as they went past and then he knew this rearing horse was the only chance he was going to get to stay alive. He ducked the flailing hoofs and as the horse came down, seized its bridle on the left side of its head.

His strange smell further terrified the horse. He whirled, and plunged away, dragging Paddock along with him. Using the horse's speed and the leverage his grip on the bridle gave him, Paddock swung to the horse's back, forced to release his rifle as he did so that he could grasp the horse's mane. Mounted, he leaned far forward and caught up the dragging reins before the horse broke them by stepping on them. Everything had happened so quickly he didn't know which way he was headed and he was relieved to realize he was headed down the Bozeman Road toward the fort.

Once more the Indians were in full and howling pursuit. But about half of them had stayed behind to strip and mutilate the body of the dead O'Mara.

Paddock found it hard to believe that he was alive. He had faced certain death there in the rocks but he had not died. Now he faced life again, finding it unbelievably sweet. He raked the terrified Indian pony with his spurs, leaning low and riding as he had never ridden in his life before.

CHAPTER 17

What had started out this morning as a routine situation, with the wood train going out, being attacked and promptly being relieved had turned into a nightmare because of one officer's insubordination. Paddock now knew that Fetterman's whole command was doomed. Grummond's cavalry, or part of it, might be saved, but only if they were reached immediately.

The stocky Indian pony was thoroughly terrified by the strange smell of his rider and ran willingly. Arrows whizzed past Paddock's head, falling to the ground in the road ahead of him. Glancing back, he saw that the pursuing Indians were less than fifty yards behind. He considered using his revolver to discourage them but gave the idea up. He only had three loads left and he might need them desperately later on.

Half a mile fell behind, a mile. And then, ahead, Paddock saw the blue uniforms of a relief force coming up the road. They were almost all on foot, but moving at double time. They appeared to be about forty of them in all. Two ambulances followed them. Paddock kept his Indian pony at a run until he was within a hundred yards of the column's head. Glancing behind as he hauled the pony to a halt, he discovered that the Indians had given up the chase. They now were trotting their ponies back up the road.

He released a long sigh of relief. He discovered, when he dismounted, that his knees were trembling so badly he could hardly stand. He grinned shakily at Captain Ten Eyck, commander of the relief column. "Godalmighty, that was close!"

Ten Eyck did not stop, but continued to double time swiftly up the road, motioning for Paddock to keep pace with him. The Indian pony, frightened by the men coming behind Captain Ten Eyck, permitted Paddock to lead him. Ten Eyck asked, "What's going on, Jess?"

"Fetterman's in trouble. He may be dead and by the time we get there all his men may be dead too."

"Fifty men?" Ten Eyck's tone was incredulous.

Paddock nodded. "Grummond and his cavalry were in fair shape the last I saw of them because of the Spencer rifles they were carrying, but as soon as the Indians finish Fetterman off, they'll turn on Grummond and his men."

"What do you think we ought to do?"

"Keep going, but don't go into anything blind. Have you got artillery?"

Ten Eyck shook his head.

"Then I'd suggest you send someone back to the fort for two or three howitzers. Artillery is the one thing those Indians fear."

Ten Eyck turned his head and yelled at a mounted civilian riding just ahead of the wagons. The man, bearded and graying, trotted his horse forward. "Yeah, Captain?"

"Ride back to the fort as fast as you can. Tell Colonel Carrington I'm going to need some artillery and if he can spare them, some more men too." He turned his head and spoke to his orderly, "Private Sample, you go with him. Borrow a horse from somebody."

The two men galloped back down the road. The fort was still visible from here and Paddock thought they

108

could have saved time with a heliograph if the sun had not been hidden behind gray and heavy clouds.

He saw Dr. Hines with the column of men behind Ten Eyck, and Lt. Matson too. Hines called to him, "Where's Sergeant O'Mara, Jess?"

Paddock waited for part of the column to pass. Abreast of Dr. Hines, he said, "Dead. His horse bucked him off and ran away. He got up behind me and caught an arrow in the back."

"What happened to your horse?"

"Arrow in the neck. I borrowed an Indian horse."

Paddock mounted, left Dr. Hines and rode his Indian pony once more to the column's head. Captain Ten Eyck was plainly nervous and searched the timber on both sides of him with worried eyes. He glanced at Paddock and asked, "How many Indians did you say there were?"

Paddock said, "I don't know, Captain. It's hard to count when you're trying to stay alive. But I'd guess somewhere between fifteen hundred and two thousand."

"How were they armed?"

"Mostly with bows and arrows and spears and tomahawks. But they've likely got all of Fetterman's Springfields, now, and maybe Grummond's Spencers too."

Ten Eyck nodded, his eyes preoccupied. He was plainly concerned about the safety of his command. Fetterman had ridden into a trap and had seen his men slaughtered. Ten Eyck didn't intend to let that happen to him if ordinary prudence could prevent it.

The road continued to ascend and, about a mile from where he had encountered Paddock, Ten Eyck ordered his command to veer right toward a high promontory from which he could better see the land ahead.

Paddock watched approvingly. Obviously Ten Eyck was not the firebrand that Fetterman and Brown were. Ten Eyck was trying to do what he had been ordered to do, relieve Fetterman's command, but he was also trying to avoid walking into the same kind of trap. He didn't have the mobility Fetterman and Grummond had, since his command was on foot, and he didn't

109

have as many men. He was painfully aware that the Indians, having killed all of both Fetterman's and Grummond's commands would probably turn on him.

The men plodded through the timber, ascending to the rocky point. Ten Eyck had earlier ordered flankers out to guard against surprise attack. Reaching the promontory, he halted and stared at the land ahead.

Even from this high promontory, it still was not possible to see the slope where Fetterman's men were engaged, nor the place farther on to which Grummond's cavalry had advanced. The firing, furthermore, had all but ceased.

Ten Eyck glanced up at Paddock. "See anything?"

"Just Indians milling around."

"Nothing of Fetterman?"

Paddock shook his head.

The Indians covered the crest of the ridge between where Ten Eyck had halted and the place where Paddock had last seen Fetterman. They seemed to be milling around aimlessly, as though uncertain as to what they ought to do.

The halt took no more than a few minutes but it accomplished its main purpose. Ten Eyck was able to see into a deep ravine lying to the right of the road and to satisfy himself that no Indians waited there to ambush him. Having done so, he gave the order to advance. He proceeded back to the road and then along it to the place where it began its descent into Peno Creek.

From here, the road dropped abruptly for about half a mile, then continued to descend more gradually for another half mile. From that point the road followed a narrow ridge for almost a mile and then dropped off abruptly into the valley of Peno Creek. At both ends of the narrow ridge were numbers of large rocks lying beside the road. Paddock was looking at the place he had last seen Fetterman but right now he couldn't see anything except the Indians milling around the nearest pile of rocks. It was an eerie experience. It was almost as though he had imagined what he had seen earlier, as though Fetterman's command, and Grummond's, had vanished from the face of the earth.

The column moved down the descending road, the

110

ambulances creaking along in the rear. Paddock watched the Indians retreat before them, and realized that the Sioux thought the two ambulances contained artillery. He said, "They think we've got howitzers in the wagons, Captain."

"Then let's hope they keep on thinking so."

While they were still half a mile from the place where he had last seen Fetterman, Paddock caught a glimpse of something white. An instant later, he saw several more white spots, and realized that they were bodies, stripped and lying on the ground. He said, "Captain, I see bodies up there near the rocks."

"How many? Can you tell?" Ten Eyck's eyes were narrowed and he was staring ahead, but he did not have the advantage of being on a horse.

Paddock now could make out a large number of naked bodies, but because of the distance it was impossible to make a count. He said, "A lot of them, Captain. A hell of a lot of them."

Ten Eyck said in a shocked voice, "Oh God! I can see them now myself. Aren't there any left alive?"

"I don't see anything but bodies, Captain."

There still were a number of Indians among the bodies and Ten Eyck ordered angrily, "Spread out and open fire! Drive those damned vultures out of there!"

The men behind him spread to right and left, knelt and opened fire. The Indians milling around among the bodies mounted immediately and galloped away down the road, not stopping until they were out of range.

Ten Eyck yelled, "Cease firing!" and the firing stopped. Paddock heard the rattling of tug chains and the creak of wagon wheels and, looking back, saw three wagons, an ambulance and about forty civilians coming down the road from the direction of the fort. Some of the men were on foot, but most were mounted. All were armed heavily.

Paddock glanced at Ten Eyck's face. It showed his relief at being thus reinforced. Ahead and well beyond the place where the bodies were, the Sioux seemed to be forming ranks again, perhaps for another attack upon the hated whites.

111

On down the road the reinforced column went. The faces of the men were white with shock, but here and there was a red and angry face. From the direction of the fort came Private Sample, galloping his horse. He reined up beside Captain Ten Eyck, dismounted and handed him a piece of paper. Ten Eyck read it as he marched, his face emotionless. Turning, he handed the paper to Paddock.

It was hastily scrawled and the paper was rumpled, but it was easy enough to read. It said, "Captain: Forty well-armed men with 3000 rounds, ambulances, etc., left before your courier came in. You must unite with Fetterman; fire slowly and keep men in hand; you would have saved two miles toward scene of action if you had taken Lodge Trail Ridge. I ordered the wood train in, which will give fifty more men to spare."

Ten Eyck said, as though trying to justify himself, "I came by the road because it was quicker and easier on the men and because there was no deep snow. And you know why I rode to that high point, Jess."

Paddock handed the paper back. "I know, Captain, and so does Col. Carrington. He was worried when he wrote this note. He'll be the first to say you did the right thing when he has all the facts."

Ten Eyck shrugged. "I hope so," he said.

They reached the first cluster of rocks at the near end of the ridge and from here they could see the entire battlefield. Nothing alive on the slope to the east of the ridge. It was strewn with the white and naked bodies of the men that had been with Fetterman. All were bristling with arrows, shot into them after they had been stripped. Captain Ten Eyck breathed, "Holy God!"

Paddock felt a little sick himself. An hour ago, these fifty men had been alive. They had headed out of the fort on a routine mission that had been safely accomplished dozens of times in the last few months.

Now, because of Fetterman's ambition and disobedience, they were dead. He let his eyes go past these bodies toward the far end of the ridge. Halfway there he saw more bodies and knew they were Grummond's men.

112

A few dead horses lay among the bodies of the slain troopers but most of the horses had disappeared. So had the soldiers' uniforms and so had their guns. There appeared to be forty or fifty bodies in an area that could not have been more than thirty or forty feet in diameter. All were savagely mutilated. In almost all cases, the men's genitals had been cut off and placed inside their mouths, a final indignity that signified both the Indians' hatred and their contempt.

Ten Eyck yelled, his voice coming out thin and strained, "Draw the wagons up here and begin loading the bodies. Keep your guns close at hand." He moved on down the ridge, followed by Paddock and two or three of his men.

Farther down the ridge, they came upon Lt. Grummond's naked body lying in the road. Off to the side, the slope was strewn with the bodies of his men, stripped and mutilated as those of Fetterman's men had been. The only living thing was a wounded horse, which one of the men dispatched with a bullet in the head.

Strangely, one body had been neither mutilated nor stripped. It was that of the bugler, Adolf Metzger. He lay on his back, fully clothed and covered with a buffalo robe. In his hand he still had the bugle, but it now was twisted and bent almost beyond recognition, and it was stained with the blood of the Indians he had clubbed with it.

Ten Eyck stared at the bugler's body. His face was almost gray and there was a film of sweat on it. He looked at Paddock and asked, "What in God's name do you make of that?"

Paddock said, "Indians respect courage above all else. Metzger must have been a tiger. I don't suppose he had a gun, but that didn't slow *him* down. He attacked the Indians with his bugle and he may even have killed one or two of them with it. He'd have to have put on a pretty impressive show to get this kind of respect from the Sioux."

Ten Eyck nodded numbly. Paddock found the bodies of Jim Wheatley and Ike Fisher in some rocks nearby.

113

Eighty-one men had died for one's man's stubbornness and stupidity. And he thought, "What an awful Goddamned waste!"

CHAPTER 18

Gathering up the bodies of the slaughtered troopers was not a pleasant task. The faces of the men working at it were white with shock. Every now and then a young trooper would run to a nearby clump of brush, there to bend double and throw up, sometimes gagging afterward for a long time before he could return, sweating, to the job.

Ten Eyck organized the men into two shifts, recognizing that no man can work at this kind of grisly task without respite no matter how tough and hardened he might be. Each shift would work for half an hour and then would be relieved by the other shift. Those not working stood guard against the possibility of attack by the Indians, who still were massed a mile away in the valley of Peno Creek.

It was now mid-afternoon. The Indians showed no inclination to attack, no doubt believing that this detachment of soldiers had artillery, but neither did they leave the area.

Paddock found it hard to believe that he was alive. He knew that only a miracle could have kept him from being killed when O'Mara was. And it was a kind of miracle that he had not been with Fetterman or with Grummond. He had volunteered to go with Fetterman and later with Grummond and had been refused both times.

There were six wagons in all. Each wagon would hold no more than eight men unless Captain Ten Eyck was willing to pile the bodies on top of each other like

114

cordwood. He was not. Obviously he felt these men had suffered enough indignity at the hands of the Indians. He would not add to it.

It was late afternoon by the time all the wagons were loaded and still nearly half of Fetterman's men lay where they had died. Regretfully Ten Eyck gave the order to return to the fort.

Half the command preceded the six wagons; about half came along behind. Ten Eyck rode at the column's head on a horse someone had given him, with Lt. Matson and Dr. Hines. Paddock rode just behind the three with one of the civilian quartermaster department employees.

Nobody talked. The only sounds were those of the horses' hoofs on the frozen road, of the wagon wheels, of the clank of tug chains and singletrees, of the slogging boots of the foot soldiers, some of whom held onto the stirrups of the mounted men to make the going easier.

They brought the fort into sight while yet three miles away, and Paddock could see men lining the stockade, standing on the banquette inside. Only their heads were visible above the pointed stockade posts.

They splashed across Big Piney Creek as the sun sank below the Big Horn Mountains in the west, those on foot not even caring now if they got wet. The wood train, loaded with logs, was arriving from the Pinery as they went through the gates. The men with the wood train seemed to know there had been a battle. They did not know how disastrous it had been until they saw the six wagon loads of bodies entering the fort.

Molly Benedict's was the first face that Paddock saw. He dismounted from the frightened Indian pony and, holding the reins, hugged her close to him. Her face was white, her eyes wide with shock as she asked, "All of them?"

He nodded. "All of them. About thirty are still out there."

He stood with her and watched the six wagons cross the parade to the post hospital. He saw Colonel Carrington talking with Captain Ten Eyck and Dr. Hines. Men came running from the barracks, and Carrington

115

detailed twenty-five or thirty of them to carry the bodies of the dead inside. Hines and his orderlies would remove the arrows and prepare the bodies for burial. The carpenters would be busy all night building coffins out of rough-sawed pine.

Paddock walked beside Molly across the corner of the parade. He left her at the stable long enough to turn his captured Indian pony into the corral. Returning, he walked with her in the gathering darkness toward her house.

They went inside and she lighted the lamp. Silently she brought him a brown bottle of whisky, seeming to know he needed this. He poured a tumbler full and drank it down as if it were water.

He stared at the bottle, wondering how long it would be before he stopped seeing those scattered, naked, arrow-filled and mutilated bodies in his mind. He had fought in the war and had seen dead men before, but there is something that is different about a man's body when it has been deliberately desecrated by his enemy.

He refilled his glass. Molly seemed to know from looking at his face and into his stricken eyes that he didn't want to talk. She sat across the table and waited patiently until he looked at her. Then she asked, "Do you want anything to eat?"

Dumbly he shook his head. He gulped the second glass of whisky but it seemed to have no effect on him. At last Molly asked, "Sergeant O'Mara?"

"Dead. I don't know what the Indians did with his body but it was gone when we came by the place tonight." He poured his glass full for the third time and sat there staring at it. Suddenly he began to shake. It started in his knees and crept over the rest of him until he was shaking from head to foot. His teeth were chattering so badly he couldn't speak.

Tears welled from Molly's eyes. She got up and put some more wood into the stove. She put on the coffeepot and it began to make its peculiar singing sound as it heated.

The shaking lasted five or ten minutes and then it stopped as suddenly as it had begun. Paddock gulped the third glass of whisky. He was beginning to feel a

116

kind of numbness and he supposed that now he probably could sleep. He got wearily to his feet. "I'm going back to my place and sleep."

She didn't protest. She only nodded silently. He knew she was wondering what would happen tomorrow and so said, "I think it's over unless the Indians attack the fort and I don't think they will. Nobody's going out looking for trouble with the Indians after this."

Relief was apparent in her face. He bent his head and kissed her lightly on the mouth. Then he went out.

The wind had begun to blow, an icy wind off the snows of the Big Horn Mountains a dozen miles to the west. It chilled him and he began to shake again. Head down, he hurried to his quarters and went inside.

He built up the fire. Still he felt little effect from the whisky he had drunk. He found a half-filled bottle and took a long drink from it. He stood as close to the stove as he could get. When he finally got warm, he added more wood, closed the damper, and got out of his clothes. He blew out the lamp and, in his underwear, got into bed.

He had been afraid he wouldn't sleep, but he did, almost instantly. It was not, however, a restful sleep. He was tormented with nightmares, not of the battle or of the bodies, but of vague and disconnected things which nevertheless were frightening. Only one thing stood out plainly from all the rest. Someone kept shouting over and over, "I can ride through them with a hundred men! I can ride through them with a hundred men!"

He awoke at dawn and though the room was cold, his body was soaked with sweat. He heard the bugle sounding reveille and he thought about Bugler Metzger, who had fought so ferociously yesterday. He wondered who was taking his place today.

The wind was howling around the eaves. It rattled the door and, when he built a fire, made it roar inside the stove.

He went to the window and stared outside. The Big Horn Mountains were hidden by swirling clouds. He dressed hastily, then took time to carefully reload his revolver cylinders.

117

When he stepped outside, he could feel the bitter cold. A storm was blowing in. He thought of the more than thirty bodies still lying out there on the hillside four or five miles from the fort. They would be frozen now. Frozen in the positions they had assumed when death caught up with them.

Paddock hurried to the teamsters' mess and ate for the first time since yesterday morning. Everybody was subdued and there was little talk. There was an air of foreboding in all the men as if they wondered what would happen next.

Outside, Paddock noticed that the sentries had been doubled on all the sentry posts. Carrington obviously thought the fort might be attacked. The Sioux had thoroughly beaten the whites they hated so. Emboldened by their success, they might now try to exterminate them all.

He hurried across the parade to Carrington's house. The Colonel had several of his officers with him. Black George admitted Paddock and Carrington shook his hand. "I was going to send for you. I want to talk to you about what happened yesterday."

Paddock asked, "Who's going out after the rest of the bodies, Colonel Carrington?"

"I am."

Captain Powell said, "You can't do that, Colonel. You're needed here."

"I won't order anyone to go. That means I'll have to go myself."

"Does anybody have to go? Can't we wait until we get some replacements from Fort Laramie?"

Carrington shook his head. "Those men deserve a decent burial." He turned his head and looked at Lt. Wands. "Lieutenant, I want you to take a detail of workmen and a twenty man guard, and go out to the cemetery to dig some graves. I want two graves, one large enough for Fetterman, Brown and Grummond, the other at least fifty feet long for the other men."

"Yes, sir. I'll get started on it right away. It looks like it might be going to storm."

"That's why I want to get the rest of those bodies as

soon as possible. If it should snow, it might be impossible to find them all."

Paddock could see that Carrington had spent a sleepless night. The colonel was still profoundly shocked by what had happened yesterday. His hands shook and his face was pale.

Captain Ten Eyck, standing on the far side of the room, said, "I'll go with you, Colonel."

Lt. Matson said, "So will I."

"Thank you, gentlemen." He looked at Paddock. "Jess?"

Paddock nodded. "Sure, Colonel. I'll go."

Carrington nodded. "Then get the men ready, Captain Ten Eyck. I'll want about eighty, all mounted, and I'll want five ambulances to bring the bodies in. In addition, I want two howitzers and plenty of cannister shot for them."

"When will we leave?"

"When everything is ready, but I doubt if that will be much before eleven or twelve o'clock."

Ten Eyck, Wands and Matson saluted and left the room. Powell also excused himself. When they had gone, Carrington looked at Paddock. "You saw part of it, didn't you?" he asked.

Paddock shook his head. "Not really. I didn't see what finally happened to any of them. I saw them under attack, though, and it looked like it was pretty bad."

"You saw the bodies. Some of them had as many as thirty or forty arrows in them. Those men were captured alive and tortured, Jess. The arrows were shot into them after their clothes had been torn off by the Indians."

Paddock nodded. "I know, Colonel."

Carrington said feelingly, "The Goddamned barbarous savages! Before we're through, we're going to have to kill them all."

The column, under Colonel Carrington, did not leave Fort Kearny until about one o'clock. Captain Ten Eyck and Lt. Matson were with him, as was Jess Paddock. About half the men, eighty in all, were civilians, the others equally divided between infantry and cavalry. Also along was Dr. Elisha Gould, a civilian surgeon in the army's employ, for Dr. Hines was busy preparing for burial the bodies of the forty-nine brought in yesterday. Each had to be identified. Countless arrows had to be removed. The bodies had to be dressed in proper uniforms and in every case the cause of death must be listed on Surgeon Hines' report.

Proceeding slowly, the column crossed Big Piney Creek, which had again frozen over during the night. The wind was bitter cold and now and then a few flakes of snow stung the faces of the men.

At intervals, Carrington left pickets behind to advise him of any Indian action at his rear or against the fort and also to maintain signal communications with sentries at the fort.

It was late afternoon when the column finally reached the place where Captain Ten Eyck had loaded the forty-nine bodies yesterday. Still there had been no attack by the Indians although several hundred of them were visible in the valley of Peno Creek and on the east slope of Lodge Trail Ridge.

The column, with Carrington at its head, moved slowly along the ridge toward the rocks where the bodies of Wheatley, Fisher and Metzger, the bugler, were. Carrington's face turned paler when he saw the remaining bodies lying scattered on the slope. He motioned for the wagons to come on and to turn around when they reached the rocks.

Before ordering the bodies loaded into the wagons, Carrington took Ten Eyck, Matson and Paddock and rode among them. The mutilations here were even worse than those Paddock had witnessed yesterday. Eyes had been torn from their sockets and laid on rocks. Heads had been split open, the brains removed and also laid out on the rocks. Arms had been severed, skulls split. There were deliberate punctures, apparently made by knives while the victims were still alive, in every sensitive part of the bodies.

Carrington was shaking, both from shock and chill, as he ordered the bodies gathered up and placed in the wagons. Today, blankets had been brought to wrap them in, and every effort was made to match up the severed parts with the bodies from which they had been taken by the Indians.

While the work progressed, Carrington rode over the battlefield, his eyes on the ground, counting carefully each place where blood had been spilled, but from which the body of a killed or wounded Indian had been removed. Paddock accompanied him, also counting the bloodspots, but only those large enough to indicate the Indian who had made it had been killed. He counted sixty-five.

He said, "Colonel, Grummond's cavalry killed at least sixty-five Indians with their Spencers."

"What about the others? What about Fetterman's infantry?"

"Well, I looked around where we found their bodies yesterday and I don't think they did as well. They had those damned muzzle loading Springfields and I doubt if any of them got off more than a couple of shots. Some probably didn't get off but one."

Carrington frowned. "But how did it happen so quickly. How?"

Paddock said, "Too many Indians. Too little experience on the part of the troops. I saw enough of it to tell that they were beaten from the start. Instead of finding cover and spreading out, they huddled together like sheep. You can see that for yourself in the way the

121

bodies are bunched. They made it easy for the Indians."

Carrington said, "There'll be hell to pay over this."

Paddock nodded. He followed Carrington back to the road.

The colonel looked at him curiously. "Why was Grummond so far ahead of Fetterman?"

Paddock said, "Eagerness, I guess. O'Mara and I tried to get through to him and tell him to draw back and help Fetterman but we couldn't make it. There were several hundred Indians between us and Grummond's men."

"Was that when O'Mara was killed?"

"Yes, sir. If you don't mind, I'd like to go back and see if I can find his body."

"Go ahead, Jess. But don't get yourself killed."

Paddock rode back along the road. Light was already beginning to fade from the sky, which had been leaden gray all day. The wind still blew strong and cold out of the northwest and the flurries of snow were more frequent than they had been earlier.

He heeled his horse into a steady trot. He passed the first of the pickets Carrington had left behind before he reached the spot where O'Mara had been killed.

His sorrel horse still lay where he had fallen but saddle and bridle had been removed. O'Mara's body was gone. The ground was covered with hoof prints, those of unshod ponies, and it was impossible to follow any single trail. It was as though O'Mara's body had disappeared into the air.

He circled around on the hillside below the road until it was too dark to see the ground. Then, shrugging regretfully, he returned to the road to wait for Carrington and his men.

They came down in darkness, the wagon wheels grating on the frozen ground, tug chains and singletrees clanking, the men cursing sourly at the cold and at the barbarity of the Indians. Paddock joined Carrington and the Colonel asked, "Find him, Jess?"

Paddock shook his head. "I don't know why they'd take his body but it looks like that's what they did."

"He'll probably never be found. There'll be nobody out on these hills for a long, long time."

Paddock nodded. It was possible that wolves had dragged O'Mara's body away during the night. It was also possible the Indians had dragged it away. At least, he thought, O'Mara had died before the Indians got to him. He had not been tortured as had so many of Fetterman's and Grummond's men.

Captain Ten Eyck asked, "What are you going to do now, Colonel?"

"Ready the fort for an Indian attack. Red Cloud probably thinks he'll never get a better chance than this to wipe us out. And I'll send a courier to Fort Laramie for reinforcements."

Paddock asked, "Want me to go, Colonel?"

Carrington shook his head. "Too risky, Jess. Mrs. Benedict would never forgive me if anything happened to you. I think I'll ask Portugee Phillips to go."

Paddock didn't argue the point with him. He knew there was little chance a courier could get through. The Indians would most certainly be watching the Bozeman Road between Fort Kearny and Fort Laramie.

But he didn't agree with Carrington that the fort was in jeopardy. He seriously doubted if the Indians would attack. Indians fought only when they could inflict heavy losses with little risk to themselves. They would not risk a frontal assault upon a fortified position, particularly when they knew how devastating the cannister shot of the artillery could be.

Still, Carrington's precautions were proper ones. The Colonel could not, in good conscience, do less than be prepared for the worst.

Once more it was a somber garrison that greeted the column's return to the fort. They lined the way on both sides of the gates, staring through the darkness at the loaded wagons. The wagons went directly across the parade to the post hospital and drew up there while Major Powell, Officer of the Day, detailed men to carry the bodies in.

It was almost ten o'clock. Paddock glimpsed Molly Benedict and rode straight to her. He dismounted and walked with her along the side of the parade toward her

123

house. He left her at the stables long enough to care for his horse, then rejoined her in the dark and bitter wind.

It had turned much colder during the afternoon. Paddock guessed it must be near zero and would probably go to ten or twenty below tonight.

Molly's place was warm. He took off his coat and sank wearily into a chair. Molly brought him coffee laced with whisky and he drank it gratefully. Her eyes were worried as she asked, "What's going to happen now? Will the Indians attack the fort?"

He shook his head. "I doubt it. They don't like that kind of fighting."

"Colonel Carrington thinks they will, doesn't he?"

Paddock nodded. "He does. But he has to think of every possibility."

"It's horrible! Eighty-one men!"

"Eighty-two. O'Mara's dead too."

"Did you find his body today?"

He shook his head.

She had some stew warming on the back of the stove and she brought him some of it. As soon as he had eaten, he kissed her and wearily went out into the everlasting wind. He could hear the shouts as the guard was changed. Otherwise the fort was dark and still.

Hearing voices, he stopped with his hand on his doorlatch. He saw two men come along the street, heading for the water gate.

They were talking as they passed and he recognized one voice as that of Colonel Carrington, the other as that of Portugee Phillips. Phillips was leading a horse, one that was instantly recognizable even in the dark as Colonel Carrington's own Kentucky thoroughbred.

Paddock called, "Good luck, Phillips."

Phillips waved a hand. Paddock went inside, thinking that Phillips must know how slight his chances were. But the bitter cold would help. Indian pickets stationed on the road would be more intent on staying warm than they would be on watching for anyone who might be escaping from the fort.

Paddock fell exhaustedly on the bed and pulled the covers over him. He was almost instantly asleep.

124

The Sioux did not attack the fort, apparently content with their decisive victory over Grummond and Fetterman. Portugee Phillips reached Fort Laramie on Christmas Day, and on January 17th, Lt. Col. Henry W. Wessels arrived at Fort Phil Kearny with two companies of the Second Cavalry and three of the Eighteenth Infantry, along with ammunition and supplies.

On January 23, Colonel Carrington, who had been relieved of his command by Brigadier General Philip St. George Cooke, left Fort Kearny for Fort Laramie, accompanied by his headquarters staff and the regimental band. The wives and children of men stationed at Kearny also went along. Sixty men accompanied the party as an escort. And in one of the wagons rode Molly Benedict and Jess Paddock.

The journey seemed endless and the hardships were unbelievable in deep snow and temperatures that sometimes reached forty below. But when Jess and Molly reached Fort Laramie they were married by the chaplain there.

And as soon as the weather moderated sufficiently, they continued southward in a light spring wagon Paddock had bought at Laramie.

There is, today, a place near Cheyenne where the grassland rolls away to infinity like the swells of a restless sea. A snug log ranchhouse nestles in a valley beside a clear and narrow stream. Here live the descendants of Jess and Molly Paddock.

Two graves, marked by small granite headstones, look out across the wind-swept land from the top of a nearby hill. The headstones face northward toward Fort Phil Kearny, now crumbled away and gone, and toward a ridge a few miles north of it where eighty-one men fought and died more than a hundred years ago. Massacre Ridge, it is called, in memory of the Fetterman tragedy.

Big Bestsellers from SIGNET

☐ CALDO LARGO by Earl Thompson. (#E7737—$2.25)

☐ A GARDEN OF SAND by Earl Thompson.
(#E7249—$2.25)

☐ TATTOO by Earl Thompson. (#E6671—$2.25)

☐ DESIRES OF THY HEART by Joan Carroll Cruz.
(#J7738—$1.95)

☐ THE ACCURSED by Paul Boorstin. (#E7745—$1.75)

☐ RUNNING AWAY by Charlotte Vale Allen.
(#E7740—$1.75)

☐ THE RICH ARE WITH YOU ALWAYS by Malcolm Macdonald.
(#E7682—$2.25)

☐ THE WORLD FROM ROUGH STONES by Malcolm Macdonald.
(#J6891—$1.95)

☐ THE FRENCH BRIDE by Evelyn Anthony.
(#J7683—$1.95)

☐ TELL ME EVERYTHING by Marie Brenner.
(#J7685—$1.95)

☐ ALYX by Lolah Burford. (#J7640—$1.95)

☐ MACLYON by Lolah Burford. (#J7773—$1.95)

☐ FIRST, YOU CRY by Betty Rollin. (#J7641—$1.95)

☐ THE DEVIL IN CRYSTAL by Erica Lindley.
(#E7643—$1.75)

☐ THE BRACKENROYD INHERITANCE by Erica Lindley.
(#W6795—$1.50)

THE NEW AMERICAN LIBRARY, INC.,
P.O. Box 999, Bergenfield, New Jersey 07621

Please send me the SIGNET BOOKS I have checked above. I am enclosing $_____(check or money order—no currency or C.O.D.'s). Please include the list price plus 35¢ a copy to cover handling and mailing costs. (Prices and numbers are subject to change without notice.)

Name_____

Address_____

City_____State_____Zip Code_____
Allow at least 4 weeks for delivery

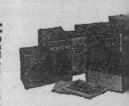